Born in Irvine, Ayrshire, John Niven read English Literature at Glasgow University, graduating in 1991 with First Class honours. For the next ten years, he worked for a variety of record companies, including London Records and Independiente. He left the music industry to write full time in 2002. He also writes original screenplays with writing partner Nick Ball, the younger brother of British TV presenter Zoë Ball. His journalistic contributions to newspapers and magazines include a monthly column for Q magazine, entitled 'London Kills Me'. Niven lives in Buckinghamshire with his fiancée and infant daughter. He has a teenage son from a previous marriage.

NO GOOD DEED

What do you do when the homeless man on the street you've just given money to thanks you by name and turns out to be one of your 'closest' friends, one you haven't seen for over twenty years? For Alan, there's no question — it's only natural that he'd want to see his old mate Craig off the streets, even if only for a few nights, and into some clean clothes. But what if the successful life you've made for yourself — good job, happy marriage, lovely kids, grand Victorian house — is one that your old pal would quite like to have too? Even if it means taking it from you? Gradually, inevitably, mayhem ensues as Craig turns Alan's orderly household upside down, threatening to wreck Alan's life for good.

JOHN NIVEN

♦

NO GOOD DEED

Complete and Unabridged

CHARNWOOD
Leicester

First published in Great Britain in 2017 by
William Heinemann
London

First Charnwood Edition
published 2018
by arrangement with
William Heinemann
Penguin Random House
London

A catalogue record for this book is available from the British Library.

ISBN 978–1–4448–3776–6

Published by
F. A. Thorpe (Publishing)
Anstey, Leicestershire

Set by Words & Graphics Ltd.
Anstey, Leicestershire
Printed and bound in Great Britain by
T. J. International Ltd., Padstow, Cornwall

This book is printed on acid-free paper

To Charlotte

'No good deed goes unpunished.'

— Old proverb

'Nothing is as obnoxious as other
people's good luck.'

— F. Scott Fitzgerald

PART ONE

Winter

1

Alan Grainger was looking for another way of saying 'disgrace', flipping through his mental thesaurus as he crossed Charing Cross Road, heading north and west from Covent Garden. He had the little Moleskine in his inside pocket, where he had already jotted down a few lines — insults mainly — while he ate the meal.

Affordable housing, better traffic management, more late-night venues, there are many things that London badly needs right now. What it expressly doesn't need is another 'pop-up' knocking out brioche-bunned designer burgers at twelve quid a throw.

Playing around with this, his main contender for the opening sentence, he cut up that little alleyway into Chinatown, the cold, late-November air suddenly full of the smell of roast duck. His plan for the rest of the afternoon was to find a quiet corner in Soho House or the Groucho and drink a pot of coffee to clear the two-beer fug out of his head while he finished writing his review. Then he'd get the train home around four, missing the worst of the rush hour. He shifted a little on his feet to try and dislodge a lurking discomfort somewhere in his bowels. Constipation. An occupational hazard.

'Ignominy'! That was it.

He stopped on the corner of Gerrard Street and took the notebook from the warm folds of

3

his thick winter coat, his fingers bony in the chill air.

'A'right, mate?'

The accent Scottish, like his own.

It was one of those very cold, very bright early-winter days, the sky above London a hard, deep blue, the chimney pots and TV antennae cartoon-contrasted against it. '*The initial ignominy . . .* ' he scribbled, crossing out 'disgrace'.

'A'right, mate?'

Close by, floor level.

'*Of the thirty-five-minute wait for a table . . .* ' The new thing — no reservations. In his late forties, this trend felt to Alan like one of the biggest backward steps mankind could make.

'A'right, Alan?'

'*Compounded by the* —'

Hang on now — why did this guy know his name?

He looked up. Or rather, down. The tramp was sitting on the pavement, his back to the wall of the cinema that formed one half of an alleyway that led into Soho proper. He was looking at Alan with intent, almost with amusement. He was eating, the tramp. Some kind of tinfoil-wrapped disgrace, some *ignominy* of falafel or kebab. Alan approached slowly, the notebook going into his side pocket, his right hand reflexively going into his right trouser pocket for his change.

Well, it wasn't so unusual really. Alan's photograph appeared regularly in the papers, passport-sized every week next to his column, even bigger next to the occasional feature or

4

interview. He was on TV and radio now and again. Maybe this guy, hunkering down in an underpass, or on some park bench night after night, had cause to read a restaurant review or two before succumbing to a few hours of Super Lager-induced oblivion. Closing the few yards between them he had time to notice that the man appeared to be about his own age. There the similarities ended, however. The tramp wore filthy jeans, burnt-out off-brand trainers, and was apparently baked, sealed, into some kind of parka, his face framed by stringy long hair. (Long and stringy but without, Alan was dismayed to note, any of the grey that had begun to streak through his own hair.) Alan formed a kind of half-smile, a benevolent 'good-luck' expression, as his fist went into his pocket and came out with a mix of warm coins.

'How've ye been?' The guy said this in a casual, upbeat tone, as though they were friends who had just seen each other last week. Yes, Scottish, and about his age. There was probably a conversation about how great Scotland was looming here. How much they both missed it, both of them having made a point of being here in London.

'Fine, fine . . . ' Alan said. He was looking for somewhere to drop the coins, for the guy's cap or blanket, or the modern begging bowl — the tattered beaker from Subway, Burger King or KFC. It felt churlish to ask after the well-being of his interlocutor, who was, after all, lying in an alleyway, begging. Except Alan couldn't see any cash receptacle. He stood there with his

5

coin-filled hand awkwardly frozen in mid-air. Cold air. Their eyes met.

'I thought you'd recognised me.'

This was the tramp speaking, not Alan.

'I don't . . . ' Alan began but didn't finish. Because their eyes were locked on each other now, Alan standing over the man, half bent with his fistful of smash. He didn't finish because the tramp's face was coming into focus, a certain glitter in the eyes, the smile lines at the corners of the mouth, the slightly crooked front teeth, but worn down to stumps, brown and rotted since he'd last seen them. Since he'd . . .

'*Craig?*' Alan said, the entire word coming out of his mouth like the squiggle of a question mark.

'Long time, pal.'

Several emotions hit him at once. Shock, obviously. Pity, the kind of deep, reflexive pity for another creature's suffering. And, most obviously, joy. Joy that, once in a while, the universe was capable of producing such a stark symbol of your own success, of how far you'd come, of how much you'd made of the hand you'd been dealt, while others had . . .

For lying there on the cold W1 pavement was one of his oldest friends. A man who, when they'd been boys, had been as close to him as it was possible to be. A man who he had not seen in the flesh in nearly twenty-five years.

And now he had to ask it, churlish or not.

'How . . . how've you been?'

'Ach,' Craig Carmichael said, spreading a gloved hand to indicate himself, his patch, the

6

thin piece of cardboard that served as his house, 'ye see it aw.'

'Jesus, Craig. Jesus fucking Christ.'

'Where are ye off tae?' Craig took a bite of his tinfoil-tubed snack as he asked this. He was carrying on the conversation, well, conversationally, as though this were just another day, as though they had bumped into each other fully pinstriped at Terminal 5, two old school friends happening to intersect at an international hub of travel. Alan? Alan was having trouble staying upright. What should he do? Sit down beside him to show 'hey, we're no different' or remain standing?

'I . . . ' Alan struggled. 'I'm just doing a bit of work.'

'Writing?'

'I . . . yeah.'

There was a pause. Wind gusted along the alley, seeking release. What else was there to say?

'Listen.' Alan looked at his watch. 'Do . . . do you fancy a quick drink?'

Later, much later, Alan would have cause to wonder about how differently things would have gone if this sentence had not escaped his lips. The tiny interstices of life, moments where we think nothing much is happening, but something always is.

★   ★   ★

Obviously, given Craig's current look, many places were out (though Alan reckoned he could probably have passed him off as a challenging

7

British artist at the Groucho), so the Coach and Horses on Greek Street it was. They crammed around one of the small tables at the end of the bar, near the toilets, Alan with a half lager and Craig with a pint.

'Cheers,' Alan said.

'Aye, cheers,' Craig responded as their glasses touched.

Cheers. Really? It sounded mockingly inappropriate to Alan as he sipped his drink and took Craig in properly. He seemed to be wearing many layers of clothing. The soles flapped off his trainers. His bundle (sleeping bag, backpack, carrier bag) was shoved under the stool next to him.

It had taken him a fair while to roll all of this up, while Alan stood there, smiling benignly, unsure of the social etiquette of the situation. (Offer to help? Or not. He went with not.) And yet Craig didn't look so filthy that the pub would have refused him entry. He wore a thick beard and his hair was a mess, seeming to go in five different directions at once, but it did look like it had been washed in recent memory. In truth, had he been twenty years younger, he could just about have earned a place on one of the old 'hipster or tramp?' tumblrs. Also, maddeningly, Craig was still thin. Maddeningly, but not inexplicably. Alan guessed one of the very few benefits of vagrant life was guaranteed calorie control. They set their glasses down and it was finally time to ask it. There was no way around it.

'Craig, Jesus, what happened to you?'

8

Craig laughed. It was as if he had been expecting just this question for the last ten minutes. 'Ah fuck, long story. When did I last see you?'

'Oh God . . . ' Alan pretended to think.

In truth he knew exactly when they'd last seen each other. He could picture the moment with total clarity right now: Craig, still dripping with sweat, wearing a fresh T-shirt he'd taken from the merchandise stall, a tumbler of white wine halfway to his lips as he waved goodbye from across the packed dressing room while Alan and the boys made their way out of the door at two o'clock in the morning. 'See ye!' he'd shouted. It had been at the Queen Margaret Union, Glasgow University, in the spring of 1993. Craig's band, the Rakes, just back from America, had played the opening night of their British tour there. It had been just before Alan moved down to London. There had been him and Charlie and Donald, the guys he shared the flat with on Huntley Gardens, just off Byres Road. Charlie, Donald, Craig and Alan had all gone to Glasgow Uni together. Craig had dropped out in second year, when his band had really started to take off, and now here he was, one of their own, headlining the QM, where the four of them had watched so many gigs together, speeding on the balcony, leaping in the mosh pit. Yes, Alan knew exactly when. So why pretend to think? *Because you don't want him to know you've often thought about him.*

'Ah . . . maybe in Glasgow? That time you played the QM?'

'Aye, aye. Maybe . . . ' Craig said, rubbing his beard.

'I mean, I've tried to find you here and there. The usual, Facebook and stuff,' Alan said.

'Don't really do any of that,' Craig said. *No shit?* Alan thought, looking at Craig's tattered belongings below the stool.

'Obviously I heard a few stories a while back, in the press and whatnot.'

Alan remembered the bits of information in the late nineties, back when he still occasionally read *Q*, or the *NME*. '*Heroin . . . rehab . . . Los Angeles . . . dropped by their record company . . .* ' They had been comforting stories at the time, when Alan had still been toiling for pennies at *Time Out*. For a while prior to this, Craig's success had seemed imminent, huge and unavoidable.

Craig took a big gulp of lager. ' 'Daybreak' was a hit in America, remember? Not a smash-hit kinda hit, but big enough. We then pretty much moved the band to LA in 1994. Just touring all the time. The album started selling off the back of all this, close to a million copies. We started getting proper royalty cheques in, you know? Not just five and ten grand kinda thing, but two and three hundred thousand dollars stuff. This was twenty years ago, mind. So, ye can imagine, you knew Davy and Tam, we all went a bit mental. Then, usual story, we're all living like guys who earn a quarter o a million dollars a year and then the next album comes out and it's 'who the fuck are you?' We sell ninety thousand. Went from nine hundred thousand to ninety overnight! No mean feat that, losing ninety per cent of your fan base from one record to the next. Anyway, we're used to living like kings, and then, the following year, your income gets cut to fuck all, but did we start reining it all in? Did we fuck. Advances from the label, trying to write another hit, no one had paid their tax bill, it was all just the usual, y'know, like every cunt before us and every cunt after us. So, about '99 I'm fucked, skint, end up working in the kitchen of a Mexican restaurant in Echo Park, trying to get another band together, still battering the nose up, bit of smack here and there. That went on for a few years, then, ach, there were a couple of women, things didnae work out. I moved back to Scotland about, what, don't know, 2005 or 2006? Something like that. Ma maw died — ' Alan interjected the obligatory 'I'm sorry', but Craig waved it off — 'and I got a wee bit of money, kept me going for a few years, but I soon got through it, and the drinking was bad by this point. I came down here to try and get out the circle I was in back in Ardgirvan, bad crowd, ye know? Smack. Ranta Campbell and they kinda boys? I was staying with a girl I knew in Tottenham. She chucked me out after a few months. I remember, the first night I slept rough — a lot of folk can always remember this — I had about thirty quid in my pocket. It was about enough for a hostel for the night or I could have got a single on the coach back to Glasgow and done what? Fuck knows. It was September, no that cold, so I walked up to the park and got in ma sleeping bag under a bush — I was steaming

11

of course — and then next thing I knew I woke up about seven in the morning. I'd got through the night, ye know? It wisnae that bad. So you just, ye know, ye find out you can do it. I went and sat near a cashpoint and by lunchtime I had about four quid. Enough for a sandwich and a couple o cans. That . . . that was about five years ago. And here we are.' Craig drained his glass.

Alan shook his head and looked at the clock behind the bar. It had taken just over three minutes for Craig to recap the last twenty-four years of his life.

'Ach, fuck it,' Craig said. 'Ye win some, ye lose some. It wisnae all bad. Had some good times along the way.'

'I'm sorry,' Alan said.

As the words came out of his mouth he realised that he meant them. He had wished ill on Craig many times when they were younger. He had envied his looks, his talent, his musicianship, his way with women, his confidence, his popularity. The young Alan Grainger had very much wanted to be Craig Carmichael. But now, today, as they both approached fifty and the results were in, he was very, very glad to be Alan Grainger.

'Ye know, I've seen ye around a few times,' Craig said.

'Where?'

'Ach, Dean Street, coming in and out of the Groucho and the like. It's a good touch there sometimes. Some steaming rich bastard handing ye a twenty-pound note, stuff like that.' Alan often noticed, and funded, the bums around the

12

doorway to the Groucho. But you didn't really *notice* them, did you? You averted your gaze.

'Why didn't you say hello?' Alan asked.

'Come tae fuck, Alan,' Craig said. 'Ye were with people. What was I going tae say? 'A'right, Al? Mind me? Craig Carmichael fae Ardgirvan? We went tae Ravenscroft Academy together? Ye got a couple o quid ye can spare us?''

'Why did you decide to say hello today?'

Craig shrugged. 'Ye were on yer own. Ye stopped near me tae write in yer daft wee notebook.' Alan smiled. But something about the quick slap of that 'daft', about the fact that, cracked and weathered though the skin around them was, Craig's blue eyes could still cut through him . . . unsettled Alan. Made him feel sixteen again, like the intervening years had not leavened all the justice that they should have. 'Anyway,' Craig said. 'Ma shout. What are ye having?'

'Craig, honestly, let me — '

'Naw. Ma round. I can get it.'

'I ken, but — '

'Fuck sake, Alan.'

'Sorry, aye. If you're sure, can ye get us a half of . . . ah fuck it. Get us a pint.'

As Alan watched Craig fight his way in at the bar, getting a couple of odd looks from some of the afternoon drinkers, but no trouble getting served (the Coach. and Horses had surely seen a lot worse), he thought to himself, *Aye? Ye? Ken?*

When had he last talked like this? Katie would be wondering what had happened to him when he got home tonight.

13

2

'Oh please, Mum.'

'For God's sake, Melissa.'

They were in the kitchen. Katie Grainger looked up from the colander of kale she was rinsing and regarded her daughter again. They were engaged in a completely normal mother-and-sixteen-year-old-daughter negotiation: the amount of flesh Melissa would be allowed to display at an upcoming fancy-dress party. Right now she looked to Katie like a cross between an underfed sex worker and Courtney Love at the tail end of a three-day bender. She was wearing a kind of witch's outfit, but one that was deeply décolleté — almost to the navel — and had a hemline that terminated just below the knickers Katie prayed Melissa was wearing. The tops of her black stockings were clearly visible. 'What I want to know,' Katie said, emptying the gleaming emerald leaves into a saucepan, 'is when did fancy dress come to mean some kind of prostitute convention? I mean — kids used to dress up as, I don't know, cartoon characters and stuff . . . '

'You want me to go as Elsa from *Frozen*?'

'Oh, it'd probably have to be some sort of sexy Elsa, wouldn't it? She'd be in a basque and suspenders.'

'Jesus, Mum, Jasmine Holland is wearing — '

'Yes, and if — ' With superhuman effort, Katie

stopped herself from saying the dread sentence involving Jasmine Holland, a bridge and some jumping. 'Look, Melissa, this is all moot. If your father comes home and sees you in that he'll hit the bloody roof.'

'I cannot *wait* to go to university . . . ' Melissa said as she stormed out, her spiked heels putting little dings in Katie's lovely reclaimed oak floor.

'Then I'd go to my room and hit the books rather than Facebook, darling,' Katie trilled after her. *Column due tomorrow*, she thought. *The oversexualisation of teens seen through the prism of fancy dress? Not bad.* She made a note in the ever-open 'Column Ideas' file on her laptop.

Katie was standing at the island in the middle of the large kitchen-cum-family room. Behind her was brushed steel — ovens at waist and head height, six-burner Viking range, the double doors of the vast Sub Zero — and the black Aga. The island itself had two sinks and a pro-kitchen coil tap. (Grohe, 789 quid.) Beyond the island was the circular dining table and chairs and, beyond that, where Melissa had just been standing, the conservatory/family area, sofas surrounded by glass and greenery, the French windows opening directly onto the tiered garden. Like many other Georgian and Victorian properties in this part of Buckinghamshire, much rearwards extension work had been done — from the wall of refrigeration behind her to the glass of the French windows was a distance of some fifty feet.

Katie looked at the clock. Nearly five. Could

15

she reach into the glass-fronted wine cooler yet and uncork a bottle of Sauvignon or white burgundy on the basis that she'd be needing it soon for the chicken? *No, have some tea and hold off.* As she turned the kettle on she heard the words '*REACH FOR THE SKY!*' and turned to see Sophie pointing Woody right at her, the last of the string disappearing into the back of the lawman.

'You. Come here,' Katie said to her younger daughter very seriously, beckoning her. Sophie trotted over, giggling, knowing that her mother was only ever very serious when she was joking. Katie plucked her up and swung her onto the counter. 'You have been found guilty of . . . ' she waited, Sophie's eyes widening in anticipation, ' . . . *being too cute!*' Katie dug her thumbs into the fleshy parts of Sophie's thighs and Sophie shrieked with delight, struggling, her bare heels thrumming against the cupboard door. 'STOP! STOP! MERCY PLEASE, DEAR MOTHER!' It was a routine Katie had taught her, she had to beg for mercy very formally. Katie relented and embraced the child, both of them giggling now. As Katie often reflected when dealing with her seven-year-old daughter straight after dealing with her sixteen-year-old: *where's the bloody aspic?* Melissa had been such good fun when she was Sophie's age. And soon Sophie would be Melissa's age, which would make Katie in her *mid-fifties* and then . . . Christ.

'Mummy? What's wrong with Mel?'

'Oh, she's fine.'

'She slammed her door.'

16

'Well, that's a bit naughty, isn't it?'

Sophie nodded. 'It's not very kind, is it?'

'No, it's not. Now — have you done your homework?' Sophie shook her head. 'Run along and do it. *The Simpsons* will be on soon.'

'Doh!' Sophie said, jumping down and running off. She stopped in the doorway. 'When will Daddy be home?'

'Soon, darling, soon. Homework.'

Today had been a London day for Alan, a review. Katie wrote her column from home, perhaps managing only two or three London days a month to Alan's seven or eight on average.

They'd been out here in Marham for seven years now, since just before Tom started secondary school. Tom — their eldest — a gap-toothed twelve-year-old when they bought this place, now a strapping, swaggering brick shithouse, a fridge-clearing wonder of appetite and disorganisation. Katie wondered what he was up to right now, up there in Glasgow. In the library hopefully. Or the reading room. (*Yeah, right*, a voice told her.) He'd only gone back a few weeks ago, after the eternity of the summer holidays. The second year of his history degree. Still, she didn't *really* worry about Tom. He had ever been a solid, fairly sensible kid. Melissa? Now that was a whole other deal. *To have children was to have your heart walk around outside your body forever.* Who said that? Joan Didion? She'd look it up later. *Mmm. Joan Didion, now there's a thought. Is it the anniversary of her death? Her birth? Her publishing something seminal or other? Her having her fucking hair done,*

17

her bush trimmed? Anything Katie could some-how wring seven hundred words out of.

Seven years out here. It had been the schools argument and the 'more space' argument and the fact that the fast train to Marylebone only took thirty minutes and whatever. Actually Katie hadn't needed much persuading. The kids had been nine and twelve. She'd turned forty. She'd felt like she'd had a fair run at London. Alan had needed a little more persuading. In the end, when their neighbours Jane and Bob had told them about their twelve-year-old son coming home from the local comprehensive, kissing his teeth and talking about 'me Nandos, seen?', that had done it.

And, like many of their generation, she and Alan had been the jolly beneficiaries of a massive, hilarious joke, one cracked by money.

Their first two-bedroom flat in West Hamp-stead: £120,000 in 1995, when they were still in their twenties. They'd scraped the twelve-grand deposit together from their savings and a 'loan' from her parents.

They sold it for £200,000 in 2001, the year Melissa was born. They'd moved to Queen's Park, buying a big three-bedroom, private-garden maisonette for £280,000. Well, Queen's Park was a bit of a joke back then.

It wasn't a joke when they sold the place five years later for half a million, using the profit to buy a run-down semi-detached Victorian house on the borders of Brondesbury Park for £750,000. They'd done the usual middle-class bits: seagrass matting, a couple of real fires, new

18

kitchen and bathrooms and slathered the walls in Farrow & Ball. (Around this time they'd also come into a nice chunk of money when Alan's first cookbook, *The Pause Button Gourmet: Cooking Like in the Movies* — a throwaway collection of recipes inspired by scenes in classic films: Dustin Hoffman's French toast from *Kramer vs. Kramer*, the pasta sauce from *Goodfellas*, Paul Newman's omelette recipe from *The Color of Money* and so forth — spiralled high into the Christmas best-seller lists.)

They sold the Brondesbury house in 2010 for 1.2 mil.

Basically Katie's father lent them six grand in 1995 and, hey presto, fifteen years later, they were property millionaires.

Their talent? Their stroke-of-genius master-plan? Being born in the late sixties and working in London with half-decent salaries in the 1990s. So here they were, not even fifty yet and mortgage-free in their five-thousand-square-foot detached Georgian with two acres of land half an hour from central London. The kids all had a bedroom, they had a huge en suite and walk-in closet, there were four bathrooms and Alan's study. Katie hadn't wanted one — she liked to work at the kitchen table, surrounded by pots and pans and cooking and the coming and goings of children and, invariably, workmen. (There was always *something* being done.)

Katie spared a thought for the average 26-year-old trying to buy a nice two-bedroom flat in West Hampstead now, trying to buy a nine-hundred-grand place on a forty-grand salary. *Mmm, seven hundred words on the difficulties of getting on the London property ladder for the young.* No, she couldn't possibly go *there* again. Editor would shoot her in the head. Balls. She turned the oven on and sat down at her laptop at the kitchen table. The clock now said 5.16. The glass-fronted wine cooler stared at her balefully.

Her phone started ringing. Alan.

3

It's all a bit different, Craig thought, looking around. Then again, he couldn't be too sure, as he'd been out of his mind when he'd been in the Groucho a couple of times before, back in the early nineties, when record companies had been romancing his band. 'My friend's an artist,' Alan had said as he signed him in at reception — Craig standing there feeling self-conscious, holding his bundle — before he went off to make a phone call, leaving Craig in a corner downstairs with a bottle of white wine in an ice bucket and a menu for bar snacks. Bar snacks? Jesus Christ, eight quid for some kind of tiny Scotch egg? Mind you, getting some food in might not be a bad idea. They'd wound up having four pints in the Coach and Horses and now here they were, starting on the white wine at five. As a rule, Craig tried not to mix his drinks these days. He generally began his slow intake of strong lager around noon, usually consuming between six and eight cans of Super Lager or Special Brew before bedding down for the night around midnight. He'd always used to wonder why tramps drank that stuff. Now that he was one the answer was clear: four 440ml cans from Tesco cost just over seven quid. Nearly two litres of a drink that weighed in at nearly 9 per cent ABV? Almost as strong as some wines? That was a no-brainer.

He tried to remember where they'd sat when he'd been here last. Over there near the piano? There had been their manager, an A&R guy and some girls from the record company and cocaine in the toilets downstairs. In fact he seemed to remember he'd ended up in the toilets *with* one of the record company girls and the cocaine. She'd been wearing dungarees (in fairness it was 1992) and he remembered her hurriedly unpopping the clasps and turning around in the cramped cubicle, her face pressed against the top of the cistern they'd just been snorting lines from. He'd been twenty-three years old and he thought it would never end.

Craig snapped out of his reverie as he saw Alan coming back to the table, weaving slightly unsteadily across the room. *Christ, the fucking belly on the cunt.* Craig still had the same size waist he'd had at age seventeen.

Alan exhaled as he lowered himself into the chair next to Craig, making a kind of moaning sound.

'Ye want to watch that,' Craig said.

'What?'

'Making noises as ye sit down. Proper pensioner stuff that, pal.'

'Ha! Right enough. Cheers.'

Craig picked up his wine glass and clinked it against Alan's. He hadn't drunk wine in ages. It was OK. 'Everything OK?'

'Huh?'

'Yer phone call?'

'Oh, yeah, fine. Just telling Katie I'd be a bit late home.'

'So, where is home?'

'Marham? In Buckinghamshire?'

In the pub they had mostly talked about Craig. Alan felt it might have been inappropriate to talk about himself. About his career, his money, his property, his beautiful upper-class English wife and his well-mannered expensively educated children. About the incredibly kind run of cards life had dealt him, kings, queens, aces. Meanwhile, there was Craig, looking at an endless succession of twos and threes, of jokers and wild cards. But he could see there was no avoiding it. 'We moved out of London, oh, seven years ago. We'd both turned forty, we'd had a good run of it here, but there comes a point you want to gear down a little, you know?' *Idiot*, Alan thought to himself. '*You know?*' Yeah, like Craig knew. Craig, who'd spent the night in an alleyway off Piccadilly Circus, using everything he owned as a pillow. Whose life had been reduced to a daily scramble to get a tenner. Ten pounds. A cab fare. A pack of cigarettes. A tip to the doorman. A couple of magazines. A single gin and tonic at the bar here.

But, if Craig was offended, he didn't show it. He just nodded and sipped his wine and said, 'So, how long you and Katie been together then?'

'God, me and Katie,' he said as he refilled his glass. Craig's was still pretty full. 'Just over twenty years? We met in '94. Right after I moved down here.'

'Kids?'

'Three. Tom's nineteen, Melissa's sixteen and

Sophie's just turned seven.' Sophie — their little afterthought. That night in Antigua. Too much local beer. Too much rum. 'You never had kids then, Craig?'

'Oh aye.'

'Really? You were married?' As soon as he said this Alan realised how incredibly 1952 it sounded.

'Fuck, naw. There's two that I know about. One in LA and one back in Glasgow.'

'And do you ever . . . ?'

Craig shook his head. 'Wouldn't be much use tae them, would I? Fuck-up like me? Naw, best out of it.'

'Christ, sorry.'

'Ach.'

'Maybe it's not too late, you could get back in touch? These days it's not so hard to track people down . . . '

'C'mon, Alan. Don't talk shite now.'

Craig reached for his wine and Alan reached for a change of gear. 'So, what about music? You never went anywhere without a guitar in your hands. Don't you ever play?' Alan remembered Craig in the common room at school, playing a note-perfect rendition of 'Sunday Bloody Sunday' on an acoustic while a ring of girls watched spellbound.

'Naw. Not in ages and ages.'

'Is it, is it too painful to play? Does it bring back, you know . . . ?'

'Nah. Just never near a guitar these days. How about you?'

'I'll pick up Tom's now and then. I was never,

24

you know, never as good as you.'

'Ach, you weren't bad . . . '

They both knew this was a lie: Alan in Craig's tiny bedroom back in that pebble-dashed council house in Ardgirvan, in the early eighties, watching Craig's fingers fly up and down the fretboard as he played seemingly everything by the Clash, the Jam, the Buzzcocks (then, later, the Smiths, Orange Juice, Lloyd Cole) on his Hondo Les Paul copy, the wee practice amp at full roar, Alan trying to emulate and follow, but each of his fingers a black pudding, a sausage roll, a flaccid penis next to Craig's trilling digits as they knocked out nimble lead runs, string bending, hammer on and vibrato. The way Alan could eventually master a simple chord sequence if he did nothing else but listen to the record and slavishly copy it for two weeks. Meanwhile there was Craig — playing along note-for-note with songs he was hearing for the first time. Alan had finally, briefly, made it into an early line-up of Craig's band. On *bass*. (And, Alan suspected, that was simply because his parents were the only ones who had the money to buy him a decent amp.)

'Aye, right,' Alan said, 'now who's talking shite?' They both laughed. Alan was enjoying talking Scottish again. 'You kicked me out of the band for Jim Rankin first chance you got!'

'Fuck, wee Jim,' Craig said. 'Good bassist but a total mental.'

'He sent me a friend request on Facebook a few years back.'

'Mind the time he shat in a Kwenchy Kup and tried tae launch it aff the window of the

25

headmaster's office but ended up wi half of it all over him?'

Alan sprayed wine across the table as the two of them collapsed, broken with laughter. 'Aye, aye, fuck! At the Christmas disco? He was stumbling around screaming, covered — '

'In his own shite! Oh man. Wonder what happened tae him?'

'I think he said he was manager of that big B&Q out by the bypass to Kilmarnock.'

A pause. They looked each other in the eye and collapsed laughing again. Craig was slapping his thigh manically, just like he always used to do, and suddenly the years had fallen away and they were sixteen again, cracking each other up in class, ripping the piss out of someone, dogging school to listen to records and make prank phone calls to random numbers.

'Oh, Jesus Christ. Man . . . ' Alan said as he reached for the bottle again and was surprised to find it empty. He signalled for the waitress, the sweet little one he liked. Clara? That was it.

'Having fun, Alan?' she said as she approached.

'Clara, yeah. Sorry, are we too loud?'

'Of course not.'

'This is my friend Craig. We haven't see in each other in a while.'

'Hi.' She beamed at Craig. 'What can I get you boys?'

'Same again please,' Alan said.

She took the empty bottle from the ice bucket and wiggled off towards the bar.

'Is there anywhere we can smoke?' Craig asked.

'Err, sure. Come on and we'll go up to the exercise yard.'

The Groucho's smoking area did indeed resemble a small prison exercise yard. The two of them staggered out, holding brimming glasses, both surprised to find that twilight had been replaced by total darkness. There were a few people scattered around, smoking, drinking, talking. Craig produced a ten-pack of some low-rent cigarettes — Raffles or Piccadilly or Mayfair or something — and proffered one of the two remaining fags to Alan.

'God — no. I haven't smoked in years,' Alan said.

Craig shrugged and lit his as he asked, 'Do you ever see anyone else from back home?'

'Nah,' Alan said. 'Oh, apart from Charlie and Donald.'

'Oh aye?'

'Aye, we go off on a golf trip once or twice a year. Gordon Miller and Alec McLean come too sometimes.'

'Fuck. All the guys ye went tae uni with?'

'Pretty much. Ye should — ' Alan was about to say 'Ye should come along sometime' — he remembered Craig as being a decent golfer when they were young. Then he remembered the situation they were in. The fact that Craig was unlikely to have a set of clubs tucked into that bundle downstairs, or a spare few hundred quid for the hotels and the green fees and the sumptuous meals and expensive malt whiskies they consumed in the evenings. He modulated it to 'Ye should see the state of Gordon these days.

27

Got to be twenty stone . . . '

'Fucking hell.'

'Ah'm telling ye.'

'Fat bastard.'

'And Charlie's bald as a coot.'

'Is that right?'

'Donald hasn't aged a day. I swear to God, there's a portrait in an attic somewhere that looks like fucking Methuselah.' He drained his glass as Craig laughed. 'You know what, can I? I'll buy some more . . . ' He reached for Craig's last cigarette.

'Sure . . . '

He took a deep puff. *Oh baby*. That was the real stuff. The headrush was considerable and he stood swaying on the balls of his feet. *Smoking — where have you been? What harm could you possibly do me?* It was bliss. Alan had been wasting his life with children and family and writing columns and books and talking crap on TV shows when he could have been attending to his true calling — hanging out smoking and drinking in private members' clubs with Craig Carmichael. The split second it took Alan to entertain this thought also gave him time to realise how very, very drunk he was. He also realised that someone was saying hello to him. 'Oh hi!'

'Alan! I thought that was you. How are you, darling?' She kissed him wetly, drunkenly, on both cheeks.

'Great, great. How's tricks?' He had no idea who the woman was. She was early thirties, very attractive. Undoubtedly in TV or publishing. Use the oldest trick in the book? Why not. 'This is my friend Craig . . . '

Craig held his hand out. 'Amanda Reed,' she said, taking it with some curiosity. That was it — Amanda. Development executive at some production company. They'd tried to work up a pilot with him a few years back. A cookery show, obviously, based around *Pause Button*. Nothing came of it. How many cheeks had he air-kissed in here? How many drunken ideas had been hatched and meetings arranged that nothing ever came of? 'Craig's a writer,' Alan said for no good reason he could figure out.

'Really?' Amanda Reed said.

'Aye,' Craig said, not missing a beat. They made an odd pair, Alan and Craig, one short, one tall. One with a pure wool overcoat draped over his shoulders. One in a filthy parka, matted jeans, stubbly beard and battered trainers. Yes, come to think of it, he really did look like a writer.

'Any good TV ideas? We're always looking.' Amanda hiked her bag up over her shoulder.

'A good one actually,' Craig said. 'Scripted reality show about oil rig workers in the North Sea.'

Alan found his eyebrows heading up towards his hairline.

'How *interesting*. Here . . . ' She produced the inevitable business card. 'Give me a call and we'll set up a meeting. Must dash — bloody dinner.' She smacked a kiss on Alan's cheek again. 'Alan, let's get together soon. Craig — lovely to meet you.' She disappeared back into the club.

29

Alan looked at Craig, who was turning the business card over in his hands. His fingernails, Alan noticed, were absolutely black. 'Scripted fucking reality show?' Alan said.

'Ach, I read about them in this bit of the *Guardian* I found in Green Park the other day,' Craig said and, once again, the two of them were falling around laughing. 'Oh man, that . . . that's too good. Right, one for the road?'

They had a whisky for the road back in the downstairs bar and another one after that, at which point Alan found himself buying two packs of Marlboro Lights and giving one to Craig and then, finally, he looked at his watch: 7.20. Shit. Where the fuck had the last five hours gone? He'd told Katie he'd back for dinner at eight. If he left right now and got a cab straight away he could just make the 7.45 fast train that got in at 8.10. 'Fuck,' Alan said. 'Got to make a move.'

'Nae bother,' Craig said.

Out on the pavement it was cold, their breath forming in silvery clouds out on Dean Street.

'Well,' Alan said. 'Look, Craig, it's been great catching up again.'

'Aye, thanks very much for all the drinks and whatnot.'

'Don't mention it.' In the distance, near the junction with Shaftesbury Avenue, a couple of hundred yards away, Alan could see the orange beacon of a cab moving slowly towards them. Craig shifted his pack onto his shoulders. What to say? What do you normally say? *Gimme your number? Let's have dinner sometime?* How do you? When someone is, when they have no . . . 'Look,' Alan said, reaching into his pocket. He brought out a sheaf of notes, fifty or sixty quid.

'Take this, Craig.'

'Naw, Alan.'

'Please.'

'Widnae feel right.'

'Come on. For old times' sake. Get a hostel or a B&B or something for the night. Get out the cold.' Suddenly Alan felt rotten and hollow. What a stupid thing to do — taking the guy off the streets for a few hours, parading him around and then throwing him back on the pavement. The cab was close now and still unmolested. Alan felt his hand automatically going into the air. 'Come on. Take it. It's all the cash I have.'

'Are . . . are ye sure?'

Alan pressed the notes into Craig's hand.

'Thanks, thanks very much, Alan. You take care of yourself now. Maybe see you again sometime?'

Walk away. Walk away right now.

'Yeah, sure, hang on.' Alan turned to the cabbie. 'Marylebone Station please.' The doors of the cab unlocked with a chunky clack. He turned back to Craig and held his hand out. 'Take care, Craig.' They shook, and before he knew it Alan had pulled him in for a hug. He *did* smell a bit.

Walk away.

'See ye,' Craig said. He turned and headed south, back towards Shaftesbury Avenue, heading into the wind. Alan stepped into the cab.

31

'Marylebone Station was it?' the cab driver said.

'Yeah, thanks.' Alan looked back out the window. At Craig, already receding into the crowd.

Walk away.

'Shit. Look, sorry, mate, can you just hang on a minute? Just, just pull up on the pavement here.'

'No problem.'

And then Alan was getting out of the cab.

4

'Sophie, it's after eight o'clock on a school night. If I hear you out of that bed *once more* there will be consequences.' Katie stood on the half-landing, ear cocked to the bedrooms above. Nothing. She went back down. Consequences. Yeah, right. Chance would be a fine thing. What consequences were there these days? Parents had long been disarmed. Being a parent was like being a cop in England. 'Stop. Or I'll say stop again.' She looked at the text on her phone once more as she walked down the long hallway back towards the kitchen, towards the smell of the chicken bubbling in white wine, vegetables and herbs from the garden: '*Sorry darling. Be half hour lat. xxc*'.

That 'lat', that rogue 'c' at the end. Alan's texts were always meticulously subbed. The very fact that he'd put three kisses too. Yes, undoubtedly pissed. She'd known he was headed there when he'd rung around five. Not that Katie minded that, Alan wasn't a bad drunk. Bit giggly and soppy. En route to the kitchen she glanced right into the small lounge, the TV room. Melissa was on the sofa, the TV on but her face lit by the glow of her phone as she scrolled and tapped away. 'Everything OK? Dad's home soon, but you can eat now if you like.'

'I'm fine.'

And what went on with that bloody phone?

Vanessa had recently discovered their sixteen-year-old son was on Tinder for Christ's sake. Mind you, the apple doesn't fall far and all that.

She checked the chicken, turned the oven down, and topped her wine up as she opened her laptop. Four hundred words into seven hundred and fifty words on, specifically, how Halloween had become a sexathon and, more generally, the sexualisation of children in society. It would be ideal if she could somehow bring in a few references to celebrities in scanty Halloween wear, give the picture editor something to work with. She googled 'Miley Cyrus Halloween outfit' and was rewarded with a link proclaiming 'Miley Cyrus Fancy Dress Grey Bear Twerk Leotard'. Katie lost the next ten minutes googling images of sexy celebrities you could dress up as at Halloween. She was so lost in this Woodward-and-Bernstein-ian wormhole (Kim Kardashian did a good Poison Ivy, you had to give her that) that the next thing she heard was the front door opening and voices in the hall and then Alan was coming into the kitchen. 'Hey!' He closed the door behind him — odd — and came over to the table. 'Sorry I'm late, bit of an, uh, situation.'

'Go on . . . ' Katie said, smiling, closing the laptop as he bent to ldss her forehead. 'Eeew! Have you . . . ?' She frowned. 'Have you been *smoking?*'

'Ah, a bit, yes. Now hang on, I'll have to be quick. He's in the living room.' Alan's voice was a stage whisper now. Thankfully they'd got some coffee into themselves on the train, had sobered up just enough.

'Eh?'

'Remember my friend Craig? The one who was in that band, years ago? The Rakes?'

'Band?'

'Yes, Christ, I've mentioned him loads of times.'

'Yes, right. What is it?'

He told her the short, short version. It took a couple of minutes.

'Bloody hell,' Katie said.

'Well, yeah. I just, watching him walk off to sleep on the fucking pavement. I couldn't do it.'

'He's not . . . he's not crazy, is he?'

'No! That's the thing. It was like catching up with someone from school, you know? Apart from the . . . '

'And how — ' here Katie lowered her voice — 'how dirty is he?'

'Pretty grubby. But just, more three-day-bender, I'm-in-the-Libertines kind of dirty as opposed to, you know, I've-soiled-myself dirty.'

'Christ. And how . . . how long is he — '

'A couple of days?'

'A couple of — '

'I just . . . I couldn't walk off and see him sleeping on the street. *Winter's coming*, you know. I thought I'd talk to Pandora, she's into all this stuff and — '

'What stuff?'

'You know, the homeless. Charity stuff. She did a big feature on it last year. Gave out sandwiches at Centrepoint and all that. See if she knows anyone who could help get a roof over his head. Come on, we can't just leave him in there.

35

Come and say hello. Honestly, he's really nice. Where's Melissa?'

'TV room.'

'Right, leave her for a minute.'

'Bloody hell, Alan.' She pushed herself up from the table.

They went back down the long hall, Katie nervously checking her hair in the big mirror as they passed it (why? — she was about to meet someone who slept in the street) and Alan opened the door to the lounge — it was the biggest room in the house, about thirty feet by twenty, high ceiling, original cornicing, what Alan's mum would have called their 'best' room — and there was Craig standing by the fireplace. He had his hands behind his back.

'Hey, Craig, this is Katie . . . '

'Hi,' Craig said nervously.

'Hi, Craig. Pleased to meet you.'

They shook hands. 'I'm, I'm really sorry about this, Katie,' Craig said. 'I told Alan this was a daft idea. I haven't sat down by the way.' He indicated the huge twin oatmeal sofas (Conran) that faced each other on either side of the fireplace, the two green leather tub chairs.

'Don't be silly, please sit down,' Katie said, thinking, *Please don't sit down*.

'Naw, I'm a bit, you know . . . ' While he spoke Katie noticed Craig refused to meet her gaze. His eyes darted around, hot with shame, picking out various spots on the floor, the walls. He reminded Katie of something. Something she'd been watching with Sophie the other day. That was it — the top ten guilty dogs of the Internet.

36

'And you and Alan went to school together?' Katie said, trying not to feel like the Queen meeting someone at a Crisis centre.

'Aye, we did. Funny, eh?Your house is lovely by the way.'

'Oh, thanks. Are you hungry?'

'Starving. It's just . . . ' He looked at Alan.

'Yeah, I was saying on the train, if Craig could just have a shower first and maybe borrow some clothes . . . '

'Of course,' Katie said. She looked at Craig, his slender frame and tiny waist. 'Although I think we're probably looking at some of Tom's clothes for Craig. No offence, darling.' They all laughed. 'Why don't you take Craig upstairs and sort out towels and whatnot. Have a look in Tom's wardrobe and see what might fit. I'll get supper ready. We'll deal with making the spare room up later.'

'Great,' Alan said. 'Follow me . . . '

Craig stopped as he passed close to Katie and looked at her for the first time. 'Thank you,' he said. 'I'm really sorry for the imposition.' His eyes were very clear. Dark, dark blue. Piercing.

'Don't be silly,' Katie said. Craig followed Alan out of the room and up the stairs. Yes. You could definitely smell him a bit. Hating herself for doing it, feeling this was a real I-have-become-my-mother moment, Katie went over to the sofa nearest to her, bent down, and examined the cushions. He definitely hadn't sat down, had he? She sniffed experimentally here and there.

'What on earth are you doing?'

Katie turned. Melissa in the doorway.

37

'I, uh, just . . . what is it, Melissa?'

'What's going on? I heard voices.'

'Your father's brought a friend back for supper.'

'Who?'

'A school friend.'

'What are they doing up there?'

From upstairs came the sound of the showerhead in the big bathroom rumbling powerfully into life. 'I think he's staying the night. I — look, Melissa, are you hungry? It's nearly nine. Do you want to eat now?'

'I'll wait till the grand tour's over upstairs.'

'Fine. And don't slouch, darling. Now listen. About your father's friend.'

She told her. Melissa's mouth went into a tiny 'O'. 'Holy. Shit. He's a tramp? A real-life *derelicte*?'

'Yes and it's not funny. There but for the grace of God go you and I, Melissa.' *Yes, 100 Mum points there*, Katie thought.

'What, what if he *robs* us?'

'For Christ's sake, Melissa, he's not going to rob us,' Katie said, shamefully thinking it might actually be an idea to hide the wallets, purses, laptops and iPhones overnight.

They ate dinner — *pot-au-feu* with new potatoes and a green salad — at the kitchen table. Craig had scrubbed up pinkly. Impressively, Katie thought, given that he'd been sleeping rough, his hair, crazy and unkempt though it was, was still very dark at nearly fifty — 100 per cent not a dye job. (And where would he have dyed it? In the fountains at Trafalgar

38

Square? Imagine the uproar in the *Daily Mail* if it transpired the homeless could afford to dye their hair?) He was wearing one of Tom's grey crew-neck T-shirts and a pair of his jeans. Impressive waistline for someone his age.

'Really nice chicken,' Craig said.

'Dig in. There's plenty of bread here.'

Alan was, again, impressed with his wife. A product of the upper classes, Katie was completely at ease with people dropping in for supper unannounced. She could whip up dinner for eight at a moment's notice from, seemingly, a potato and some stock. Alan tried to imagine how his mother would have coped with a stranger suddenly appearing for supper at eight thirty in the evening and found he couldn't get very far with the scenario — mainly because his mother would have eaten supper three hours before. She also wouldn't have known what the fuck 'supper' was.

'What was Dad like at school?' Melissa asked. She was fascinated by his teeth. They were awful. Little yellow pegs. Also his accent. Her father was Scottish, but you could barely tell. This man, however. Melissa reckoned she was getting one word in five.

'A pain in the erse,' Alan said.

'Clever. Always did well in exams.'

Alan tapped his head with a piece of bread to indicate 'not so dumb' to his daughter.

'Yeah, exams in *Scotland*,' Katie said.

'Hey, you, ya wee snob,' Alan said.

'Dad? Why are you talking like this?' Melissa said.

'Like what?'

'Like this. 'Erse'. 'Ya wee'. You've gone full Scottish since Craig's been here.'

Katie snorted. 'You have actually.'

'Ach, get it up yese,' Alan said. They all laughed.

'Maybe I'm a bad influence,' Craig said.

5

Alan woke up and blearily checked the clock next to the bed: 7.12 a.m. He ran the damage check. Limbs? Not aching. Head? Not pounding. Mouth? Mildly dry, nothing drastic. Stomach? Fine. What a result. He did the thing of counting his drinks. Two halves and one, no, two pints in the pub. Two bottles of wine between two of them in the Groucho. Oh — and a couple of whiskies. But he'd stopped early, stopped drinking really at about 8 p.m. — that coffee on the train had been the turning point. He'd just sipped a single glass of wine with dinner and they'd gone to bed very soon after. Not bad. Right on the cut-off point of having a proper hangover, thank God.

He was aware of Katie moving around the darkened room, gathering things. Dressing. It was one of her London days. 'Morning,' Alan mumbled from beneath the duvet.

'Morning yourself, there's tea there.'

He saw the mug steaming on his bedside table, the yellow *Balamory* mug, a mug it was well known he hated. *Balamory* — the kids' TV show much beloved of Sophie a few years back (and Melissa before her, it was after Tom's time). It was aimed at preschool children and dealt with the comings and goings of folk in a fictional island in Scotland. All ethnic groups were represented — black, white, fat, thin, gay (the

41

town policeman was absolutely *flaming*, to the point where Alan had wondered if he might not be part of a brilliantly ingenious BBC scheme to actively promote homosexuality to children behind the government's back), disabled — and everyone got along famously. The plotlines all dealt with stuff like helping someone else do some fucking thing. As a family they had visited the island where the programme was shot, when holidaying up there a few years back. Alan had got in with some locals at the hotel bar, where, over a bracing round of malts, he had been delighted to learn about which of the cast members were raving alcoholics, which were utter shits and which would literally do it with the coalman behind the bus stop for 50p. Initially, of course, he was driven to murderous tears of rage by the programme and used to survive the repeated early-morning viewings only by imagining the wonderful, appalling things he could do to various cast members had he the use of a soundproofed basement and some surgical instruments. Had he been apprehended mid-flaying, he often thought, all he would have to do by way of mounting a defence would be to show the court a video of the average episode and the 'acting' it contained. No judge in the land would convict him. (Convict him? He'd get the George fucking Medal.) But, over time, a funny thing happened. Alan found that he would be tuning into *Balamory* before Sophie even asked for it. He found his heart lifting as that boat sailed over the sparkling water towards the green place where no man or woman was hated on account

42

of their appearance or sexual preference. He enjoyed the visual fabric of island life: the sunny harbour, the windy high street, the battlements of Archie the Inventor's castle (a local landowner, English, obviously, very possibly also gay and involved in something with the copper), and when Sophie finally started saying 'NO!' when he tuned to the show in the mornings (having intellectually bested its screenwriters somewhere around the age of four and moved on to violent cartoons), it was with a heavy heart that Alan realised a troubling fact: like a kind of modern-day Winston Smith with tears of Victory gin running down his face — he loved *Balamory*. Katie had bought him the mug — ironically — as a parting shot in the island gift shop and it depicted PC Plum looking jolly (no doubt having recently had, or being in the act of planning, a buggery). Why did Alan hate the *Balamory* mug? He just did. We do not enjoy dispassionate relations with inanimate objects, do we? This bowl or plate, that knife or grater or peeler is a favourite. That other is banished to drawer Siberia. Nowhere is this more crystallised than in the field of mugs. Just something to do with the shape of it, the feel of it in the hand, the volume of tea or coffee it will contain (mustn't be too much or too little) and the colour the inside of the mug will turn the beverage. The mugs tremble in their hierarchy in the cupboard as the master or mistress approaches and there are some — like the fat kid with the cola-bottle-bottom glasses at school — that will never know the joy of being picked. We do not consciously go through all of this. We just know we like 'him' and we don't like 'him'. Just as Alan did not go through the rich history of mug theory right now, he merely looked at it in the half-light and said, 'I hate the fucking *Balamory* mug.'

'Everything — and I mean *everything* — is in the dishwasher,' Katie said.

He sat up and sipped the weak tea. Katie made terrible tea.

It was still dark outside. 'Right, I'll be back around four. So, tell me, what are your plans for the day?'

'Plans?'

'With our guest.'

'Oh. Well, I — ' Of course he had no idea. Somewhere in his head Alan had thought this would be simple. That they'd have breakfast and share a few amusing memories from their youth, Alan would then give Craig his dry, clean clothes back (he'd perhaps even throw in a few new sweaters, from the Mum drawer; the vast collection of woollen oddities that had come his way as presents over the years, all testimonies to how strangely the simple words 'a crew neck or V-neck in plain black or navy' could be interpreted) before slipping him a few quid (how much was a vexing question, true. A few hundred would seem about right. Anything less might be insulting, anything more might open the door to Craig saying something like 'You know, with a few thousand . . . ') and sending him on his way.

It was also possible that Craig would just wake

up, thank him for a lovely evening, tell him how nice it was to catch up, and see you around. But really, Alan had no idea how it was going to go. Not that he could say this to Katie. 'I'll let him sleep in a bit and then see what he wants to do. I thought I might take him shopping for a few bits and pieces. Maybe some new shoes . . . '

'And you're going to talk to Pandora?'

'Yes, I'm in town tomorrow.'

'Don't get me wrong, he seems very nice and we've got plenty of space and all th — '

'EVERYTHING IS AWESOME!' and a pair of knees were headed for his chest. Alan just had time to set his mug down on the bedside table before Sophie smashed into him. Sophie always woke up somewhere around 7 a.m. Never later. Holidays, weekends, it didn't matter if you kept her up until two in the morning or she went to bed at 7 p.m. She would be awake — fully, screamingly awake — by 7 a.m. Alan sometimes thought about conducting an experiment where they kept the child up all night until 6.59 a.m. to see if she'd fall fast asleep for one minute to reboot before snapping awake again at 7 on the dot. Right now, however, he was grateful for the distraction.

'Look,' he said to Katie while wrestling with Sophie over the remote control for the TV, 'we'll figure it out. Play it by ear.'

'Mmmm, I thought you might say that . . . '

'SOFIA THE FIRST!'

'I'll call you after I — no chance, Soph — talk to — '

'I'm not saying just kick him — '

45

'We're watching the news. I know you're not, Ka — '

'*HORRID HENRY!*' Alan was thumbing through the channels now. Infuriatingly the TV had come on on one of the kids' channels. He had to get out of here quick, before something really juicy caught her eye.

'Soph, please, Mummy and Daddy are — '

'OK then.' Katie went through into their en suite.

'*AVENGERS ASSEMBLE!*'

'Sophie, do we have to do this every morning?'

'What?'

'Every morning you come in here and demand kids' programmes on our TV and every morning I tell you that, during the week, we watch the news first.'

'NO! CHILDREN'S TV!' He could solve this. Sophie's iPad, her seventh-birthday present, was in his bedside drawer, but they'd agreed her access to this extravagant gift would be heavily policed — a good balance of educational apps and no handing it to her just to obtain yourself five minutes' peace. He found BBC1 — the girl who did the stock market looking very serious about something. He turned the volume up. ' . . . who announced record profits this quarter.' Supermarket profits. Some fucker at *BBC Breakfast* was absolutely obsessed with supermarket profits. Every other day it seemed there was a long feature on the subject.

'THIS IS BORING!'

'Oh for God's sake, go and get ready for school!'

46

'BORING!'
'Oh here . . . '
He gave her the iPad.
'YAYYY!'

6

Ten o'clock found the house at peace (the girls off to school, Katie off to London, Craig still sleeping, and the only sound Petra the cleaner moving around somewhere towards the back of the place) and Alan hunkered down in his study over his review of Grease and Fire, yesterday's burger joint.

Increasingly, after twenty years in the game, he felt there was little place for the one thing people probably (rightly) expected in criticism: reason. Only two kinds of review really played these days: the five-star rave and the one-star panning. The latter was all too common. Understandably so, because most things were bad, weren't they? Most architecture, most books, most films, most music, most food, and, consequently, most restaurants, were bad. In fact, most *criticism* was bad. (If you wanted validation of this theory all you had to do was to see what the amateurs were up to — click onto the comments thread of pretty much any review and behold the sightless monsters that lived beneath the waterline, all stumbling around screaming about the short-comings of the piece they had just read, shortcomings that could usually be summed by saying: 'THIS IS NOT EXACTLY WHAT I WOULD HAVE WRITTEN. WHY IS NO ONE LISTENING TO ME?')

Also, and this was something he felt he had to

48

whisper, certainly to his editors and most of his peers, who really gave a shit about the food in restaurants? In the kind of restaurants he ate in at any rate. Once you were somewhere in central London where the cost of the meal rose much above fifty quid per head, it was unlikely that you were actually going to get a gurgling abortion served live at the table. If you were in a reasonably pleasant environment, surrounded by people you liked, with access to as much booze as you needed and it didn't take three-quarters of an hour between courses, then who really gave a fuck about the nuances of the food? (Yes, if you were going to eat in places where a roast dinner cost £4.99, or where they had pictures of the food on the menu, some chain place called 'TEXAN BOB'S CRAZY GOOD TIMES FUN FOOD EMPORIUM', then obviously your dinner prep would consist of some teenage Pole throwing a plastic sac into a microwave and fuck you for expecting otherwise.) Maybe two or three times a year Alan ate something that genuinely made him think, *How on earth did you do this?* Most nights he'd be perfectly happy to eat a thickly buttered baked potato straight from the oven. Sadly 'who really gives a fuck, let's all have a baked potato' wasn't paying the bills. Strong opinions of between seven hundred and fifteen hundred words were what paid the bills.

So here he was — with the *Chambers* and the *Roget* cracked open on the desk, trying to come up with a new and interesting way of saying 'viscous'. He wriggled uncomfortably in his chair a little. Blocked. And not in the writer's sense. When had he last had a proper . . . two, three days ago?

Alan's study was every inch the ideal of the writer's den. Three of the walls were lined with handmade bookshelves, crammed with heavy hardbacks. There was a sofa and his 'reading chair', a low comfortable armchair with matching footstool and side table for coffee or whisky, and the fireplace, where a log was already burning on this cold morning. Then there was his desk: a Victorian partner's job in dark-stained oak with green leather inlay, a green banker's lamp sat in the corner, his MacBook Pro in the middle. The main desk was abutted on the right by a sleek glass table that made an L-shape and that housed his printer and whatever books he wanted to hand. Behind his desk French windows gave onto the front lawn. Perhaps it was because the room was so much the ideal writing lair that Alan sometimes found himself playing with uncomfortable thoughts in here. His eyes drifted towards the top right-hand corner of the bookshelves on the wall facing him, the section devoted to his own work. There, next to a row of paperback editions of *Eating Out, Speaking Out*, the first collection of his restaurant columns, was a single copy of *The Eagle Banquette Murders*, his novel.

His agent had obtained a deal for him to write a novel fairly easily following the success of *Pause Button*. And, for a time, when he was working on it, Alan had felt like what he always fancied he might become: a real writer. He'd lost himself in crafting his plot (a fabulous young chef called Stephan — hot-headed, flamboyant, basically Marco Pierre White — wrongly becomes a suspect in a murder that takes place in his happening new gastropub. He must solve the crime himself in order to clear his name. They'd pitched it as Agatha Christie in the world of celebrity cooking), he'd sweated over his dialogue, loading it with just enough kitchen jargon to make it feel real, but hopefully not too much that the research clanged on the page. He'd gradually come to truly care for and believe in his characters. There was a problem, however.

No one else did.

The book was eviscerated in the review sections. He got a nod for the bad sex award (the scene where Stephan fucks Rachel, the detective in charge of the investigation, in the dry-goods store. He could still remember writing the scene, late one evening, lost in a frenzy of what he believed at the time was the Muse incarnate, but what he now realised was a tantrum of drink-fuelled false artistry) before the novel sold fifteen hundred copies in hardback then vanished without trace.

It seemed that when Alan was venting spleen about the length of time it took someone to bring him a cocktail, or how could it be so difficult to cook a piece of tuna properly, then people believed him. They bought his tone. When he tried to reach for the higher voice of fiction, to create characters and a world that rang with life and vitality, the response was 'No thanks. We're all right.' So he'd gone quietly back to restaurant reviewing, cookbooks and the TV and radio appearances, sadly filing the role of 'novelist' under something he'd given a go but would never be comfortable with. Like French. Or skiing. Or anal sex.

From somewhere two floors above him in the house (the spider detecting something at the outer reaches of its web) he heard pipes juddering, the high-pitched squeak of water being forced through old plumbing. Craig was finally on the move. (To be fair, who knew how long it had been since he'd experienced clean, snow-white sheets and a warm toasty room.) Alan took a moment to complete his final (scathing) paragraph before he headed into the kitchen, where he put the kettle on, took some bacon out of the fridge, and started busying himself with mugs, coffee and cafetière.

He was just pressing the plunger down where he heard 'A'right?' and turned to see Craig in the kitchen doorway, scratching his head sheepishly in Tom's old T-shirt and jeans.

'Excellent timing,' Alan said.

★   ★   ★

'Mind that time Big Murdo made the homebrew cider? It was jist water wi an apple pulled though it. And Mad Marky drank aboot four pints o it and spewed up all over the couch at Rab's party?'

'Aye! Rab's party. Fuck,' Alan said. 'That was the wan where his big brother shot the record player wi an airgun after we played 'Tom Hark' by the Piranhas for the third time in a row and Wee Sammy got caught finger — '

Both of them together — 'FINGERING FAT SENGA IN THE BOG!' They shrieked with laughter, Alan pounding the table with his fist. They were back in fourth year at school. Sixteen years old. Everyone was 'Big' or 'Mad' or 'Wee'. Both of their accents had thickened back into full, broad Ardgirvan. If Katie had walked into the kitchen right now she wouldn't have been able to understand a word her own husband was saying.

The plates in front of them — bacon rind and toast crusts and a smear of egg. 'Here,' Alan said, picking up the empty cafetière and heading for the sink, 'what do you think happened tae Mad Marky?'

'Christ,' said Craig. 'The jail?'

'Or ho — ' With a flash of horror Alan realised he was about to say 'homeless'. Improvising quickly he said, 'Or how about Murdo? That mad pervert.'

'Probably a pillar o the community now,' Craig said.

'Hang on,' Alan said, 'why guess?' He put the kettle on and grabbed the family iPad from its magnetic holder on the fridge-freezer. A couple of taps brought him to Facebook where he typed in 'David Murdoch, Ardgirvan'. A bunch of possibilities came up before there it was — a face both of them had known so well over thirty years ago. 'No way, man . . . ' Alan said, 'check it out!' He went over and put the iPad in front of Craig. There he was — Big Murdo. And 'big' wasn't quite covering it these days. 'Gargantuan Murdo' would be nearer the mark.

'The . . . the fucken state o it' was all Craig could manage. There he was — in a wetsuit of all things, on some beach somewhere, like a mammoth seal, giving a grinning thumbs up to the camera. They both fell about laughing. ' "Married to Leanne, lives in Ardgirvan.' He still fucking lives in Ardgirvan,' Alan said, shaking his head as he read on. ' "Works at Henderson's Forklift Trucks.' Fuck — was that not where he started right after school? The cunt's been there for thirty-two years?'

'Mental,' Craig said, taking the iPad as Alan went back to finish making the coffee. 'Christ, ye can see everything he's been up to on this . . . '

'You're not up on the social media stuff then?'

'No much use for it the past few years, Alan.'

'There's probably stuff on there about your band, you know.'

'Aye?'

'I bet there is. Here, type it in.'

'How do I . . . ?' Craig fumbled with the device.

'Here.' Alan came over. He tapped on the 'search' box and typed 'the Rakes band'. Up it all came — a picture of the 23-year-old Craig, glaring moodily at the camera, a black Rickenbacker cradled in his hands.

'Fuck,' Craig said.

'Look, you've got a Wikipedia page . . . ' He clicked on it. ' "The Rakes were an indie-rock group from Glasgow, Scotland,'' Alan read. ' "They were formed in 1989 by Grahame

54

Walker, Craig Carmichael, David . . . ' blah blah blah. 'They enjoyed a minor US hit in 1993 with their single 'Daybreak' . . . '' Craig read on as Alan sat down and started pouring the coffee.

'Christ, some of this is just bollocks,' Craig said.

'Aye, well, that's the Internet for you, mate.'

'Jesus, these photos . . . '

'Here, there's a thought,' Alan said. 'Do you not still get any royalties off that song?'

'I wish. Nah, we signed some daft publishing deal, took a load of money upfront and gave away all the rights. I think. Fuck knows.'

'You should look into that,' Alan said, thinking.

'Aye, maybe. Look at Grahame there. For fuck's sake, he's — '

Suddenly Craig broke off and was quiet.

'What?' Alan said.

'Och, nothing. Jist, you know . . . '

Alan looked at the iPad, at the photograph of four boys with spiked and slicked-back hair, in black leather jackets and striped tops, holding black guitars, full of hope and defiance and youth, their eyes glittering with the certainty that kingdoms would be conquered and why would the world not give you everything that you asked of it? They were eyes that had only experienced good things and saw only the promise of good things to come. Then Alan looked back up, at one of the four faces from the photograph, the face now lined and drawn, the eyes dull and cloudy. Alan sipped his coffee and watched Craig clicking through photographs of himself from a quarter of a century ago and he thought about how very glad he was that he hadn't experienced the crazed rush of success in his youth only to find out that it was a mirage, a phantom gone off to dance on another mountaintop, leaving you alone and bereft, leaving you twenty-five years old and with only leftover life to kill.

'Come on then,' Alan said, hitting the home button, the screen going black. 'Let's go for a wander round town. Show you the sights.'

'Sights?'

'Well, I'm using the term loosely.'

7

'How odd,' Vanessa repeated, draining the bottle of Gavi into her glass and signalling the waiter for another, shaking the empty bottle in his direction with a mad grin and a thumbs up. 'How very odd . . . '

Katie was lunching with Vanessa, Camilla and Emily. They were in the courtyard of 76 Dean Street — coats buttoned up against the cold — so that they could smoke. Each of the girls had a different approach to smoking. Katie was very much of the 'two drinks and I'll have a couple of fags' school. Vanessa smoked constantly and unrepentantly — somewhere in the region of forty a day. When she wasn't smoking a cigarette she was wielding a vape the size of a clarinet. Camilla also seemed to smoke all the time although no human being had ever witnessed her engaged in the act of actually *buying* cigarettes. Emily was of the 'just give us a puff, I don't want a whole one' school, very much believing that if she never took full possession of a smouldering Marlboro Light then she could never possibly get cancer. This meant that with the four of them smoking full tilt (as they were now, deep into the third bottle) it was costing Vanessa a whole pack an hour — or fifteen pounds an hour at Soho House prices, including Vanessa's generous tipping policy It vaguely troubled her that this was more than she paid her cleaner.

'How very, very odd,' Vanessa said once again.

'That's one word for it,' Camilla said.

'You think it's mental?' Katie asked.

'Well, duh!' Camilla said.

'I think it's sweet,' Emily said.

'Oh do shut up, Emily,' Vanessa said. 'Right, let's just recap. Alan meets this guy in Soho. He's literally on the streets.'

'Yep.'

'They go drinking in the Coach and Horses.'

'Yep.'

'Why did they go to a *pub*?' Camilla said, doing a very good job of making 'pub' sound like 'Belsen' or 'anus'.

'Trampy too smelly for club?' Vanessa.

'Yep.'

'How come they went to Groucho later?' Emily.

'Pissed by that point?' Vanessa.

'Yep again.'

'So then they rock up at yours, pissed, you have supper, Trampy is — '

'Stop calling him Trampy, Vanessa,' Katie said, 'his name's Craig and there but for the grace of God and all that . . . '

'OK, OK. Craig is perfectly pleasant and then this morning Alan implies he's going to be staying a while.'

' 'A couple of days' were the actual words.'

'Yes, how very odd,' Vanessa repeated.

'Is Tram — Craig hot?' Camilla.

'Well . . . '

'What was the name of his band again?' Emily.

'Oh, the . . . something.'

58

'Can you be just a little more specific, Granny?'

'Began with an R. The Rifles, the Ramps . . . '

'The Rapists?' Camilla.

'The Rakes! That was it.'

'And how well did Alan know him back in the day? Oh, thank you, darling!' Vanessa addressed this last comment to the waiter who had arrived with a fresh bottle of wine.

'They were at school together. Then uni for a while.'

'Here we go!' said Emily.

Camilla snatched the phone from her and lowered her glasses to scrutinise the screen. 'Mmm,' she said. 'Would. Definitely would.' She passed the phone around — the same photograph Alan and Craig had been looking at earlier.

'Bear in mind this is, what, thirty years ago?' Vanessa said.

'And that Camilla would do Fred West Dominic West?' Katie put in.

'In a heartbeat,' Camilla said.

'Well, I hate to be the Dowager Boring,' Vanessa said, 'but you do have Melissa to consider in all this . . . '

'I know . . . ' Katie said.

'Who?' Emily said.

'Her sixteen-year-old daughter?' Vanessa explained.

'Eh?'

Vanessa spelled it out, as you would for an infant. 'Trampy. Man. Insert. Penis. In. Hot. Teenage. Daughter.'

'Eeeewww!' Emily said.

'Oh, don't be ridiculous, V,' Katie said.

59

But, of course, the thought had flashed through her mind. Not just about Melissa, about Sophie too. For this is what the mind seems to like doing when you are a mother — it finds time to invent awful, appalling galas of torture for your children. Your child is quarter of an hour late home from school, or vanishes on the beach for three minutes, and the mind has already fashioned a convincing basement, with restraints and gags. It has come up with a terrible Central Casting paedophile. It has worked out its bleak indie-movie ending (the funeral), its middlebrow ending (the years of therapy with the broken child) and its blockbuster ending (the dramatic, last-minute rescue by SWAT team). Working in media, Katie's mind had already written the headlines, and the subheaders, and the pull quotes:

'GIRL OF SEVEN RAPED BY FAMILY FRIEND.'

'The girl, who cannot be named for legal reasons . . . '

'A source said friends had raised concerns about the unusual living arrangements . . . '

And then the child suddenly appears with some excruciatingly convoluted (and utterly innocent) excuse for the delay, sweet reason and sanity prevail, and you realise that your son or daughter is most likely not going to be abducted by a monster in much the same way that they are unlikely to be eaten by a shark, or die in an air disaster, or be struck by lightning. But then you read the newspapers: 'the five-year-old was raped on multiple occasions by . . . before disposing of

60

the body . . . the girl, fifteen, was subjected to . . . a long history of sexual violence . . . stabbed twenty-three times . . . discovered wrapped in a tarpaulin in the attic . . . '

These are all real. Who stabs a child a couple of dozen times? Who would rape a five-year-old? Who would cut a teenager's body into pieces and hide them in their attic?

Where were sweet reason and sanity when all of this was going on?

'I have to say,' Camilla said, looking at the photo again, 'when I was sixteen I'd have fractured my fucking pelvis opening my legs for that.'

'Jesus,' Emily said.

'Oh well,' Vanessa said. 'There's a good column in this.'

'Mmm. Alan might not be keen.'

Katie and Alan had a sort of uneasy détente about the degree to which she could use their private lives as grist for the column mill. Vanessa accepted no such restraints on hers. Consequently, Vanessa's Sunday column enjoyed a huge readership and she was paid a colossal figure for writing it, a fact that very much made her queen bee in this particular circle.

'Then maybe,' Vanessa said, 'I could — '

'No, Vanessa. If I can't write about it you're not bloody chiselling in there . . . '

'Fair enough,' Vanessa said, breaking the seal of the fresh pack of cigarettes.

8

While Katie lunched Alan and Craig had not been idle. In downtown Marham (their nearest conurbation and train link to London, a market town of about fifteen thousand people, mentioned in the Domesday Book) they had visited the newsagent's, then Costa, then Water stones, Alan as ever discreetly checking that at least a couple of his titles were on the shelves (they were: two copies of *Eating Out* and one of *Pause Button*), and finally the butcher's, where Alan bought some sausages, a duck and a large cut of brisket he intended to poach with some root vegetables for dinner that evening (Craig had marvelled that it was possible to spend over fifty pounds on these items), before arriving at 3.30 at the school gates to collect Sophie.

While they waited Alan introduced Craig to the other parents who came up to say hello, or to invite Sophie on the various play dates that seemed to consume much of her — and, with the driving, their — free time. (When did the play date become a thing? He'd never gone on a fucking play date when he was a kid. You just went and played.) Craig, Alan had to admit, had scrubbed up well. A good night's sleep and fresh clothes (he was wearing an old Barbour of Alan's now) had left him looking like he had every right to be waiting at the gates of a cripplingly expensive private girls' school in Buckinghamshire on a sunny winter afternoon. And by 'introduced' we should clarify that Alan simply said 'this is my friend Craig' repeatedly. He, of course, had no idea what the other parents' names were. The number of times, over dinner, in the kitchen, in the car, when Katie would say 'at Megan and George's place' and Alan would say 'who the fuck are Megan and George?' and Katie would sigh and say 'Emily's parents? Sophie's friend Emily?' And Alan would say 'oh yeah' while privately thinking something like, *Emily? Well, fuck her too.*

'DADDY!' He turned and saw Sophie's black-cloaked figure bounding towards them. (The girls all wore cloaks during the winter months.) 'Daddy, can we — ' As ever, Sophie was about to embark on a torturous request: 'can we go ten-pin bowling/miniature golfing/for sushi/to insert-name-of-friend's house' etc. But Alan cut her off by scooping her up and saying, 'Wait, Sophie, listen, this is my friend Craig.'

Sophie regarded Craig. 'THAT'S MY DAD-DY'S COAT!' she shrieked. Craig laughed.

'Yes, I know,' Alan said. 'Craig's just borrowing it. He forgot his. Say hello.'

'Hello.' Then, to Alan, 'You're a poo-bum.'

'Sophie . . . ' but she was already shrieking with laughter at her own wit.

'Right, let's go.'

'Where are we going?'

'Home!'

'Aww — home's boring, Daddy!'

'Do be quiet, Sophie. We have to make dinner.'

'Are you coming to dinner?' This was

addressed to Craig.

'Err, aye. I think so.'

'You're Scottish.'

'I am. Yeah.'

'My daddy is Scottish.'

'I know. I knew your daddy when he was your age.'

'Seven?' Sophie seemed incredulous.

'Yep.'

'Was he good?' Sophie asked.

'He was a poo-bum,' Craig said.

'AHHAHAHAHAHAHAHAHAHAHA!' Sophie shrieked. 'You *were* a poo-bum!'

'Yes,' Alan sighed. 'I was a poo-bum. Now get in the bloody car and calm down.'

★ ★ ★

The brisket went in the oven.

Sophie did her homework.

Melissa came home. ('Hi, Dad. Hi, Craig. Hi, Bum Face,' then off to her room.)

Around six they opened some wine.

Katie came home.

Dinner happened.

By 10.30 the girls were in their beds. Alan, Katie and Craig were in the living room, watching the news with their drinks: Craig was finishing the last of his red wine from dinner, Alan cradled a powerful tumbler of Talisker and Katie sipped a mug of green tea. (She'd looked a tiny bit the worse for wear when she'd come home earlier, Alan had thought, and she had drunk very little with dinner.)

'Right,' Craig said, yawning. 'I'll hit the sack.'

'Night, Craig,' Katie said.

'No nightcap?' Alan asked, brandishing his tumbler.

'Nah. Thanks. Would one of you mind giving me a shout in the morning? It's just . . . I don't have an alarm or anything.'

'Sure,' Alan said. 'What time?'

'As soon as you're up. I wanted to get off early.'

'Off where?'

Craig was hovering in the doorway now. 'Well, you know. It's been really nice catching up and all that, but probably time I was on my way.'

On your way where? Alan thought.

'It's Friday tomorrow,' Alan said. 'At least stay the weekend, eh?' He looked at Katie.

'Yes, of course. Stay the weekend,' she said.

'Ach, that's really kind, guys. But I think I'll get off. See you in the morning.'

They both waited until Craig's footsteps had retreated well into the upper reaches of the house before speaking. 'I'll talk to him again in the morning,' Alan said. 'I mean, on his way where? Where's he going?'

'Alan, darling, have you really thought this through?'

'How do you mean?'

'I mean — what's the long game here?'

'Well, I . . . '

'He can't just stay with us forever, you know.'

'Of course I know that. I just thought . . . till he gets on his feet a bit.'

'And how's that suddenly going to happen?'

65

'Oh, I don't know.'

'By you giving him some money, I suppose?'

'No. I — '

'And I wouldn't mind that. Honestly. A childhood friend who's wound up on the streets? I get it. It's sweet that you want to help him. But you can't give him the sort of money he'd need to turn his life around. That's assuming he wants to. I mean, you can't pay his rent for the rest of his life.'

'He just needs to — '

'I know how you think, Alan. You have this old-school Protestant work ethic where I can see you thinking if we just get him off the streets, he'll find some kind of job and sort himself out. Not everyone's built like that. I know it's like having your old pal back, and he seems very nice, but to end up where Craig did . . . he has to be quite damaged in some way.'

'He can't just have been unlucky?'

'He could be both.'

Alan sighed and twirled the glass in his palms. He looked up at the ceiling, fifteen feet above them, at the smooth white plaster, the ornate cornicing and the heavy brass-and-glass chandelier that had been a house-warming gift from Katie's parents, who had brought it back from France in the 1960s. 'It's just . . . when we're talking away. He seems just like the guy I knew thirty years ago.'

'But he's not.'

The fire crackled, the last log dying down, as both of them tuned into the TV again, where the weather lady had taken over from the newsman.

She was magically saying, ' . . . and temperatures are set to plummet over the weekend, reaching minus two in London and the southeast and as low as minus six degrees in parts of the Scottish Highlands . . . '

Alan looked at Katie, who was already imagining sleeping on the pavement in *that*.

'Look,' she said, 'I'll talk to him in the morning. He probably thinks I don't want him here. It's fine for the weekend, but just think on. We can't have him forever.' She got up and kissed him on the head. 'It's not your job to fix this, you know.'

'I know.'

'You're in town tomorrow, aren't you?'

'Yep. Editorial meeting.'

'Don't stay up too late.'

He sipped the last of his whisky and stared at the fire. Of course Alan, an inveterate fixer, was already thinking about fixing this.

★   ★   ★

Two floors above them Craig stretched out, still enjoying the feel of a soft bed for the first time in a long time. He listened to the creaks and sighs of the house around him. He couldn't hear any voices, the place was too big for anything to carry up here from the ground floor, but he knew they'd be talking about him down there. 'Poor' this and 'how sad' that. Oh well, he could take that. He'd take it. A little pity might go a long way here. She seemed very nice, the wife. The kids too. He opened his journal and started making a few notes. Some ideas.

9

In addition to his column, cookbooks and restaurant reviews, he was the editor of the *Standard on Sunday*'s Food Quarterly section. The job involved him being in the London office a few days every month, listening to pitches for feature ideas, deciding on photographers, approving layout and so forth. But what he was really paid for was the use of his contacts book to chisel celebrity faces into doing food-related things. For this small (and hardly time-consuming) sideline to his main job Alan was paid several times the national average salary. Shocking really, but there it was.

It was an odd thing, he thought. The four times a year the Food Quarterly appeared always saw an increase in the paper's circulation. (Admittedly the paper's circulation was now next to nothing compared to what it had been when Alan first started writing for it twenty years ago. The Internet. Free, it turned out, had been a pretty big incentive for many people when it came to deciding that newspapers were another essential they could get along well enough without, thank you very much.) People loved reading about food, in the same way that they loved buying cookery books and watching food on TV. And yet every quantifiable survey you could get your hands on showed that people cooked less and less. The figures for people who routinely made their own fresh food from scratch were tiny. Show someone on TV making a fish pie — lovingly photographed flakes of white cod gleaming in dollops of thick creamy sauce flecked with parsley and so forth — and the British public were there in droves. Actually making a fish pie? This was an activity for a tiny segment of the middle classes. Sweating off vegetables, peeling and boiling and mashing potatoes? Get bent. Most people would rather have their fish pie in a plastic tub, into which it had been lovingly pumped from a vat in a factory somewhere in Lancashire by someone in a boiler suit and a hairnet. The marketing department had once shown Alan a survey that said that if you regularly had a box of fresh vegetables delivered to your doorstep rather than a reeking slab of pizza then you were basically in the 0.01 percentile of the population.

In the meeting now in progress in the paper's glass-walled conference room with (just) a view of the Thames they were discussing the spring edition. Present along with Alan was his deputy editor Pandora, Arabella the PA they shared, and three freelancers called (he thought) Rory, Calum and Poppy. Alan rubbed his forehead as the conversation rambled on.

'But why a *bicycle*, Calum?' Pandora was saying.

'Well, everything else has been done to death, hasn't it? Cars, motorbikes . . . '

'France? Feels a bit . . . meh.' Poppy.

'He likes it there.' Calum shrugged.

'What about . . . India?' Pandora.

'Never go for that.'

69

'Or, oh oh, Holland! That's a very bicycle culture.'

'What fucking food comes out of Holland?'

'Bacon?' This was Arabella.

Alan suspected that Rory was actually asleep.

That morning Katie had taken tea up to Craig just before Alan left to get the train. She'd been up there a while and when she came back down to the kitchen she'd said, 'He'll be happy to stay the weekend. I told you — he thought I was pissed off.' 'And you're not?' Alan had asked. 'No. Definitely not. Promise.' And she'd kissed him on the nose, his marvellous wife.

'France would be so beautiful in terms of photos.'

'Pandora, have we actually budgeted this thing?' Alan finally asked.

'Well, we can get a freebie on the Eurostar — first class — if we mention them in the piece. I'm sure we'll get a deal on the hotels as long as —'

'Yes, yes, but the fee, photographer, expenses . . .'

'Probably about ten K. Ish. Whistles and bells.'

'Right, enough,' Alan said. 'Sorry, Calum, we are not spending ten grand so Alex James can spend a weekend cunting around the Ardennes on a bicycle eating nicking cheese.'

Calum looked chastened.

'What else do we have?' Alan asked.

It began.

Deep-sea fishing in Ireland with an Irish celebrity. ('Graham Norton?' Arabella volunteered.)

Al Murray on pies.

Cooking the perfect steak with Gérard Depardieu. (Someone seemed to throw this one

70

in at every meeting.)

Wine tasting with Ashley Cole.

Oysters in Whitstable with a seafood-hating celebrity.

A wild-food weekend in Scotland where three foodie celebrities caught, shot and foraged their own food.

What does Richard Branson eat on a long balloon trip?

My weekly shopping basket with Richard Osman.

My favourite restaurant: Colm Tóibín wasn't available but Jonathan Coe was definitely interested.

Alan looked through the glass wall and across the office to the news section of the paper, where serious men of his age were doubtless debating the hot, breaking political stories. And here he was — up to his teats in pure monkey tennis. He glanced around the room and guessed that, collectively, the money spent on the secondary-school educations alone of the five twenty- and thirty-somethings in here — the fees to Westminster and St Paul's and Wycombe Abbey and God knows where else — probably totalled well over a million pounds. Throw in prep and university and you could triple that. Yes, it had taken a few million quid — and a whole bunch of nepotism — to put this room together, a room that was now focusing its discursive powers on 'The Best Music Festivals for Food with Hugh Fearnley-Whittingstall'.

'Oh, Latitude would be *fantastic*,' Poppy was saying.

'OK,' Alan said, looking at his watch. 'That's lunch. Poppy — Hugh doesn't know the first thing about music. You might as well send Anthony Bourdain to a vegan restaurant. Arabella — Graham Norton deep-sea fishing? Are you on crack? A general note — if I hear Depardieu's Perfect Steak in here once more I will *flay* some fucker. Pandora — let's look into this wild-food hunting and foraging thing in Scotland. See who might be available.'

As Alan went to leave the room Rory suddenly sat forward and made his one contribution to the meeting. He held a finger in the air as, with great deliberation, he said the words, 'Clarkson cooking a full English breakfast on the bonnet of an Aston Martin in Death Valley.'

Alan nodded. 'See you all after lunch.'

He caught up with Pandora in the corridor.

'Hey. P.'

'I thought Rory was on excellent form today,' Pandora said. He laughed.

Alan and Pandora. Pandora and Alan.

There had very nearly been a mishap there, a couple of years back. They'd both been at the Cheltenham Literature Festival, Alan promoting the paperback of *More Eating Out, More Speaking Out* (hey, if ain't broke . . .) and Pandora covering the event for the paper. They'd been very drunk and Pandora — ten years his junior — had magically produced a wrap of coke from somewhere and said, 'Shall we be very naughty?' It had been on their third trip to the hotel bedroom that night — both of them at the desk with the CD case, the rolled-up twenty,

72

the little pile of powder and their excited yabber about *what a cunt X was and how this stuff was actually really good and that you often got better cocaine outside of London these days and could you believe how long Y waffled on for in that Q&A and did you see the look on* — when they'd shared an 'aren't we having a great time?' hug that had lingered on a fraction too long and suddenly Alan's eyes had drifted down to her cleavage and he'd felt lust pounding thickly through his veins and their lips had moved towards each other before they'd jumped apart and Alan had spent the rest of the evening with the mantra '*I love my wife and kids, I love my wife and kids*' playing on a constant loop in his head.

He and Pandora had never spoken of it and never repeated their joint cocaine experience. And he did love Katie and the children of course. Alan, almost uniquely for his milieu, was faithful. (Part of this was to do with a sense of his wife. You know that some girls will stand for that kind of thing. They will wear it. Katie, he felt, would not.)

Of course many people in their circle coped perfectly well with this stuff. Take Vanessa — an inveterate shagger-around and maintainer of many concurrent affairs.

Then again, dealing with all of this was part of Vanessa's genetic make-up. The aristocracy traditionally couldn't afford the scandal of divorce and, besides, being the product of places like Eton and Westminster and the offspring of long lines of utterly amoral bastards, they had no problem with the concept of infidelity. Vanessa's forebears were no strangers to creeping along the cold halls of mansions in the middle of the night, shoes in one hand and cock in the other, people who were familiar with the routine of funding a tranche of bastards. It seemed as though infidelity, like smoking in your own home, was fast becoming the sole province of the very upper and lower classes. If you were minted beyond belief much more became doable. Similarly if you lived on a sink estate where everyone was banging everyone and a pregnancy only meant another form to fill in, more queuing in some appalling benefits office, where a scandal just meant a drunken fight in some blighted pub (the wife and your lover throwing themselves at each other in a flurry of sovereign rings and 'you fucking slags'), again much more was permitted. It was the stolid middle classes who generally soldiered on unfucked. They couldn't *afford* to get divorced. Alan's friend Connor had been caught with his hands in the till a few years back. Three kids, all in private schools. Out on his ear. He'd wound up in a bedsit. A fucking *bedsit*.

What was she to do, Vanessa argued, stranded there in the sexless desert of a twenty-year marriage? (What was it Amis said? Eventually most marriages become sibling relationships, broken by the odd, embarrassing bout of incest.)

Alan's near miss with Pandora had happened three years ago, when he was still (just) in his mid-forties. It was a time, a friend had explained to him, when you were 'randier than a dog with two cocks'. As randy as you were at seventeen. It perhaps had something to do with the hormones having a last hurrah, a final farewell to all that, to the fuel that had powered you for the last thirty-odd years. It all started calming down a bit at the end of your forties, he'd said. Who had told him all this? That's right — Connor, there in his bedsit, nursing cheap Scotch and the diminishing libido that had cost him everything.

'Christ. Rory,' Alan said. 'Whose cock did he suck to get in here?'

'His dad's brother's on the board.'

'Listen, remember you did that homeless feature last year? Have you still got a contact for anyone at that charity? I've got a friend who's in a bit of a jam.'

'They're homeless?'

'Pretty much.'

'God. I'll dig her number out and email it to you. What do you fancy for lunch?'

'Just get the work experience to get us a crayfish and rocket from Pret.' He handed her a fiver. 'I'll be in Graham's office. Thanks.'

He made his way along the corridor, yawning and stretching. What was it with all this tiredness as you got older? This exhaustion that sleep didn't seem to touch the sides of? Sleep — there was another thing. Or rather, there it wasn't. There was Alan — staring at the dark garden at five o'clock in the morning (the underfloor heating insanely luxurious on the pads of his toes through the wide oak boards) as the kettle began its symphony somewhere behind him. Nabokov believed you could divide the world neatly into two camps: the sleepers and the sleepless. Those who 'went out like a light' the moment their 'heads touched the pillows' (and the cliches here are fully meant to imply that such people are simple-minded buffoons) and those who tossed and turned in brutal insomnias that ended in full consciousness somewhere around dawn. (These people being, naturally, geniuses.) Alan was still within enough touching distance of his youth to remember the days of the great sleeps. Of indeed the Big Sleeps. If we were to characterise sleep as Nazi Germany then one's teens were 1933 through to the spring of 1941: a time of incredible, seemingly endless triumph, a time when all of us are naturally Hitlers — grandmasters, dons, Obi-Wans — of unconsciousness, a time when you'd basically go into a coma for twelve to fourteen hours, the kind of hyperspace-cryo-sleep his son Tom enjoyed, that could only be broken by something like an elephant with a bell strapped to its trunk rampaging through the bedroom.

Alan knocked on an open office door. 'Hey there, fella,' Graham said. 'Come on in. How's tricks?'

'Well, other than the roomful of Oxbridge halfwits I'd quite like to kill, it's all good, Graham. How do we end up with these people?'

'Mummy and Daddy worked here.'

Alan liked Graham. A Belfast lad who went to Trinity, he was now the paper's head of Legal and Business Affairs. Alan caused Graham the odd headache in terms of libel, but he was always helpful in getting him into hard-to-book restaurants, so Graham liked Alan. Alan sat down on the small sofa. 'Got a minute?'

'Just about . . . ' Graham tapped at an email.

'There's a friend of mine who was in a band. Briefly quite successful about twenty-five years ago but he's never really seen any money. I was wondering, if he was due any back royalties or anything like that, would there be a way he could find out?'

'Ooh, not really my area. You'd need a music industry specialist.'

'Yeah. He says he signed away all his publishing rights back in the day.'

'Common enough in that racket from what I hear. What was his band called?'

'The Rakes.'

'Never heard of them.'

'Well, like I said, 'briefly' and 'quite' success-ful.'

'And what's his name?'

'Craig Carmichael.'

'Craig Carmichael . . . The Rakes . . . ' Graham was writing this down now. 'And when were they . . . active?'

'Kind of '92, '93. Around then.'

'Tell you what.' Graham finished writing and stuck the Post-it on his computer monitor. 'I've got a mate from university who's over at Harbottle & Lewis now. They do a lot of entertainment law. I'll give him the details and see what he thinks. Fair enough?'

'That'd be great. Thanks, Graham.'

'Not at all.'

Alan gazed across the hall at the toilet door — someone coming out looking well pleased with himself. The fucker. If this didn't resolve itself soon he'd have to go and see the doctor. Four days now. Maybe have to get back on the Ex-Lax.

10

Friday was a day of heavy domestic activity at home. Petra came at nine, when she commenced the biggest of her tri-weekly onslaughts on the house: dealing with all of the laundry as well as the usual cleaning chores required for the place to be lovely for the weekend so they could trash it in time for her to start again on Monday. Petra was Russian, in her thirties, thin as a credit card, and aggressive when it came to her territory of cleaning. (*'No! Niet! Ecover no good! I tell you before! Is garbage!'*)

Barry the gardener came on Fridays, though only every other week in the winter. He pruned and tidied and cleared branches and leaves and burned stuff in his incinerator. Barry had come with the house. He'd tended the garden for the previous owner, Dr Rosen, for twenty years. He was in his sixties, silver-haired and, despite smoking like a laboratory beagle, seemed incredibly fit and supple. In summer he was forever up a tree, tearing off dead branches with his bare hands.

Friday was also deadline day for Katie, so that was one of the three days Cleo, their part-time nanny-cum-housekeeper, came too. She dealt with getting Sophie off to school and picking her up and cooking lunch and dinner. Cleo was of Caribbean descent, a larger lady (when she stood next to Petra it was impossible not to be reminded of a multi-racial Laurel and Hardy), a fabulous cook and much loved by the kids — she'd been with the family for over a decade, after they'd poached her from Melissa's nursery when Melissa was five, Tom was eight and Sophie was still a drunken dinner away from ever existing.

A TV engineer from Sky was also there that day — installing another box in the small living room, finally giving in to the kids' demand that they have the capability to watch completely different TV to their parents at any given time.

Craig sat sipping coffee and scribbling in his journal in the kitchen. He regarded all of the activity around him: Petra's shrieks, cackles and curses from the utility room adjacent to the kitchen (the 'futility' room, Katie called it, a reference to the endless mess of washing and ironing in there), where she was watching some soap opera on her iPad while she ironed. (Some of the exclamations were in Russian — 'PIZDA!' featured a lot — and some were strange bastard-ised English swears — 'PIG OF WOMAN!' for instance.) Cleo humming as she unpacked some shopping she'd done after she dropped Sophie at school. (Cleo, Craig had learned, had a car and a credit card on the family.) Through the French windows he could see Barry piling branches into the smoking incinerator. Down the hall the Sky man was on the phone to his HQ discussing some technical issue with the installation. Music, late-seventies Dylan, played softly through the Sonos system that was wired through the entire house.

Just then Katie came bustling in, making for the kettle. 'Hello, all!'

'They didn't have that type of almond milk you wanted,' Cleo said. 'I got this stuff.' She held up the offending carton.

'Oh, that'll be fine.'

'I just made some coffee,' Craig said.

'Ah! Herbal tea for me. Too much coffee in the morning and I get a bit stabby.'

'I hope that's OK,' Craig said. 'The coffee I mean.'

'Of course! Please, Craig, help yourself to whatever you want.'

'Right,' Cleo said, closing the fridge. 'I'll be back with Sophie around half three. I'm gonna do you jerk chicken for tonight, Kate.' Cleo was the only person who called Katie, Kate. She didn't mind it.

'Ooh, fantastic,' Katie said. 'Alan will be over the moon.'

'Bye!' Cleo disappeared down the long hallway.

After the front door shut, as Katie was pouring boiling water into her mug, Craig said, 'Christ, all this must cost you guys a fortune, eh?'

'How's that?'

'All this . . . ' he gestured around him, meaning Petra, Cleo, Barry, Sky Man, ' . . . staff.'

'DIRTY SHIT YOU MAN!' came from the utility room.

'Don't mind Petra. She's watching some mad soap. Well, it's not quite Downton,' Katie said (Katie who had grown up in a place not completely dissimilar to Downton), 'but, yes, it

81

takes a few bob to keep the wheels on the wagon.' She bobbed her tea bag (three ginger) up and down in her mug ('I HEART MARHAM', a mid-ranking mug). 'God, do you find all this terribly offensive, Craig? Given, you know, recent circumstances and all that?'

'Don't be daft.' Craig found himself moderating his accent around Katie's incredible poshness.

'SOOKA! PIZDA!'

'It's nice you guys have done so well yourselves.' The idea of 'doing well for yourself' was admittedly an odd one for Katie, coming as she did from a world where everyone had always done, and, as far as she could see, would always do, well for themselves, but she played along.

'Yes, well, we've been very lucky.'

She sat down at the table across from him, noticing that Craig had closed the A4 pad he'd been writing in and put his coffee mug on top of it. Katie was wearing jeans and a sweatshirt that had the face of a tiger embroidered on it. Her hair was tied back. Her body toned by marathons of yoga and Pilates, her complexion smoothed by the litres of water and pounds of vegetables she consumed daily, she looked girlish, nowhere near her forty-eight years. Craig reflected on the girls he went to school with in Ardgirvan, girls who were the same age as Katie but who could comfortably pass for old-age pensioners now. Poverty really took it out of you.

'YI-BAT, YOU ASSHOLE.'

'Here,' Craig said, handing her a sheaf of envelopes. 'Your post came.'

'Thanks,' Katie said, taking the stack of mostly brown bills.

'I think there's a couple of wrong deliveries in there,' Craig said. 'Something for Renegade Limited?'

'Ah, no. That's the name of Alan's company.'

'He's got a company?'

'Oh, everyone does it. You have a limited company and you can put a bunch more expenses through it, reduce your tax bill and all that.'

'Oh aye — tax dodgers, are you?'

'No, no. It's all legit. Well, there might be a few grey areas, let's say no more than that. And have you got any plans today?'

'Thought I might walk downtown and have a wee nosy around.'

'Oh, you should go into the Pantry. Brilliant coffee and cakes. Listen, tomorrow night, Saturday, we've got this bloody birthday party for my dad, over at my parents' place. It's just down the road towards Oxford. Cleo's going to stay to watch the kids. So, I was wondering, maybe you'd like to come along?'

'NO! PIZDA!'

'Katie, you don't need to take me to your parents' party . . . '

'No, no. There'll be loads of people there. They're very much of the 'more the merrier' school. Dad can be a bit fearsome, but he's all talk. It'll be fun. We won't be there that long. Leave here around seven and back before midnight I should think.'

'SHIT. DIRTY SHIT. NO. YOU FOOL BITCH.'

83

'Come on. What am I going to talk about when people say 'What do you do?' and I say 'Nothing'?'

'You'll fit right in, believe me. You'll be among people who've never worked in their lives. They think we're utter vulgarians.'

'Ach, we'll see,' Craig said.

'Fair enough. Offer's there. Right.' Katie pushed herself up from the table. 'Better get back to it. You don't have any strong views on the recent MP sexting scandal, do you?'

'Afraid not.'

'Oh well. Have fun in town. See you later.'

Petra appeared in the doorway, removing her headphones. 'Meez Katie, I should change sheets in guest room also?'

'Yes please, Petra.'

Petra looked at Craig, the source of this extra work.

'Oh, that's OK,' Craig said. 'I'm fine.'

'I change sheets.' She withdrew back into the lair of the futility room.

'There you go,' said Katie.

11

'I don't think it's fair.'

'Oh for God's sake, Melissa, you don't think anything's fair. Here, be a darling and find me the hairbrush.'

Katie was at her dressing table in the bedroom, damp from the shower in her underwear, putting earrings on. Melissa was sprawled on their bed in a teenage torpor.

'Everyone else is going.'

'One, I'm sure they're not, and two, I've told you: you *can* go. But you're not staying the whole night. One of us will collect you at midnight.'

'Great . . . fucking Cinderella.'

'*Don't* swear, darling. Have you seen my necklace? The little gold paperclip Katie Hillier one?'

'I'm wearing it.'

'Off. Now.'

'I never get to do any — '

'Oh, Melissa, honestly, I'm trying to get dressed. Can't you talk to your father about it? — ALAN!'

Alan was in their dressing room across the hall, tying his tie, the final third of a pleasingly strong gin and tonic on the table in front of him. He was involved in a negotiation with their other daughter. 'Maybe next year, Sophie.'

'That's what you always say.'

85

'If you want a different answer ask a different question.'

'You always say that too!'

'I know — it's boring, isn't it?'

'Yes!'

'So wouldn't we both be happier if we discussed something else?' Downstairs Cleo was making supper for the girls in the kitchen.

'You said we could have a puppy one day.'

'I said 'maybe'.'

'Maybe always means no. Oh, Daddy! Look at this one!'

Sophie held Alan's phone up to him as he marvelled afresh at her attention span. There were gnats somewhere marvelling at the shortness of it. She was scrolling through a Twitter account called *Hold My Beer*, a Sophie favourite. The account collated gifs of people falling off roofs, crashing cars, walking into walls and so forth. Basically a twenty-first-century *You've Been Framed*. ('The Falling Down Programme', Tom had called it when he was small, before the thing Sophie was holding existed.) Sophie loved *Hold My Beer*. On the screen now a youth of about fourteen was preparing to jump from the roof of a garage onto a small trampoline. Two seconds later he seemed to have pretty much destroyed his entire house. While Sophie shrieked delightedly Melissa appeared in the doorway.

'Dad, why can't I stay the night at Jade's party?'

'Because the last time I dropped you off at a party it looked like Sodom and Gomorrah by way of *Animal House*.' He recalled pulling into the driveway of the huge house over in the Chalfonts — half a dozen barely dressed teenage girls staggering about, one vomiting, a surly teenage boy looking at him evenly, sucking casually on a joint.

'What's *Animal House?*'

'Before your time. Here, make yourself useful — ' Alan waggled his glass — 'and go and get your dad another drink.'

'No way.'

'A pound.'

'Dream on,' Melissa said.

'*Two* pounds.'

'I'll do it!' Sophie squeaked.

'You *can't* do it,' Melissa said.

'Can so.'

'Girls, please. Melissa, show your sister how to make a G&T.'

'Come on, dumbo.'

'Dad!'

'*Melissa.*'

'OK . . . Hi, Craig.'

The girls trudged off down the hall, to be replaced in the doorway by Craig, who was still in ragged jeans and a T-shirt. Alan turned from the big mirror. 'You not dressed yet?'

'Och, thought I might give it a miss.'

'Piss off. If I have to deal with Katie's folks you're suffering too. Come on — I left a shirt and tie in your room for you.'

'Christ, what am I going to talk to these people about?'

'It doesn't matter, they won't understand a word you say anyway.'

87

'Cheers.'

'Or me either. Listen, unless they can trace your family directly back to William the fucking Conqueror you're fucked. Seriously, they're the kind of people who ask you where your father has his shoes made.' Often, when having to describe what he did to one of Katie's old friends or family, Alan had, like Richard Tull meeting Demeter's father in *The Information*, felt the urge to tug on his forelock as he said, 'Yes, sir, I ply the scrivener's trade . . . ' He sprayed a light mist of aftershave onto his wrists and said, 'Anyway, come on. It'll be a laugh and we won't be there that long.'

'What will you tell people?'

'Eh?'

'About me?'

'Just . . . you're an old friend from university' Alan used the last gulp of his drink to wash down two tabs of Ex-Lax.

'Should you be taking so much of that stuff?' Craig asked.

'Probably not. Occupational hazard. Anyway, if they ask you anything just tell them you work in music. Honestly — that'll do it.'

'Ach fuck — OK then. Lemme get changed.' Craig wandered off down the hall. Alan went the other way and into their bedroom, where Katie was fully dressed now — in a black wrap dress and silvery heels — and applying make-up. 'Hey, doll, you look gorgeous.'

'Thank you. What was all that about?'

'Craig's coming.'

'Oh good.'

'It'll be all right, won't it?'

'Of course.' Katie was dabbing at her lipstick with a tissue, peering into the mirror over the battlement of costly creams, ointments and unguents she seemed unable to survive without.

'We'll just say he's an old friend from university.'

'Ah.'

'Ah? What does 'ah' mean?'

'Well, I may have let a couple of the girls know a bit of the real backstory.'

'Who?'

'But don't worry, I told them to keep it on the down low.'

'*Who?*'

'Well, Vanessa . . . '

'Vanessa? Oh for fuck's sake! You might as well have taken an ad in *The Times*. Or *The Lady*.'

'Oh, she's not that bad.'

'Daddy swore!'

He turned to see Sophie coming slowly into the room. With tiny, trembling hands she was holding the crystal tumbler of gin and tonic in front of her, like a priest performing a sacrament. 'Here, Soph, I've got it . . . ' He took it gently from her.

'Using the children as slave labour again?' Katie said, not turning from the mirror.

Sophie held out her hand.

'Oh, right,' Alan said, rummaging in his pockets.

'I made it!' Sophie said. 'Melissa just helped.' Alan regarded the beverage: one tiny ice cube and no lemon.

'Here.' He handed Sophie two pound coins.

'Hmmm, not *quite* slave labour then,' Katie said. 'Though I don't know which is worse, bribery or slavery.'

'I'm putting this towards a puppy!' Sophie said, marching off proudly to her bedroom, and her Homer Simpson piggy bank.

Alan sipped the drink. Then embarked upon a coughing fit. 'Jesus Christ . . . ' He guessed the proportions of the cocktail would have to be about 98 per cent gin to 2 per cent tonic. 'Melissa! What are you thinking!'

'Well,' Katie said, 'you get what you pay for, eh?'

12

'*Fuck me*,' Craig said as Katie turned the Range Rover into the driveway.

And 'driveway' felt inadequate. Yes, 'driveway' wasn't quite doing it justice. The gravel pathway they were on was wide enough for three cars and stretched ahead of them in the headlights as far as you could see. You were dimly aware of the shapes of giant trees rising above you in the dark on either side. After what felt like some time a large house of pale stone came up out of the darkness on the left-hand side. 'Is this it?' Craig said.

'Staff cottage,' Kate said.

They drove on. And on. Just when Craig was about to offer the observation that they had surely got lost, they came over the crest of a hill and there it was below them, bathed in floodlights and with many windows blazing — Gresham Park. Built in the late eighteenth century and designed by Robert Adam, the house had seventy-two bedrooms and over two hundred acres of gardens originally landscaped by Capability Brown. 'Fuck me,' Craig said again. 'Who lives here?'

'Just the folks. They don't live in all of it obviously, and they have to let the public in now. Guided tours, you know? To help cover the costs? But my brothers and sisters are all still in London and they use it a fair bit on weekends

91

and hols,' Katie added, as if the occasional addition of ten or twelve people made for a fair use of space.

'What does your dad do?' Craig asked.

'The usual,' Katie said. 'Property, stocks and shares.'

'Though funnily enough they got this place in a card game,' Alan said. 'Didn't your great-great-grandfather win it in something like 1880? Playing fucking whist or something in White's?'

'Well, that's the family legend,' Katie said as she pulled up on the gravel near the front of the house, parking the car next to several others. It seemed like the assembled company here was single-handedly keeping Range Rover in business.

'OK, watch out for Woodford, getting on a bit, something of a law unto himself these days.' Katie got out of the car and headed up the steps, saying brightly, 'Hello, Wooders!'

'Woodford?' Craig said to Alan as they too got out.

'Butler.'

They followed Katie up the steps, the massive neoclassical house towering over them, towards where she was standing with the tuxedoed Woodford, who seemed to be about two hundred years old. 'You remember my husband Alan, don't you?'

'Good evening, sir.' Woodford inclined his head slightly.

'And this is our friend Craig Carmichael.'

'Mr Carmichael,' the old retainer said.

'Pleased to meet you. Craig's fine,' Craig said,

92

extending his hand. Woodford had known Katie since she was a little girl but he was disconcerted by the appearance of these gentlemen: ties, lounge suits. It only seemed like yesterday — but was probably the late 1970s — when Gresham on a Saturday evening always meant black tie. It had been explained to him many times that things had changed in this department. Still, the gentleman in front of him now actually looked like a *thief*. Woodford looked at Craig's madly proffered hand briefly before turning and leading them through the door.

'You are expected. Your mother and her party are in the old library,' he said.

'And how have you been, Woodford?' Katie asked, walking off with the butler, taking his arm, leaving Alan and Craig following, Craig still looking at his blanked, unshaken hand.

'Eh?' Craig said.

'You don't shake hands with the staff, dude,' Alan said.

'Of course not, silly me,' Craig said, already feeling the Red Clyde rising within him.

They followed the stiff-backed Woodford through a hall the size of a couple of tennis courts (tiled floor, dark wood rising all around them, candles flickering in an enormous wrought-iron chandelier, the only sign of human habitation a cluster of brightly coloured children's toys beside a radiator) and into the old library (and what was the 'new' library like? Craig found he just had time to wonder), where they were greeted by the sight of the English upper classes at play. There were about thirty or forty people gathered around under the towering shelves of books, a good-sized public library of books in fact. Some sat on sofas or armchairs, most gathered in knots of half a dozen or so, chatting and laughing. Portraits of ancestors in deep oils glowered down from high on the walls, the bastards and bitches whose industry, whose abuse, enabled the generations below to live so well.

Several young waiters moved through the throng, carrying trays of champagne and canapés.

The reactions of the trio to entering this environment varied enormously. For Katie it was walking into her own living room. As someone who grew up in such surroundings she did not really see the grandeur, she knew about the leaking roof and the water running down the east staircase, and the mice that teemed behind the walls and the miles of rotten wood and missing lead that could not be replaced. And the astronomical heating bills and the fact that probably only 10 per cent of the vast living space was regularly in use, that there were bedrooms above them where the furniture was covered in dust sheets and the crumbling curtains were almost permanently drawn, rooms that only saw life for a few weeks in high summer, when the house might, briefly, be full of guests.

Craig's reaction was a simple, reflexive '*fuck a dog*'.

Alan's was more complex. He, like Craig, had grown up in a terraced pebble-dash council house that would have fitted comfortably

94

— garden included — inside this room. He had not seen garlic until his twenties. These were not his people and this was not his milieu. However, he had been moving in these circles for over twenty years now, and had been fully a part of them since marrying Katie. The marriage was accepted by Katie's family with resignation, tempered by the fact that Alan had just started on a respectable broadsheet. He might yet make something of himself, although there was obviously, as they used to say, no blood there. He had learned how to deport himself with a certain ease in these surroundings, when to hold forth and when to nod knowledgeably and remain silent if the conversation teetered off into areas of toff where he was unqualified to follow (the filigrees of individual Mayfair gunmakers, the long bond curve, the finer points of point-to-point). He was familiar enough with the handful of schools, shops, clubs and restaurants that these people's lives had revolved around for centuries. He knew his White's from his Wilton's, his Pratt's from his John Lobb's. The other thing he had learned, and this was the thing that was causing Craig to look at him now with frank astonishment as they began to be introduced to people, was this —

Alan had learned how to moderate his accent.

In the early days of their relationship, when he met Katie's friends or family he very quickly became used to the response whenever he contributed to the conversation: a stark 'What?' (these were the first people Alan had met who did not say 'pardon'. Just as they did not say 'toilet' or 'settee') accompanied by a sort of stunned stare from the ruder end of the spectrum (her father and most of the guys) while at the more polite end of the scale (her mother, the ladies) he got a strained, nodding, rictus grin, as though a severely handicapped child were being encouraged to express itself. Understandably enough, the appeal of this soon waned and Alan embarked on a war on his mangled speech, the accent he deployed in their company finally modulating itself into a more middle-class Scottish burr, something closer to the Morningside accent that the aristocrats had at least heard, some of them having been to Edinburgh once or twice, or known someone who went to Fettes or Gordonstoun.

It was this accent Alan was now using (to Craig's increasing bewilderment) as they were hailed by a man in his late thirties, who turned from his group of friends to greet them. 'Katie! Hello, darling. And Alan! Alan — just the man. We're talking about the festival.'

'Hello, Henry. What festival?' Alan said.

'You know, the one I'm going to do here. Help pay for the bloody roof.'

'Oh, I see Vanessa, back in a minute, boys,' Katie said, disappearing across the room.

'Ah, sorry, Henry, this is Craig, old friend from back home, he's staying with us for a few days. Craig, this is Henry, Katie's brother.'

'Pleased to meet you,' Henry said, extending his hand.

'Actually,' Alan said, 'talking of festivals, Craig's in music.'

'Really?'

'Ach, ah ewes tae bee,' Craig said, taking a glass of champagne from a proffered tray.

'What?' Henry said.

'Ah used tae be, a while back,' Craig said.

'*Sorry?*'

For Alan it was like watching a video of himself, twenty years ago. For his third attempt Craig slowed it right down, putting a hard end stop to each word. 'I. Used. To. Work. In. Music.'

'Ah! Marvellous. Then you'll know the festival circuit. What we're looking to do is, kind of a boutique thing obviously, some cool bands, dee jaaayys, comedians, writers.' Fresh from marvelling at Alan's 'posh' accent, Craig was now free to marvel at Henry's Etonian drawl. 'Food will be a big thing of course, I must bring you in on this, Alan, you know this stuff, the whole organic burger, artisanal ice cream, handcrafted cheese nonsense. Fitzroy I went to school with started one on the family estate over in Norfolk a few years back. Had ten thousand punters last year. Bloody coining it in. Lining up in droves for six-quid bacon rolls in the morning! Bit of that wouldn't go amiss round here. Anyway, how are you, Alan? How's the world of celebrity food?'

'Oh, fine.'

'Saw that thing you did in the paper recently — grass sandwiches with . . . '

'Bear Grylls and Kylie Minogue?'

'That's it. First rate. What's she like then?'

Across the room Vanessa lowered her glasses (pointlessly — they were clear glass, non-prescription) and peered through the throng to

97

where Henry was talking to Alan and Craig. 'Mmmm. Would. Definitely.'

'Actually, he's perfectly nice,' Katie said. 'Just a bit . . . lost. Always scribbling in this journal.'

'Don't get too attached, darling.'

'Eh?'

'Well, not to put too fine a point on it, isn't he going to have to go back to, you know, the streets at some point? Ah, hello, Connie!'

'Hello!' Mwah, mwah! The three of them air-kissed. 'Katie darling!'

'You make him sound like a puppy,' Katie said.

'Eh?'

'Craig. 'Don't get too attached.''

'Oh. Well, you know what I mean.'

Back across the room Alan was finishing his Bear Grylls anecdote — ' . . . and I said, 'I'll stick to my own bloody piss if you don't mind'' — to general acclaim when a fearsome seventy-something figure in tweeds approached their party. 'Henry — are we having bloody dinner or what? Long past eight.'

'Hello, Hugh, happy birthday,' Alan said.

Katie's father, Hugh De Havilland, the 11th Duke of Gresham, stared Alan down.

'It's Al, Papa,' Henry said. 'We watched him on the television not long ago? Katie's husband?'

Some faint light seemed to seep into the Duke's eyes. 'Ah, yes. Al. How are you?'

'Very well. This is my friend Craig . . . '

'Hi, happy birthday,' Craig said, proffering his hand.

The Duke regarded it with frank astonishment.

'Craig's Scottish too,' Henry offered.

The Duke's eyes narrowed. 'Scottish?'

Craig confirmed the description.

'Do you know the Balfours?'

'The . . . '

'Borders. Marvellous shooting.'

Craig realised that here was a man who, when he thought of Scotland, thought not of pebble-dash post-war council houses, but only of rivers teeming with salmon and the brains of deer spraying across sun-bleached heather.

'Ah, I don't . . . no, I don't think so,' Craig said.

'Do you shoot?'

'Not . . . no. Not really.'

This exchange really signalled the end of Craig's relationship with the 11th Duke of Gresham. One of Henry's friends asked, 'Where's the loo?' The question seemed to anger the Duke. 'Across the hall on your left, but do be bloody careful and not shove too much paper down there. Plumbing is on its last legs. Hasn't been touched since about 1850.'

'One square to wipe and one to polish?' Craig said.

'Exactly, just like school,' Henry said, speaking from the experience of Eton. Craig had been speaking from the experience of a Stephen Fry book he'd read.

'Now,' the Duke said, 'where the bloody hell is Woodford and why haven't we been called into dinner yet?'

'But it's only just gone eight, Pa . . . '

'Really? Bloody watch . . . '

And then, magically, Woodford appeared in the doorway and announced that dinner was served.

★ ★ ★

Dinner was served in the Great Hall — a vaulted, draughty space that could easily have contained three times as many as the thirty-odd guests who were there. Alan found himself halfway down the table, seated between Tara something and Andy someone, almost opposite Craig, with whom he exchanged the occasional astonished glance. By the time the starter plates were being cleared away (some kind of pâté or terrine) and the grouse was being served, Craig wondered if he'd ever heard the word 'what?' quite so much in his life. He calculated he'd said every (short) sentence he'd contributed to the conversation at least three times. He watched Alan across the table, shifting uncomfortably in his seat. Finally, with an 'excuse me', Alan got up. 'Excuse me,' Craig said. He got up too (without waiting to hear the 'what?') and headed quickly out through the curtain, beating Alan to it by a few seconds and heading swiftly for the toilet. He turned round as soon as he heard Alan's footsteps behind him on the ancient flagstones. 'All right, mate?' Alan said. 'You surviving?'

'Just about. No one understands a fucking word I'm saying.'

'Told you. Can I ju — '

'You after the toilet?' Craig said, hooking a thumb at the door.

'Yeah, but on you g — ' They did the dance of

100

'no, after you' for a minute before Craig said, 'Actually I only need a quick piss.'

'Yeah, I might be . . . longer.' Alan shifted uncomfortably from foot to foot.

'Haha. Gotcha. I'll be really quick,' Craig said, getting in there and locking the door behind him.

Craig was as good as his word.

He worked really fast.

About ninety seconds later he stepped back out with a cheery 'All yours!'

'Ta,' Alan said, slipping in there pretty sharpish and locking the door behind him. Craig smiled and wandered back off down the draughty corridor towards the dining hall.

Alan unbuckled his trousers with the frantic excitement of a soldier who has come home from a three-year campaign to find his wife naked on the bed and planted his cold, naked buttocks on the toilet. Or rather, what constituted a toilet at the height of the Edwardian era: an old box-and-chain affair.

He strained and grunted, alone there on the freezing ox-collar, eventually ending up biting the back of his fist and stamping his feet on the floor in a frenzied attempt to cajole his bowels into some sort of action. Finally, with tears streaming down his face and his forehead dotted with perspiration, he was rewarded with a tiny 'plop' as something small disappeared into the icy waters of the pan.

'Are you fucking kidding me?' Alan said.

It was like going through childbirth and producing a marble. Worse than this, his bum

101

seemed to have pulled off some kind terrible kind of *turdus interruptus*, unaccountably breaking off what was promising to be a rather substantial delivery before it even got started. If the load he was trying to get rid of could be defined in terms of a jumbo jet it was as though he'd just succeeded in passing the nosecone and cockpit. Everything else — from first class right to the back of economy — was still up there. He strained again but it was clear that this round was over for the time being. Another unfortunate aspect of this situation — Alan wearily realised he would be some time in the wiping.

Perhaps half a roll of toilet paper later he was finally in a position to stand up and buckle up. As he did so something in the very act of standing up, some rearrangement of internal piping and wiring, some untangling or unblocking took place and Alan was suddenly scrabbling at his belt again and pulling his trousers and pants back down as he hurriedly thrust himself back on the toilet. (What was it with the human arse? What did it *want*? It was there to help you. And here was his — spending half its life trying to fuck him up.) And just in time too — for here came the remainder of that 747.

In terms of a pure logging experience, part two was to part one what comparing a balloon popping was to Hiroshima.

Soon enough he was simply hanging on for dear life as the atrocious torrent of filth cascaded from him. He found himself engaged in a commentary whereby he was simultaneously congratulating and abusing his own arse: '*Oh go* on, *oh Jesus that's . . . oh you fucking animal, you disgraceful bastard you . . . oh yes, that's the stuff, that's, CHRIST, you fucker . . .* ' and so on.

Eventually it subsided. Alan took a moment to get his breath back and then, with trembling hand, he reached for toilet paper for the second time, calculating that the remaining half-roll might *just* be enough to take care of the horror. (There had been a good deal of splashback.) Seven or eight minutes of wiping followed before he was able to stand up again. Pink-faced and unsteady on his feet, he peered into the bowl, the flushed mother in a post-partum glow, tenderly inspecting her newborn.

Jesus. Wept.

Alan pulled the chain and turned to wash his hands. From behind him came a throaty gurgling, a kind of low growl, as the ancient plumbing moaned into life. Then came a juddering, almost as though the floor beneath his feet were shaking. He turned around. Without wishing to ascribe anthropomorphic qualities to something as mundane as a toilet bowl, it looked to Alan was as if the very apparatus itself was retching, was trying to cry out in protest at the horror that had just been pumped down its very gullet. The water level, or rather the sewage level, in the toilet was rising. Fast. As he stood there, not quite sure what to do next, he realised that within seconds the horrific flood would soon be over the rim. Panicking now, he tugged on the chain again. The devilish bowl gave another gulping bark of protest as it, briefly, sucked the horror back about half an inch before it started rising again, faster this time, actual terrible chunks brimming to the top. He pulled the chain again. Hard.

Obviously it snapped off in his hand.

It was clear that with this third tug Alan had administered some kind of deathblow to the system. There was a thump, a kind of muffled bang that seemed to come from deep within the ground, and then a disgraceful froth of hell was foaming, pumping, over the rim and cascading onto the floor.

On and on it went. This . . . this couldn't all be him. There were whole turds, bits of turds, some of which he imagined had been down there since the Victorians. Vintage turd. Antique turd.

Before he quite knew what was happening Alan was actually up to his ankles in raw sewage.

He burst out of there and slammed the door behind him. A torrent of water and pulped excrement poured under it and cascaded down the passageway, seeking its lowest level.

Which was, of course, the Great Hall.

Faintly, in the distance, he could hear the clink of glassware, the clatter of cutlery and the murmur of polite conversation, the diners blissfully unaware that a hellish tsunami of faeces was headed their way. Alan quickly balanced his options.

1) Go straight in there and confess.
2) Run away.
3) Try and front it out.

Moving at a half-jog — his sodden feet squelching horribly at every step — he found he could outpace the stream. He pushed through the thick velvet drapes that covered the passageway and back into the Great Hall. He calculated that he had perhaps thirty seconds before Hurricane Jobby went public. He saw they had followed the old Edwardian custom of swapping seats for dessert and coffee and that — who else? — the Duke himself was now sitting next to him. *Attack is the best form of defence*, Alan said to himself. He sat down next to the Duke and, before the reek from Alan's shoes could hit him, said — 'Oh dear. What is that dreadful smell?'

'Smell?' the Duke said.

The first scream rang out from the bottom of the table, the end nearest the velvet drapes to the passageway.

Within moments the place was in uproar. Pandemonium.

As though in the beach-onslaught opening of *Saving Private Ryan*, Alan looked around — a whooshing in his ears — and caught individual vignettes of horror: a young man vomiting. A woman slipping in her haste to escape and falling into the reeking miasma. A dowager countess type seated near where the avalanche had come in staggered around dumbfoundedly clutching a large human log.

In the insane melee Alan was naturally one of the first and most vocal proponents of outrage. (*'Oh dear God! This is disgusting!'* etc., etc.)

Except for those actually staying at Gresham

Hall the party had almost immediately broken up. As they left, taking their coats from Woodford along with the other coughing and retching guests in the excrement chamber of the hall, Alan caught a glimpse of the Duke and several members of tire staff — all in Wellington boots now — gathered in the doorway of the small lavatory, some of them openly gagging as they regarded the bowl, the torrent pouring out of it now slowed to a mere gush, the effluent it was producing now presumably dating back to the Middle Ages.

The Duke was holding the broken handle like a smoking gun and there was a streak of shit across his face. He looked up to the heavens and cried, 'WHY?'

Craig was still laughing as they pulled into the driveway of their own house an hour or so later. Katie and Craig were in the front. Alan was stretched out on the back seat, his bare feet out of the window, his socks, shoes and trousers tightly sealed in a plastic bag in the boot.

'It . . . it's a *poo*!' Craig said as he again mimicked the reaction of the Dowager Countess. (Apparently she'd thought she was retrieving her fallen spectacles case.)

'For God's sake, you two!' Katie said. 'Have you any idea what it's going to cost them to fix that?'

'They should have had it fixed ages ago!' Alan said. 'All that money and the plumbing's out of the Dark Ages.'

'Someone must have put a ton of bloody paper down there,' Katie said.

'Mmmm,' Alan said.

And so to bed.

★　★　★

Later, after he'd finished laughing for a very long time, still quite drunk, up in his room in the attic, all silence and darkness around him, Craig opened a new section in his journal; this one was called 'Katie family?'. It joined several other sections, stuff like 'Work colleagues?' and 'Finances?'. He made a few notes about the evening.

13

Sunday mornings always followed the same pattern, even after an evening that had concluded as horrifically as the previous one had. (The only substantive difference this morning being Katie's concerned phone calls to Gresham Park. Her father, she was told, was spending the day in bed, having been utterly drained by the trauma. A team of plumbers were now working in the catacombs deep below the house, at incredible expense.)

It being a Sunday morning Sophie's internal alarm clock would obviously wake her at 5.30 a.m. when she would come bounding into their bedroom. Alan would blearily put the TV on and allow her free rein on the children's channels while they dozed for another hour or so. The first one of them up would rub the sausages with a little oil and put them in the oven in the heavy cast-iron skillet — the one they'd got at that little flea market in the Dordogne years ago (Alan once heard himself saying this sentence out loud and found he had time to reflect on the fact that he had become the world's biggest cunt) — while they made the tea. The sausages went on the lowest possible heat for an hour or so while they all remained in bed with tea. Towards the end of that hour the rest of the full English was assembled. There would be bacon, tomatoes, black pudding — occasionally haggis — toast, mushrooms cooked with black pepper and a cubic foot of butter (what did the mushroom *do* with butter? Where did the fucker put it all?), and finally the eggs, usually scrambled, just after Alan or Katie drove round the corner for all the Sunday papers. The enormous meal would be leisurely consumed with frequent trips to the teapot and many an 'Oh my God, have you seen what X is saying?' as Alan or Katie commented on the brilliance or otherwise (more often otherwise) of what one of their peers was saying in whatever column, interview or think piece. After the children had left the table (which didn't take long: Melissa was well into a phase where eating more than three forkfuls of food was described as 'stuffing her face'; Sophie had the attention span of a gnat and could barely sit in a chair long enough to eat anything, and was often to be found dancing or hanging upside down from the chair after one mouthful) the quality of these exchanges escalated in their viciousness as the wisdom/fidelity/morality/sexuality/sanity and indeed appearance of almost every broadsheet writer in the UK was called into question.

'She says what? Fuck her.'

'Oh, he and his wife are 'blissfully happy since they both gave up drinking', the utter pair of fucking cunts.'

'He tried to get off with Emily at Hay last year.'

'Look at the arse on that cow . . . '

'Coked off his nut. Got his cock out in the lift.'

'Why doesn't she just write 'I AM BOTOX' on her face?'

' . . . banging on about food banks, he's on 250 a year now.'

Craig was still sleeping, somewhere above them.

'The best fish in London my fucking hole.'

'Surprise surprise — it turns out that this place in the Maldives that gave them a *completely free trip* gets a really great review . . .'

While doing all of this both of them would be on their phones/tablets scanning social media to see how the story about the weekend's most outrageous statements/claims/ banalities was taking shape, additionally Katie would have three or four private chats going on within Twitter and Facebook where the commentary would get about as dark as it was possible for commentary to get in a hermetically sealed, libel-free world. Which is to say very. Katie's private chat made the banter she was having with Alan across the breakfast table sound like the stuff you'd say if all the children's friends AND their parents were in the room.

'*That photo in today's ST mag? She must have Aids.*'

'*Apparently his is tiny.*'

'*Couldn't get it up.*'

'*Obs mag p. 17. Do we think he's clearly in the midst of a deep homosexual panic?*'

Katie, Alan knew, had chats that splintered off from the private group into sub-private chat groups into sub-sub-private chat groups until sometimes all that was left was Katie and Vanessa destroying the whole world.

Alan was reading a 'Day in the Life' piece by

the ageing supermodel Amber Gris, about her daily routine and diet. The article was accompanied by a photograph of Gris, taken on the deck of her house in California with the ocean sparkling behind her and a holocaust of green salad in hand-carved wooden bowls spread out on the table in front of her, the honey-tanned skin on her perfectly flat stomach shown off by a white cotton blouse knotted at the midriff. The article could fairly accurately be summarised thus:

I get up at 4.25 a.m. when my wind chimes activate an air purifier that gently wafts a chilled breeze across my face. This is great for your pores and also contains nutrients called 'oxygen' that really help your lungs. I got the purifier at a place called Donkey Walloper in Santa Monica.

I drink a small glass of turmeric-infused algae before I do half an hour of hot burlap yoga. I learned this on an ashram in Kilmarnock. You're basically going mad inside a hessian sack so it really helps with getting the toxins out. I have breakfast around 6 a.m. with my son Dangleberry who's three. On a working day I'll have a small piece of dehydrated root vegetable (no fruit! Sugars!) which I chase with a cup of seawater and some pebbles. Dangleberry has whatever he likes. Usually chia seeds in menstrual blood. I weigh 48 pounds and so I stopped menstruating in 2002 so we get the blood from this great store in Topanga Canyon called WE SELL THE MENSTRUAL BLOOD OF

IMMIGRANTS. It's awesome.

The business calls start at 7 a.m. and I'm pretty much flat out until lunchtime.

I grab lunch at my favourite deli Fritzl's Dungeon in Brentwood, usually just a seaweed wrap with something like alkalised snow peas and maybe a side of toasted organic spirulina if I'm really hungry.

I love to cook properly in the evenings, when my husband Strap On gets home. We never have red meat, flour, sugar, caffeine, white meat, wheat, dairy, alcohol or nightshades in the house. So that means no tomatoes, eggplant or peppers. (Also no actual nightshades on the lights. Just bare bulbs.) The family loves my no-egg omelette that I make from tofu, linseed oil, kale and semen. But sometimes, if it's been a really busy day, I'll whip up a plate of actual nothing. We just sit staring at bare china plates (they have to be plain white, from Bone Rapist in Malibu) until around 8.30 when it's time to go to bed. Before retiring Strap On and I both drink a glass of chilled Alsatian's urine infused with lavender. It's rich in melatonin, a natural relaxant.

We live by the ocean and we fall asleep with the sound of the waves and the gentle, rhythmic crying of Dangleberry from the next room until the purifier goes on at 4.25 and the whole crazy circus starts again . . .

Reading this Alan experienced all the usual things. Like any sane person he certainly wished a good deal of harm upon Amber Gris and her immediate family. He playfully visualised himself sawing her head off, for instance, ideally while she was forced to watch her son and husband consume enormous plates of rare beef and refined sugar as they chugged down pints of whisky. He imagined locking her in a branch of Kentucky Fried Chicken with nothing but the Colonel's thickly battered poultry standing between her and starvation. He pictured her gagging and crying as he mercilessly kept his gun trained upon her while she was forced to gorge her way through a colossal plate of chips fried in beef dripping.

Suddenly his mobile rang. A London number he didn't recognise. Ignore, or . . . Sunday morning? Weird.

'Hello?'

'Alan? It's Graham from work.' A spasm of fear: was he getting sued again? (It was surprising how may restaurateurs thought that not liking their food — or the fact that you had to wait forty-five minutes for a glass of wine — constituted reasonable grounds for legal proceedings.)

'Hi, Graham. Everything OK?'

'Yeah, sorry to bother you on a Sunday, but I saw Tim last night — the music business lawyer I told you about? — and I thought you might want to know about your friend's thing. It's quite interesting — can you talk for a minute?'

'Sure . . . ' Alan wandered into the conservatory.

Ten minutes later he came back in. Katie had the *Sunday-Telegraph* travel section spread out in front of her as she typed a reply on her phone.

('. . . *grabbed my tits at that party* . . . ')
'Graham?' she said, not looking up. 'We're not getting sued again, are we, darling?'

'Ah, no. No. Any sign of Craig yet?'

Katie shook her head, eyes still on her phone. ('. . . *at Tate Modern that time* . . . ')

'Lazy bastard. Well, this is interesting.'

'What?'

'Phone down please.'

'OK. Sorry. Just a sec . . . ' Katie finished her atrocious anecdote defaming a well-known novelist and gave Alan her full attention. 'Go.'

'Remember I told you how I'd asked Craig if he really had no money left over from the band and all that and he said about how they'd signed away all their publishing in some dodgy deal or other?'

'Mmm, *vaguely* . . . '

'I mentioned it to Graham and he said he'd ask his friend who does music law about it. It turns out that even if he had given away all the publishing there's still money out there from mechanicals, something called PPL —'

'Mummy! I can't get Sky Movies to work!' Sophie, from the living room.

'Be there in a minute!' Katie trilled before turning back to Alan. 'What's PPL?'

'I think it's a bit like PLR.' (PLR — the few pennies an author automatically got when someone borrowed one of their books from a library. Alan's amounted to a couple of grand a year — a nice wee bit of pocket money. God knows what, say, J. K. Rowling's looked like.)

'Wow. So what does this mean?'

114

'Have you seen my schoolbag?' Melissa, in the doorway.

'It's in your room,' Katie said.

'It's not.'

'It bloody is, Melissa. Please, use your eyes.'

'It's not.'

'If I come up there and find it . . . '

'Fine, I'll look again. But — '

'Darling, please — Mummy and Daddy are talking.' Melissa stomped off. 'Sorry,' Katie said, 'go on.'

'He took Craig's name and the name of the band and all that and he looked into it and, well, cut a long story short, it seems Craig might be due a decent bit of money. Could be five figures?'

'Really? Gosh. He'll be over the moon.'

'Well . . . ' Alan said, (needlessly) lowering his voice and glancing up towards the ceiling, as if he were looking up through two floors to where Craig was sleeping. 'I'm not sure we should tell him right now. Graham's friend's got to make a few phone calls and he said it'd probably take a while to actually get the money in. I don't think it's a good idea to get his hopes up until things are a bit clearer. Thing is . . . ' Alan leaned forward. 'To actually deal with this properly, to get paid he'd — '

'MUMMY! Sky Movies!'

'Oh for God's sa — I'll be there in a minute, Sophie!'

'Graham said he'd need an address, a bank account . . . '

Katie looked at him. 'Right . . . '

'I was thinking, you said before, 'what's the

115

end game here?', well, this could be it, couldn't it? With the money, even if it is at the lower end of the scale Graham mentioned, he'd still have enough for a rental deposit on a flat, maybe enough for the first year's rent. He . . . '

'Alan, wh — '

' . . . could get a roof over his head again. Get . . . '

'Yes, but — '

' . . . back on his feet.'

'Alan!'

'What?'

'What if he doesn't want to do any of that stuff?'

'Eh?'

'What if he just wants to bugger around, sleeping rough and drinking beer in the street?'

'But . . . why would he do that if he didn't have to?'

Katie sighed. 'Not everyone's built the same way. Some people, some men particularly, they can't deal with responsibility, with the idea of running their own lives. Gas, electricity, rent, mortgage, council tax, phone bills, water bills . . . they just can't keep it all on track. Anyway, where are you going with this?'

Alan fiddled with his teacup. 'Well, I was thinking, maybe, I mean, don't go nuts, I know this is an ask, but maybe . . . '

Katie: 'If we offered to put him up until he gets . . . ' Katie spotted Melissa slouching across the hallway. 'Find it?'

Melissa, flatly: 'Yes.'

'Where was it? Just out of interest.'

Something mumbled.

'Sorry, Melissa?'

'IN MY ROOM,' then, under her breath, 'Jesus.'

'Thank you.' Back to Alan. 'Until he gets this money.'

'Well, yeah.'

Katie sipped her tea. 'How long, realistically, how long is that likely to take?'

'Graham says we'll have a better idea tomorrow. But, the thing is — '

'He's meant to be moving out tomorrow.'

Of course Katie was already several steps ahead of Alan. She'd landed on the square marked 'extend Craig's stay' about four seconds after he'd said the words 'might be due some money'.

'Here's the thing, Alan, and I've got nothing against Craig, he's perfectly nice and if it was an old school friend of mine who'd found themselves down and out then of course I'd want to help them as much as I could too . . . ' (and here Alan tried to picture one of the girls Katie went to school with — one of the Arabellas or Emilys — finding themselves sleeping round the back of Euston Station. He found it couldn't be done) ' . . . and, if it's a question of just a few weeks, maybe even a couple of months, then, yes, we can probably live with that. If it's going to be closer to something like six months then I think you'd need to find another solution.'

'Such as?'

'Well, if it were definite he was getting this money maybe we could advance hi — '

'MUMMY! DADDY! *FROZEN* IS START-
ING AND I CAN'T —'

This is what every adult conversation becomes
in a house filled with two or more kids: a battlefield of interruptions, of half-finished sentences,
a graveyard filled with lost trains of thought.

'MELISSA, WILL YOU PLEASE HELP YOUR
SISTER WITH THE BLOODY TELLY?! Sorry,
where was I? Yeah, advance him the rent on a
small place, get him off the streets for the worst
of the weather —' behind them a sharp, wintry
breeze was growling along the glass of the conservatory — 'and he could pay us back later. But —'

'That's a possibility . . .'

'*But*, as I said, he might not want that. Who
knows what he wants to do? He might just want
to bugger off.'

'He did say he wanted to get back on his feet.
Find a job . . .'

'That can all change when someone gets
handed a big cheque, you know . . .'

Faintly, from the living room, the sound of the
girls having some sort of debate became audible.

'Yes, I know.'

'But anyway, about tomorrow, here's what I
think — you're right, don't mention anything
about this money until you get a clear idea of
what's happening. Then we can decide what
we're going to do. Do you have any way of, um,
entertaining him tomorrow until you hear from
Graham?'

'Well, I've got to have lunch at this new
Mexican place I'm reviewing off the Strand.
Thought I might take him.'

'OK then.' The sound of feet on the stairs. They resumed 'casual' positions, leafing through the papers. 'I'm going to have a bath and then take the girls shopping. Soph needs new shoes. Morning, Craig! Sleep well?'

'Aye, thanks, Katie. Any word on Poo Gate?'

Alan busied himself with the teapot.

'Oh don't, it's a nightmare. Right, bath for me . . . ' Katie said.

'There's bacon and sausages in the oven,' Alan said to Craig as he sat down. 'Want me to do you some eggs?'

'Nah, sarnie will be fine. What's happening in the papers?' Craig started leafing through the mountain of newsprint on the kitchen table.

'Oh, the usual shite, pal. The usual shite. Here, read this Amber Gris interview if you want to get your heart rate up.'

Sophie appeared in the doorway. Or rather, she collapsed through the doorway. She was broken and gulping for air, unable to catch a breath, her face completely soaked with tears.

Alan held her and soothed her as he asked what on earth had happened. It was a good minute before the child regained the power of speech. 'Me-Me-Melissa p-p-put *X-Men* on.'

14

'So what, what kind of thing are you looking for at this place we're going to later?'

'Well, it's not like you're 'looking' for something specific — '

'Craig? I'VE GOT A PAMPER PARTY THIS WEEKEND.'

Alan was in the driver's seat, Craig in the passenger seat, Sophie in the back. They were dropping her at school and had joined the long fine of cars causing a tailback so that their precious contents didn't have to walk a couple of hundred yards in broad daylight, surrounded by dozens of other children and in full view of many passing motorists.

'Have you now? What happens at one of those?'

As Sophie filled Craig in on the finer points of the seven-year-olds' pamper party, Alan looked at the line of cars in front of him (Audi 4x4, Lexus 4x4, Range Rover), and then in the rear-view mirror at the cars queuing up behind him (Mercedes 4x4, Porsche 4x4, Nissan Micra: obviously someone's nanny) and reflected, not for the first time, on how very many middle-class parents were convinced that the world's population outside of their immediate family was comprised of 96 per cent paedophiles. The other 4 per cent was comprised of potential paedophiles.

Their neighbours, Theresa and Malcolm, had twin girls (Chloe and Claire) a year younger than Sophie. They'd been over playing one evening in the summer and, when home time had come, Alan had told Sophie to walk the girls the two-minute stroll from her own front door back to their house. She had returned five minutes later — task happily completed, the ever-bossy Sophie pleased to have been entrusted with this mammoth responsibility — and they were in the kitchen when the doorbell rang. Alan opened it to find Theresa on the doorstep.

Now, being a restaurant critic, Alan had experience of people presenting themselves to him in a state of pre-enragement. He had seen chefs and restaurateurs materialise before him at parties and book launches already fairly fizzing with rage because of something he'd written, or said on TV or radio. He'd been accosted by members of the public (in the street, walking from the stage to the backstage bar at literary festivals) who were pre-enraged over something he'd written in the paper months before. So he knew the signs: the set jaw, the balled fists trembling by their sides, the fixed look in the eyes. It was in such a state that he found Theresa when he opened the door to her that summer evening.

Theresa was in her early forties. A prim, stick-thin Home Counties type who drank very little alcohol, ate no fat or spices and was known to Alan and Katie as a monument, a colossus, of joylessness. If you talked to Malcolm about something he and Theresa had done — a trip, a hotel, a meal, a holiday — it was a twenty-four-carat, gold-plated certainty that Malcolm would begin the conversation with the words 'Well, Theresa wasn't happy because — ' before going on to reel off a catalogue of his wife's complaints.

'Hey, Theresa, what's up?' he'd said, beaming, throwing the tea towel over his shoulder. (With the joyless he found it was often a very good riling tactic to give off an air of invincible good humour.)

'I . . . the girls just came back. With Sophie. You . . . you *cannot* let Sophie walk them home alone.'

'Eh? Soph knows to check for cars.' (They had to cross a narrow private lane that ran between the two houses. A vehicle, usually an Ocado van, moving at around 3mph did occasionally pass through.)

'It's not the cars, Alan.'

He nodded seriously as he stepped closer to her and whispered conspiratorially, 'Is . . . is it the paedos, Theresa?'

She almost reeled back on her heels at his audacity in actually saying the word, as though the very utterance might summon an actual sex offender, *Beetlejuice*-style. Theresa said, 'I don't think it's appropriate for children of six and seven to be out unaccompanied by an adult.'

'Out?' He gestured along the lane, towards her own house, blatantly visible over the hedge.

'I . . . the distance doesn't matter.'

'It's the paedos, right?'

'Look, Alan — '

He sensed she was on the verge of genuinely losing her temper, something Alan wouldn't have minded seeing, indeed would have paid some money to see, but Katie had recently told him off for baiting the neighbours. He held up his hand. 'Come on. I'm just messing with you, Theresa. Of course. My apologies. I'll never let the girls walk home on their own again. Fair enough?'

He enjoyed the sight of someone prepared for battle having the fight juice instantly sucked out of their system. 'I . . . well, yes. Thank you. Tell Katie I said hello. See you later.'

Fuck you, you joyless life-sucking cow, Alan thought as he said a cheery 'Bye!' and closed the door.

'It's more that you . . . ' Alan tailed off, trying to answer Craig's question as he guided the car through the school gates, the parking sensors beeping crazily at the proximity of the gateposts. 'Fucking sensors,' Alan said automatically.

'Daddy,' Sophie said warningly from the back.

'Sorry, darling. No, it's more a case, with this kind of restaurant, not a three-star Michelin-type place, of can they do the fundamental things right? They're not going to be reinventing the wheel. It's not El Bulli. It's just, can they do the basics properly and — here we are, darling. Kiss please.'

Sophie unbuckled and came between the two seats to plop a kiss on her father's cheek. 'Craig too!' she said, giving Craig a quick peck before she scampered out of the door and — with a quick shout of 'Amber! Boo Boo!' — joined a group of girls, all in their scarlet blazers, heading

123

into the grand old building.

'No boys here?' Craig said.

'Girls only,' Alan said.

'How much does it cost then, this place?'

'You don't want to know.'

'I do. Go on.'

'Oh . . . five or six grand?'

'A year?

'A term, mate. *A fucking term.*'

'Holy shit. How many terms a year?'

'Three.'

'Man, and if you've got two or three kids here . . . '

'Well, exactly.'

'Fucking hell.'

★　★　★

They were in a corner booth of El Cantina, where, over Modelos with slices of lime, Alan was (sotto voce) filling Craig in on some backstory: it was a new, achingly hip Mexican restaurant opened by the very hot chef from Centrino and a trio of bankers who fancied playing 'we're not just total dickheads who rob people' for a while. The basement room was dark, cave-like, with sand-coloured walls. Some kind of ambient whale music played softly. It was late for lunch, nearly three o'clock, and there were only half a dozen other diners scattered around the room: a drunk couple who were clearly embarked upon an affair of some sort and a four-top of City types, very probably friends of the 'we're not just dickheads' men.

The reason Alan was speaking so softly was that he was pretty sure he'd been made. You could usually tell this by the way there was a certain extra zing in the service, everything from the greeter's (as they had increasingly American-ised *maître d'hôtel* into) 'Right this way' to the fast, slightly nervy appearance of bread and water, and the way the waiting staff positively *ran* to the kitchen. It was a by-product of becoming tolerably well known, this loss of anonymity. 'Funnily enough,' Alan was saying to Craig now, 'when they've sussed out who you are, it doesn't always make for improved food and service. You know, when their nerves are jangling things are almost more guaranteed to go tits up.'

'What a power to wield,' Craig said.

Alan scanned for sarcasm as the waiters — whose alacrity in bringing out the food confirmed Alan's suspicions that he'd been recognised — started bringing out the chef's selection of platters. Alan hated ordering, hated reading menus. If he were in a new place he'd always say, 'Just feed us — bring us your best shot.' How well the restaurant coped with this disarming request was often a fair barometer of how good the place was. You generally wanted the signature dishes and the special of the day. They looked at the array of food piling up on the table. There were standards like steak burrito with chipotle salsa, tiny black-bean tostadas, refried beans with avocado and fresh tomato salsa, a spicy slaw and some chunky guacamole. Nestling among these were a couple of slightly more ambitious offerings: something that looked like mushroom quesadillas and a piece of grilled fish served with green rice and . . . were they pork scratchings? It turned out they were *fennel* pork scratchings and they were delicious.

'What happened to chilli and tacos and big cactuses and sombreros on the walls?' Craig asked.

'Mexican left all that behind some time ago, my friend,' Alan said. 'You had Bodega Negra, Coya, Peyote, all these places doing the hip Mexican thing.'

'Guess I wasn't thinking too much about hip Mexican a few years back . . . ' Craig said.

'Fair point,' Alan said.

More food appeared. Medallions of lamb in dark jus, a seafood cazuela — a paella-like dish with squid, prawns and clams in a creamy, tangy sauce — a ceviche of octopus in a light broth with watercress and slivers of red onion. Beef in tamarind and shitake mushrooms. 'Are we really going to fucking eat all of this?' Craig said as he reflected upon what the average Mexican scarfing down some forty-peso guacamole and tortilla chips at a van in a Juárez side street would reckon to some London ponce hole knocking out (a probably inferior version of) the same thing for ten fucking shitters.

'So,' Craig said. 'Tomorrow, I think I'll probably get off.'

'Where are you going to go?'

'Might head up to Islington. Got a few pals there. It's not a bad pitch, outside Angel Tube?'

'But — '

'It's not your problem, Alan, honestly. It's

been good to catch up, don't get me wrong. I mean, it's been weird, but you . . . you've got a lovely family and all that. It's great to see you've done so well for yourself.'

'I've just been lucky.'

'Nah. I always knew you'd do well for yourself. Even when we were thirteen, fourteen . . . you could tell even then.'

'How?' Alan did not ask this disingenuously, he was not fishing for compliments. He was actually curious as to why the teenage Craig thought Alan was going to sail through life while he struggled. They both came from much the same background.

'Just . . . you were, not that you were that much cleverer than anyone, just, you were, you know . . . you had that air of someone who was going to get on.'

Alan sensed there was something he wasn't saying, but he didn't have time to pursue the question because his mobile started buzzing on the table. Graham. Literally at the eleventh hour. 'Look, I've got to take this, sorry,' Alan said. 'Get yourself another beer. I'll be back in a minute.'

He bounded up the steps into deep and dark December, his heart pounding as he hit 'accept' and said 'Graham?' over the roar of traffic from the Strand.

He listened to what Graham had to say, smiled, thanked him, hung up and wandered back down the stairs to the restaurant. He stopped at the foot of the stairs and looked down across the room. In the darkest corner the couple were now openly snogging, the banker quartet

127

were braying loudly. He watched Craig fiddling with the label on his beer bottle, Craig Carmichael, who had taught him how to play guitar, who had been the coolest guy in his class, who had once, very briefly, had the world at his feet. Alan was about to change his life.

'Craig?' he said as he sat back down. 'I've got some good news . . .'

Some fifteen minutes later — over a third round of beers — they were still sitting there as Craig once again said, '*Thirty-two fucking grand?*'

Alan nodded. 'Give or take. You'll need to sign some forms authorising Tim, Graham's mate, to deal with the various collection agencies on your behalf, and it might take a few months to get the money in, but, yeah, that's about the size of it. Congratulations, mate.' Alan felt like Santa.

'I . . . fuck. Fucking hell. I thought, because we gave away the rights back when — '

'Apparently it doesn't matter. Some of the money should still go to the band and songwriters individually. He said that every year there's millions that goes unclaimed. It all goes into one big pot. The fact is that you had this song that still gets played on the radio here and there, not a huge amount, but over the last twenty years, a few grand here, a few there. Obviously you'll have to pay Tim some legal fees, but he'll do you mate's rates, maybe a couple of grand? A case of wine for Graham would be a nice gesture . . .'

'This . . . ' Craig said, 'this isn't real.'

'So, I've talked to Katie and here's what we

128

think. You can stay with us for the next couple of months, over Christmas, and when your money comes in you'll have enough to put down a deposit, get a flat sorted out and all that. If it looks like it's going to take a bit longer than that then I'll lend you the money to sort it and you can pay me back when you get paid. In the meantime, I'll advance you a wee bit to live on. You can pay me back when you're rich.'

Craig looked at him. 'Fucking hell.'

'What do you think?'

'Are you sure? I . . . I'm just worried that, what if something goes wrong and we don't get the money?'

'Graham says this guy's pretty good. Even if it all goes tits up you'll still be off the streets for the worst of the winter, won't you?'

'Aye, but . . . are you sure? Is Katie su — '

'Actually it was Katie's idea.' Flushed with beer and the triumph of his detective work, Alan felt the situation could support this slight embellishment.

'Well, I guess, aye then. Fuck. OK. Thanks, man. I mean it. We should celebrate.'

'Get the cocaine in?' Alan said.

'Coke?' Craig said, surprised.

'Kidding,' Alan said. 'All that stuff does now is turn me into a crazed mute zombie sex offender. Let's get these down us and get home to tell everyone the good news . . . '

15

It was the week before Christmas and all across London a riot of conspicuous consumerism was raging. Alan looked at his own contribution to all of this — a tangle of shopping bags from Liberty and Selfridges. He'd spent several thousand pounds in the hour and a half he'd allocated for his Christmas shopping. Katie, of course, had long since taken care of her own end of things. For the last week or so packages from Amazon, John Lewis, Net-a-Porter and the like (the glassy squiggle of your signature a mad blur across the tiny screen) had been arriving at the house as the fruits of Katie's many hours of organised online shopping were delivered. He'd got Craig a Bose digital alarm clock for his room, to save them constantly having to give him a shout in the morning. (And how quickly that had become standard parlance in just a few weeks: 'Craig's room'.)

'What did you get Katie?' Pandora asked. They were in the office she and Alan shared at the paper, waiting for a conference call to happen.

'Kinda clutch bag thing from Hermès. Blouse she fancied from Alexander McQueen.'

'Ooh, very nice.' Pandora had her feet up on the desk, ankle boots and tight black jeans.

The speakerphone on the desk between them finally burbled into life. They had the paper's managing editor Rose from her home in the

Cotswolds and Steve the head of digital for the paper, who was in LA on a job. 'Hi, guys,' Steve said.

'Run this expensive bloody thing past me again,' Rose said.

'Right,' Alan said. 'For the cover of the summer edition: a 'Going Wild' cook-off. We've got Bear Grylls taking three celebs into the wilds of Scotland where each of them has to catch and cook something out in the open.'

'We're thinking,' Pandora jumped in, 'of one doing something like rabbit, one doing fish — trout or salmon — and one doing a vegetarian dish using foraged wild veg and stuff.'

'What if none of the buggers catches anything?'

'Well, obviously we'll have backup,' Alan said, picturing the boot of a Volvo estate filled with game, fish and rustic veg. 'But we're doing it on part of Katie's family estate. From what I can gather it's pretty well stocked in terms of edible wildlife.'

'And who's in?'

'Miles Warren is definite, he's got a new book out. Fergus Marks is a very strong possibility — his people say he's back from LA around then to promote some film or other. We might get him shooting, doing the rabbit or pigeon, and for the vegetarian we thought a woman, maybe Chrissie Hynde — '

'Although we don't know if she'll agree to be photographed near animals being killed.' Pandora.

'Or Lauren Laverne, or Ellie Goulding.'

131

'And how much is all this going to cost?'

'Photographer, writer, assistants, hotels, transport, eight to ten grand tops.'

'What are digital saying, Steve?'

'I think if you can get Fergus it's much more attractive for us. He does very well online. I'm assuming you'll be filming all of this for the website, Alan?'

'Oh yeah. Course.'

'And you say 'cook-off'? Is someone going to win this thing?'

'Oh yeah. We thought Bear could judge the results.'

'Could you get a 'surprise' guest to appear just to judge it? Maybe — '

Don't say it, Alan thought.

' — Jamie Oliver?'

'Good idea, Rose,' Alan said. 'We can try. You know how busy Jamie is.'

'How about Gordon Ramsay?' Steve said.

' We had him a few issues ago,' Pandora said.

'Let me think about it,' Alan said. 'I don't think the idea needs to stand or fall on throwing another celeb into the mix though.'

'And the photos would be . . . ?'

'You know, one of them fishing, gutting the thing, frying it on a little camping stove in a field near the babbling brook. I was going to get Archie to photograph it. It'll look great. Bruce is writing it.'

'Bruce?'

'Chatwin? Freelancer. He did Johnny Marr on vegan desserts in the summer issue? He's great.'

'Ah, Alan,' Rose said. 'Not being funny, but

why don't you write it?'

'Me?' Oh fuck. The last thing Alan wanted to do was spend a couple of days in the wilds of Scotland with some pack of celebrity bastards. 'Well, Bruce is good and I'm — '

'Come on,' Rose said. 'We're up against it financially. You're already on the payroll, not paying a fee to a freelancer would save a chunk of the budget. And you could stay with Katie's folks!' *You penny-pinching cow*, Alan thought.

Times were indeed tight at the newspaper these days. A recent interview and photo session with one of the most famous actors in the world had been conducted in what was basically a community centre in Acton. The catering had been some Tesco sandwiches cut into fingers and an urn of stale coffee. Pandora was looking at him expectantly. Sometimes you had to support the staff. 'I, oh well . . . I guess I could do it.'

'OK,' Rose said. 'Then I think if you can get a 'yes' from Fergus Marks then this is a goer.'

'If we can't?'

'Who else is on the list?'

'Jonathan Ross, Stephen Fry, Graham Norton . . . '

'All a wee bit . . . old for us,' Steve from digital said.

'Who'd work for you, Steve?' Alan said. 'Fucking Zoella?'

'Well . . . ' Steve said. *Yeah*, Alan thought, *good luck with getting her stomping about a Scottish moor picking mushrooms or firing a shotgun at rabbits.*

'Ah, does she like food? Does she cook?' Rose asked.

'Fuck knows,' Steve said. 'I do know that everything she does gets a billion hits and I heard she has a new book coming out.'

'Rose,' Alan said, 'I do think it's essential that whoever we get is at least a bit of a foodie. Why don't we draw up a B-list? We should know for definite on Marks soon, right, Pandora?'

'Yep. The press officer for the movie is desperate for him to do it as long as it's the cover and we tag the film.'

'If he's a yes and I write it then we're good to go? If he's a no we'll reconvene with some other contenders?'

'Yep,' Rose said.

'Great, thanks, guys.'

They all said their goodbyes and hung up.

'Alan, you took one for the team!' Pandora said. 'I'm genuinely impressed.'

'Fucking great, a wet weekend in Scotland with a bunch of egomaniacs,' Alan said.

'Me and the guys are off down the pub in a bit if you fancy a pint?'

He did rather fancy a pint, but there was that tangle of shopping bags to get home. And, there was no getting away from it, that image of their lips moving close to each other, white powder stinging their nostrils, did flicker through his mind. *Are more hours lost over the people we didn't sleep with than the ones we did?* 'Ach, better not, P. I need to get this bloody lot home. We've got the Christmas party day after tomorrow anyway.'

'Fair enough. I'll let you know as soon as I hear back from Fergus's people.' She turned back in the doorway. 'Oh, also — Zoella?'

Alan shook his head. 'Fucking digital.'

16

He caught a taxi at King's Cross, then the train out of Marylebone, then another taxi home. (Respective fares: £12.50, £22.30 and £6. Receipts all neatly folded in his wallet. The taxman cometh, every January. Throw in a six-quid shoeshine at the station on his way in, the taxi he took to the office, three Pret coffees at two quid a throw and another five pounds something for the new issue of *GQ* and you saw how it seemed impossible for Alan to set foot out of the house without dropping a hundred quid.)

The house was blazing with light in the dark night (the fifteen-foot Christmas tree in the bay window of the lounge) and he was greeted by another pleasing sight as he came up the gravel drive — his son's VW Polo. Alan sighed as he glanced at the mess in Tom's car — it always looked like he was living in there — and slipped around the back of the house, coming in through the futility room, carefully hiding his gifts under a pile of clean towels, reflexively remembering as he did so that he'd forgotten to get something for Petra.

He came into the kitchen. 'DADDY!' Sophie cried, running across the room. Melissa was at the table, doing homework, Katie at the Aga, stirring something. 'Hey, guys,' Alan said, picking Sophie up.

'I got a merit badge in spelling!' she squealed.

'Did you now? Hey, Mel, how's tricks?' He leaned down and kissed his elder daughter's head. A noise of some kind was audible from somewhere above them.

'It would not be possible for me to care less about the constitution of the United States,' Melissa said, referring to the books and pad spread out in front of her.

'Then you'd make an excellent lawyer over there,' Katie said, coming across to peck Alan on the cheek on her way to the sink with a colander full of knobbly, oddly shaped carrots from the Abel & Cole box by the back door. (Was there any middle-class cliché they didn't tick off? Alan sometimes wondered.) 'How was town?' she said.

'Oh, fine. I might have to go off to Scotland for a couple of days in the new year though, on this bloody wild-food feature. Where's the prodigal son?'

'Upstairs,' Katie said. 'He got back this afternoon.'

'He's, uh, 'jamming' with Craig . . . ' Melissa said.

Alan cocked an ear and indeed the noise from upstairs did resolve itself into some kind of twelve-bar blues motif.

'Come and see, Daddy!' Sophie said. 'They're really good!' She stomped off, turning round in the doorway and putting her hands on her hips. 'But they're *too loud*!'

'Tell the guys dinner in about twenty,' Katie said. 'Mel, you'll need to clear your books off, darling.'

Alan reached into the fridge and took out three bottles of Corona then followed Sophie up the stairs and down the hallway to Tom's bedroom, right at the back of the house. The music got louder, rock and roll, something like Elvis or Carl Perkins. Sophie pushed the door open and wagged her finger at them. 'YOU BOYS ARE TOO LOUD!' she shouted before running off down the hall towards her own room.

Craig was cross-legged on the floor playing Tom's black Telecaster copy, a seventeenth-birthday present. It was plugged into Tom's little practice amp through a cream-and-blue pedal. Tom was sitting on the edge of the bed strumming his acoustic guitar. They kept going for a minute or so while Alan — whose musical talents had never progressed much beyond the anti-rhythmic stabbings at the bass that had caused Craig to fire him from their first band all those years ago — looked on amazed and not a little jealous. Tom had started playing guitar at school when he was about twelve and had progressed into a decent, basic rhythm player; he could hold down chord patterns and play simple riffs. Now, with Craig playing over the top, he sounded transformed. Tom was knocking out a three-chord progression with energy and excite-ment while Craig filled in with little licks and fluid lead passages, his guitar drenched in a kind of swampy reverb or echo.

Seeing Craig on the floor like this instantly transported Alan back over thirty years, to the council-house bedrooms and creosote-scented garages of their youth, when Craig had seemed like a superman capable of anything, rather than an enfeebled tramp. Alan could see him now: his Peavey amp with the black grille and jagged silver logo *('Bandit')* and his sunburst Shergold Masquerader, the same guitar Barney played in Joy Division, as they all drank Strongbow or Kestrel and called out for songs while Craig's mum screamed up the stairs to 'turn that bloody thing down!' The hours, uncountable, that Craig had spent in his teenage bedroom playing along to records, putting the needle back again and again as he tried to get this or that exactly right, peering at photographs in the music papers to try and work out chord shapes, standing in front of the guitarist at gigs, trying to get it all. ''Eton Rifles'!' someone would say. Or 'Do 'Pretty Vacant'!', or 'Gie us 'Safe European Home'!' (a short year or two later — a year being a century in your teens of course — it would be ''This Charming Man'!' or ''Felicity'!' or ''Walk Out to Winter'!') and Craig would knock it out, not just the basic chords, not an approximation, but the *exact* part, the precise notes, making you think that Mick Jones or Roddy Frame himself was standing there. His amp had been so loud in those small rooms, the cider so sweet as the smoke of roll-ups and cigarettes stained the Artex ceiling above them, and their futures had seemed limitless, even in those dark days of Ayrshire under Thatcher. 'The Touch', Alan's dad had called Craig, a reference to his guitar playing, when once at a Hogmanay party, rather than bringing forth the usual punk-rock stylings,

Craig had silenced the room with a note-perfect acoustic version of Simon and Garfunkel's 'Feeling Groovy'. Alan's dad had pointed heavily, drunkenly at Craig. 'Aye,' he'd said solemnly. 'That boy's got the touch . . . ' The nickname had stuck for a while.

'Hey, Dad,' Tom said getting up.

Alan's initial thought as he hugged his son was, as ever when he hadn't seen him in a couple of months, *You little fucking bastard*. Because, and this didn't seem fair or possible, Tom had grown some more. The boy would soon be twenty and there was no longer any point in trying to deny it, or outflank it with a teased-up hairstyle or those boots Alan had with the quite high heels, because the results were definitely in: Tom was now taller than his father.

And this was real hinge-of-life stuff. Alan remembered how shocked he'd been to find some of his own graduation photographs, years back, when they'd moved out of London, and to see that his father was so much shorter than him in them. He'd never thought of himself as being taller than his father until the very end, but there he was: towering head and shoulders over the old man back in the early nineties. Would Alan and Tom look like that by the time graduation came along in a couple of years? Would Alan be a frail, teetering Yoda next to this hulking Skywalker?

And yet, strange though Tom's continuing growth was, it never failed to astonish Alan how your children always seemed to be the right age, the correct age for maximum love. When you a have a three-year-old and you look at parents with, say, seven-year-old children you think something like *Yeuuch, how can they love such giant brutes?* Yet, when your child reaches seven this seems exactly the age they should be. And the same thing at ten, twelve and twenty.

'Hey, Craig,' Alan said, handing one of the three beers to Craig, the other to Tom. 'So you two have met?' Tom had been filled in about Craig on a couple of Skype calls over the past few weeks, when either he or Katie succeeded in pinning him down on a Skype call. ('Wow,' he'd said. 'You're quite literally helping the homeless?') Mostly, like many long-distance parents, they kept up with his activities via stalking him on the social media profiles he had not yet succeeded in blocking them on. The Instagram account Katie still had operational under a false name showed a relentlessly hedonistic series of images: Tom and some mates suited and booted in some awful student kitchen, holding beers towards the camera, Tom and a bunch of girls doing shots in a nightclub, Tom and mates doing shots at a pool-side bar on his lads holiday to Greece the previous summer, Tom and his mates doing shots at a bowling alley, doing shots at a gig, doing shots in tuxedos at some university ball, doing shots at . . . whatever.

'Yeah,' Tom said. 'Craig got my delay pedal working again.' Tom nudged the wee cream-and-blue box with his foot. Craig pressed the pedal down with the flat of his palm and snapped off a riff on the guitar. 'Rockabilly?' Alan said.

'Aye, classic slapback echo you can do on the DD-3. It just needed soldering. Your boy here's

141

no a bad wee player,' Craig said, switching the amp off, standing up. 'Cheers.' The three of them clinked beers. Alan lowered himself onto the overstuffed beanbag Tom had had for years.

'And how's tricks, Tom? Term end OK?'

'Yeah, all good. I changed a subject.'

'Eh? How come?'

'Couldn't stand the psychology module.' Tom was reading PPE at Glasgow, his father's alma mater. They'd bought a flat for him in the West End.

'Eh? You can do that?' Trying to understand the make-up of degrees these days was far beyond Alan. In his day you picked a subject, did it for three or four years and then sat your finals. Nowadays, modules, dissertations, continuous assessment . . . who had the attention span? Still, he felt he should make some comment here. 'Shouldn't we have discussed this?'

'OK then,' Tom said, playing along, knowing well his father's monumental laziness when it came to anything education-related. 'What do you think about the move from psychology to criminology within a PPE degree, Dad?'

'Fairs,' Alan said, using one of Tom's favoured expressions to admit defeat.

'Anyway, I told Mum. She said 'fine'.'

'Oh good.' Alan said this in a 'we're all done here then' tone.

'Did you two meet at Glasgow?' Tom said.

'At school,' Alan said.

'I dropped out of uni,' Craig said.

'To become a pop star,' Alan said.

'Ach, hardly.'

142

'I googled your band,' Tom said to Craig. 'There's a few songs up on YouTube. Pretty good.'

'Ach, it was a long time ago.'

Sophie appeared in the doorway, hands planted on hips again. 'MUMMY SAYS YOU HAVE TO HAVE DINNER NOW!'

'Jawohl, mein Führer,' Alan said.

'I am NOT mine Fewreerr,' Soph said. 'I'm sitting next to Tom!'

'I thought Craig was your favourite?' Alan said, getting up, draining his beer.

'Tom,' Sophie said firmly, taking her brother's hand.

'That's me told,' Craig said.

* * *

All six of them around the kitchen table, Katie, Alan, Craig, Tom, Melissa and Sophie, the rain lashing off the windows now as they ate winter food: pork shoulder braised in cider (broccoli bake for Melissa) with dollops of mash and carrots slowly cooked in butter and sugar. Wine all round, even a splash for Sophie, topped up with 80 per cent sparkling water — her 'special' cocktail, to celebrate Tom's home-coming. Lana Del Ray played softly — a compromise choice following fierce debate between the kids, with Tom wanting an indie compilation, Melissa some hip hop and Sophie arguing passionately for either *Minecraft* songs or Katy Perry. (Though to be honest her 'argument' amounted to shouting the words '*MINECRAFT*' and 'KATY PERRY' over and over.)

143

The conversation ranged over guitars (Tom and Craig), to the unfairness of not getting to stay the whole weekend at her friend's house for some party (Melissa), to whether Applejack could beat Twilight Sparkle in a race (Sophie, with a spirited contribution from Tom), to Katie and Alan discussing their upcoming meeting with the accountants about their joint tax bills.

Tax. A difficult area. While neither of them could be described as Tax-Me-Daft Red Clyders, it was fair to say neither Alan nor Katie were entirely comfortable with the concept of tax dodging. Minimising the amount you paid within the law was their preferred route. They'd never have an offshore trust but they'd happily put through any conceivable claimable expense. They'd never set up a Dutch shell company but there had been that thing the other year where — on advice from their accountants, after Alan had received an unexpectedly large royalty cheque — Alan had set up a new limited company and then sold some 'assets' (his books) to the company as a way of deferring tax or something. (A bit like asking directions, Alan always zoned out after the accountant's third sentence.) They were assured it was all perfectly legit but it had felt like sailing as close to the edge as they wanted to get. They'd bought the flat in Glasgow's West End for Tom through the company. And with an unexpected windfall from Katie's father. Some dividend or other.

'Tax-dodging scumbags,' Tom said jovially.

'Hear, hear!' Melissa said.

'For the millionth time, Tom,' Alan said,

144

'there's a difference between tax *avoidance* and tax *evasion*.'

'Mmmm,' Tom said. 'A legal one. If not a moral one.' Under siege, from their own bright children.

'You'll find those distinctions get blurred as you get older,' Katie said.

'Aye, true enough,' Craig said. 'I remember back in the band days. We got offered all sorts of money for adverts at one point. Laughed at them. Turned them all down. No way were we selling out. God, I could have done with that money recently I'll tell you.'

'What products was it for?' Tom asked.

'Och, nothing nasty. A car. Some juice drink. It was hardly banks or the *Sun*.'

'Dad did an advert,' Melissa offered, helping herself to a second glass of wine. Bold for a sixteen-year-old.

'Did you?' Craig said.

'A few years back. Just a cameo. Supermarket Christmas ad.'

'You were rubbish,' Melissa said.

'Sell-out,' Tom said.

'As I have no interest in becoming an actor your words cannot hurt me. Anyway, Tom, how's things with the flat?'

'All fine.'

'No crazed mass-invite Facebook parties of late?'

'No. Well . . . '

'That's our money, remember.'

'Grandad's money more like,' Melissa muttered. It was a rare, and slightly too savage,

145

reference to the fact that Katie's family wealth was occasionally helpful to them.

'We earn our own money, Melissa,' Katie said.

'Yeah, sure.'

'And what's that supposed to mean?' Alan said.

'Come on. Grandpa gave you the money to buy Tom's flat.'

'That's not entirely the whol — OK. Enough wine for you.'

There was an edge to the conversation now. Craig kept his head down and concentrated on his food. Sophie said 'No arguing!' and wagged her tiny finger at them. Alan had noticed this recently — Melissa got a little more belligerent, a little more aggressive, every time Tom came home. It was as if this was increasingly the way she defined herself in his presence: Tom was laid-back and gregarious, by some distance the easiest of their children (so often the prerogative of the first-born), so Melissa cast herself as the spiky, provocative one. *The roles that the order of our birth assigns us,* Alan thought. There was also, clearly, a showing-off-in-front-of-Craig element that had crept in in the last couple of weeks. Although it would, of course, be suicide to mention this to a teenage girl.

'Oh, calm down, Dad,' Melissa said.

'Don't do that, Melissa,' Alan said.

'Do what?'

'Attack someone and then, when they defend themselves, accuse them of losing their temper. It's a really tedious tactic.'

'Oh, I'm tedious now, am I?'

146

'Jesus, Mel,' Tom said, exasperated now.

'I said the tactic was tedious, not you.'

'OK, let's move on.' Katie. 'Craig, can you pass the carr — '

But Melissa: 'Uh, maybe it wasn't, like, a tactic?'

'Uh, do you come from, like, the Valley? Are you going to, like, the mall?' Alan said, using the rising inflection at the end, his standard tactic when someone of Melissa's generation did the American sitcom-speak thing.

'People talk this way now.'

'What people? The people on a dumb American sitcom?'

'Oh yeah, everyone's dumb except you.' Melissa, it seemed, was absolutely determined to have the last word, a trait Katie would no doubt have pointed out she shared with her father.

'OK, Mel, that's *enough*.' Alan caught some kind of *smirk* passing between Melissa and Craig. This touched something primitive and patriarchal within him, something ludicrously Victorian, him, the provider, being disrespected here at his own table. *Fuck this*, he thought as he reached for the suicide button. 'For Christ's sake, stop showing off in front of Craig.'

'Oh PISS OFF!' Melissa said, cutlery clattering onto her plate.

'HEY!'

She pushed herself up from the table and stomped off. Alan got up to follow her but Katie said, '*Leave it, Alan*,' in a tone that brooked no argument.

'Melissa's mad,' Sophie said.

147

'Oh, Melissa's always bloody mad about something,' Alan said with far more casualness than he felt, draining his glass.

There was a fractional pause before Tom said, 'Bloody kids, eh?'

Alan grabbed some plates and carried them to the dishwasher. He began stacking the machine, continuing to do a very good impression of someone who was wryly amused by what had just happened. In reality the blood was pumping behind his eyes and he felt light-headed with rage. That smirk they'd shared. He struggled to remember the last time he'd been this enraged at his own dinner table. The last time he'd been this enraged full stop. There was something unnerving about the experience, about what he was feeling right now. That sense of being belittled and outmanoeuvred and made to lose your temper, it . . . it was like being a teenager again. It was like he used to feel around Craig.

★ ★ ★

Sitting outside the Costa the next day, out on one of his walks, wrapped up warm in one of Alan's parkas, sipping a macchiato, Craig turned the page in his journal (the last section he'd begun was headed 'Cocaine?') and began a new section called 'Tax?'. He'd need to read up on this a bit more.

17

'Now this, this, I think you'll find this has a lovely transparency and lightness. It's just 12 per cent ABV. Very floral, you should be getting pink peppercorns, sweet cranberries, fynbos herbs and a trace of soil . . . '

'Mmmm.' Alan swilled it around his gums, getting nothing much of anything apart from watery red wine.

New Year's Eve and he was standing in Turnbull's, their local wine merchant, trying to choose a couple of cases for their party that night. Tom was off seeing some friends, Katie and the girls were still in their pyjamas at home, and Craig had popped into London for a 'wander about'. Something he was increasingly doing these days.

'Whereas this, the Italian, is made from the *falanghina* grape, grown in the south. Very refreshing, with a tinge of orange and saffron. This is an excellent example. The producer makes very limited amounts, the vines were planted in the fifties and he nurtures the grapes with the utmost care. We were very lucky to get a dozen cases this year.'

Nature versus nurture.

Before Alan had children he'd cleaved to the latter as being the primary factor in terms of determining someone's personality. You could take a baby born to an alcoholic serial killer and

149

an unrepentant paedophile and, if you raised the child in an atmosphere of love and serenity, you'd end up with a perfectly well-adjusted adult. Conversely, you could take the child of a judge and a nuclear physicist and throw it into the world's worst sink estate to be brought up by a pair of crack-dealing junkies and you'd get a pretty bad human being. But this didn't explain the blips and glitches you encountered as you went through life: the son of loving, middle-class parents who was sent to the finest public schools in the land and stumbled into adulthood as thick as mince, doing something undemanding in advertising at the paper. The daughter of a cleaner sent to a comprehensive that was a notch above a borstal and yet who breezed out of Oxford with a double first and wound up running BBC2. As he watched his own kids grow up he was increasingly unsure about the wisdom of 'nurture'.

Tom and Melissa had all, or so he thought, been raised in exactly the same way. The same attention had been paid to them, they'd had the same educational opportunities and the same encouragement of after-school clubs and activities. Yet you could not — even allowing for the differences of sex — have produced two more dissimilar teenagers.

Tom was laconic, laid-back and friendly. He was easy to talk to, comfortable in adult company and had, as the cliché went, never given them a moment's bother. He'd always been a solid student rather than a stellar one. He'd got two As and a B in his A levels which

150

had got him into a decent Russell Group university where he was dependably scoring in the 2:1 region.

Melissa was highly strung, argumentative and truculent. She was often prickly and hostile in adult company. Where Tom hadn't really bothered much with girls during his schooldays, Melissa had been boy-crazed since the age of fourteen. At school she did appallingly in the subjects she had no interest in and incredibly well in the couple she cared about — English and history.

Then there was the phenomenon of Sophie. Sophie was ever-cheerful and noisy. She was insanely confident, would take centre stage in any room, talk to any stranger and instantly befriend any child that crossed her path. In the minus column was the fact that Sophie had zero powers of concentration. Even the shortest, flimsiest cartoon could not hold her attention for more than a couple of minutes. She would tune out ten minutes into any movie, could not sit at the table to eat dinner for more than two seconds before she was striding about the room or hanging upside down in her chair, and she could no more sit and read a book on her own for half an hour than she was likely to successfully perform open heart surgery. Her teachers were at a loss. She was described as by far the friendliest, chattiest, most open and confident child in the classroom but she would have absolutely nothing to do with concentrating on an exercise. Alan often found himself wondering where this heady combination of insane overconfidence and zero attention span would take Sophie. TV presenter? Radio DJ? Banker?

So, three children, all raised in much the same manner, with three utterly different outcomes. When all three were babies, if they had been, say, looking to stick their fingers in an electrical socket, and you'd shouted at them to stop, Tom would have obeyed you instantly, Melissa would have looked you in the eye as she defied you and Sophie wouldn't even have heard you. She'd already have been clambering into the fuse box and taking it apart with her teeth. Nature, Alan felt more and more, was encoded. Hard-wired. It would out.

'What do you think?'

He snapped out of it to find Turnbull (fiftyish, fat, florid) grinning at him, holding the label towards him. 'You should be getting cherry, ripe tomatoes, rosemary, thyme, basil, pure Tuscan hillside.' Alan stuck his nose further into the enormous balloon glass. He was certainly getting a headache.

Because you liked food and found you could write about it in an entertaining manner everyone assumed that when it came to wine you had a cultured palate and an encyclopedic knowledge of every varietal grown from Sonoma to southern France. 'You know what?' Alan said. 'These are all nice. You can choose, Richard. Just do us two mixed cases, fifty-fifty red and white, about thirty quid a bottle max, and a case of that champagne we had the last time. Oh, and can you throw in two bottles of Hendrick's? I'll pop

152

back in half an hour.'

'Sure, Alan, you going to be on the telly again soon?'

'I hope not.'

He came out onto the high street — the afternoon staggeringly sharp and clear — and consulted the list of chores on his iPhone.

Puff pastry
Olives
Cheese
Wine
Gin
Logs
Light bulbs (small, bayonet)

He'd left the deli bag with the olives, cheese and pastry with Richard, he'd ordered the wine . . . that left just the hardware store. Tonight would be the usual affair they'd hosted for the last few years — a few of the neighbours, some of Tom's and Melissa's friends.

He huffed and puffed along Marham high street, conscious of the extra weight he was hefting around his middle.

The period from Christmas Eve until today had been spent in the usual kind of somnambulant food-induced coma: an endless parade of snacks and sandwiches and movies and drinks and huge meals. There was a long-established house rule that from Christmas Eve until New Year's Day they would eat whatever they liked. This had had the standard result — in just under a week Alan had gained six pounds. He could feel his stomach straining at his belt. It cracked Alan up when you heard actors banging on about how difficult it was to gain weight for roles, how much praise they got for piling on two stone. Left utterly to his own devices Alan would put on two stone for you in a fortnight. But Katie kept them on the straight and narrow: low carb, lots of greens. It has often been said that without women life becomes a pub. But it also becomes a restaurant — an all-you-can-eat buffet, with a line of sweating, gasping fat men clutching their trays. He'd have to get some exercise in soon.

If this bright, clear weather held up overnight he might try and get out on the golf course tomorrow. Yes, it wasn't quite a 5K run, but walking four or five miles and carrying your own bag (as he always did) so you had a twenty-kilo pack on your shoulder, it was a good way back in, a first step out of holiday indolence. It would be winter greens but that was OK, it would still show this belly he meant business. Maybe take Craig with him, give him a thrashing. They hadn't played since university. Craig, maddeningly, had been eating non-stop too and didn't seem to have gained a pound.

The end of the year marked the one-month anniversary of Craig's residency with the family. There was no question that he'd integrated pretty seamlessly. He didn't get under anyone's feet. He took himself off for walks on his own, read in his room quite a bit and helped out with any chores, happily washing the dishes and taking the bins out. Two mornings a week he

154

went to a basic IT course at the local library that Katie had found for him after he'd expressed frustration at being so far behind with the world of the Internet. He'd been looking at flats online. Studios and one-beds in zones 3 and 4. Alan found the idea of Craig moving into a flat pleased him now for reasons that weren't entirely altruistic.

That smirk.

18

New Year's Day dawned bright and clear, with a crazily unseasonable temperature of fifteen degrees. Consequently, noon found a *slightly* hung-over Alan and Craig in the locker room at Alan's golf club, Royal Marham.

The club had been established in 1902 and was, like Alan's house, the product of a supremely confident Empire. The main building was a late-Victorian mini-castle, with an impressive columned porch and several well-proportioned, high-ceilinged rooms in which the good members (the usual array of doctors, dentists and self-made bastards who formed the core groups at most affluent golf clubs) ate, drank, played snooker or billiards and gossiped. Two more modern annexes flanked outwards from the main structure to the south and the east. The southern extension, built in the late 1990s, housed the swimming pool and gymnasium. (The latter mainly used by the younger membership, those under forty, who had grown up in the post-Tiger world of the 'ripped' physique and the 300-yard drive. The older members were a generation who wore their wealth around their waists and had 300-yard driveways.) The eastern extension, where Alan and Craig were now changing into their shoes, had been built in the 1950s and refurbished every fifteen years or so since then. It contained the changing facilities, a thickly carpeted, oak-panelled warren of lockers, deeply upholstered armchairs and benches. There were Cowshed products in the showers and by the sinks, and the Golf Channel played softly on the several plasma-screen TVs dotted around.

'Fucking hell,' Craig said, looking around as he slipped into one of Alan's Polo shirts, 'far cry from old Ravenscroft, eh?'

'Aye, just a bit. Morning, Jim,' Alan said to a passing member, some silver-haired captain of industry.

Ravenscroft Golf Club back in Ardgirvan, where they had both learned the game as kids; a municipal club, a drab one-storey pebble-dash building where the locker rooms had a cracked concrete floor and the showers a block of carbolic soap the size of a house brick, the clubhouse of tacky carpet and cheap linoleum flooring where their fathers had spent their post-round hours in a thick fug of cigarette smoke by the fruit machines. 'Hey,' Alan said, 'did ye catch any of that business a few years back with Ravenscroft? That boy Irvine who — '

'Aye!' Craig said. 'He near won the Open! Mind his brother?'

'Aye. Madman. He hooked me at the school disco one year.'

Nearly ten years ago a kid from their school, Gary Irvine, had nearly won the Open at Royal Troon. Craig and Alan had been in the same year as his big brother Lee: a total maniac.

'OK, ready to rock?'

'Aye, I suppose so,' Craig said. 'Does this look all right?' He was wearing a pair of Tom's old chinos, one of Alan's sweaters that had shrunk a little in the wash, and a pair of ancient golf shoes Alan had found in the shed.

'Aye, you'll be fine,' Alan said.

'What you playing off these days?' Craig said.

'Thirteen point four,' Alan said nonchalantly.

Back in their youth Craig had been the more regular winner in their golf matches. He had a natural physicality and grace — evident in his guitar playing, his walk even — that lent itself to sport. Although completely untutored he would run rings around Alan at tennis and golf. That was then, however. In the intervening years Alan had sunk the many thousands of pounds and many thousands of hours into his golf game that only being well-off and self-employed allowed you to. A few years ago, just before Sophie was born, his handicap had got as low as 10.3: tantalisingly close to the single-figure mark that had been a lifelong goal. It had gradually slipped back to its current, still respectable level in recent years. But Craig? Craig had been sleeping in underpasses and eating out of bins until a month ago.

'Fucking thirteen?' Craig said. 'Ach come on. I've no swung a golf club in years. You'll need to give us a few shots.'

'Aye, sure. How about we put you off twenty? Match play with full handicaps. I'll give you seven strokes at one to seven.' This meant Craig would get a single stroke taken off his score at the seven hardest holes on the course.

'Fair enough,' Craig said, shouldering the bag containing the makeshift set of clubs they'd assembled for him from some of Alan's old cast-offs and half of Tom's irons.

158

'Let battle commence,' Alan said.

Alan's drive left the first tee, a long downhill par four, with a clean, clear snap. It faded to the right in the air, finishing in the light right-hand rough just over 250 yards down the fairway. 'Pushed it a bit,' he said, picking up his tee.

'Right,' Craig said, taking his place in the spotlight. 'Come on then.' He took a few practice swings just off the tee box and Alan was pleased to see that his swing bore no resemblance to the controlled, punchy three-quarter shot Craig had been known for back in the day. It was wild, looping, his feet moving all over the place. 'Oh man,' Craig said. 'This feels bad . . . '

'Keep your head still,' Alan offered.

Craig sighted down the fairway, drew the club back, and lurched at the ball like a Highland warrior swinging a claymore on the battlefield. He barely made contact with the top of it, sending it skittering along the ground, scarcely making it past the ladies' tee some seventy yards ahead of them. 'Ach well,' Craig said. 'We'll maybe just enjoy the walk, eh?'

'That's the spirit,' Alan said, as the two old friends set off down the first fairway of a golf course together for the first time in . . .

'Hey,' Craig said. 'When was the last time we played golf together?'

'God,' Alan said. 'Fuck knows. Would I have been . . . aye, hang on. I was still at university. You were living in London with the band and we were both back in Ardgirvan during the summer, mind? We played at Ravenscroft?'

'Aye, that's right,' Craig said.

'Would have been '89, '90 at the latest, I reckon.'

Craig whistled.

They had already reached Craig's ball. He took out a five-iron. He still had a good three hundred yards to the green. 'Right, come on, Craig,' he said, settling down into the shot. 'Give this ball the message . . . '

He hit a horrible duck hook into thick rough about another hundred or so yards along the fairway. 'Bastard,' Craig sighed, picking up his bag. 'Who won?' he said, as they set off again.

'Eh?' said Alan.

'Who won that time? When we last played at Ardgirvan.'

'Christ. Cannae remember.'

They parted and went their separate ways, Craig heading off to the left-hand rough, where he would hack out and then take another two shots to make the green, where he would three-putt for an eight, a dreaded snowman. Alan wandered over to the right-hand edge of the fairway where he sweetly hit a nine-iron onto the green and two-putted for a par to convincingly win the hole.

Alan had been somewhat disingenuous in his reply concerning their match in Ardgirvan. Of course he had been. No true golfer ever forgot a round. Jack Nicklaus could give you chapter and verse on what shots he had hit in tournaments from the early 1960s. Alan was no Nicklaus, but well he remembered his overhit approach shot that flew the fifteenth green, the foozled chip and the three putts that followed it to hand Craig a victory of four up with three to play. Yeah, he could still recall the pain.

The first seven holes went exactly as the evidence of the first hole suggested they might: Alan won all of them except the par-three fourth — where he'd stupidly three-putted and Craig had thinned a chip from just off the green that would have been on the adjacent fairway had it not hit the flagstick and dropped in — with the result that he stood on the eighth tee box five holes up. A near-invincible lead.

With this lead Alan was feeling chatty, expansive, as they walked down the eighth fairway towards their drives. (Alan's pleasingly on the fairway, Craig's in a bunker.) 'How are you getting on with the flat-hunting?' Alan asked.

'Seen some nice ones. Seems mental though — a grand a month for some wee studio miles from the Tube?'

'That's London.'

'I might see about just getting a room in a house.'

'Be cheaper.'

On the ninth tee, feeling good about his game, feeling relaxed and swinging freely, Alan made a great powerful arc with the driver . . . and sliced the ball into thick woodland where it would never be found. Cursing, he fished another ball out of his bag and managed to put it on the fairway. Three shots off the tee on this long par five.

Craig stepped up and settled over his drive. He drew the club back slowly. Something seemed to happen. Craig locked into position at the top of his backswing, his shoulder pointing directly down at the ball, and then there was just the slightest of pauses before he uncoiled and — smack — hit a lovely drive straight down the middle of the fairway. The first proper connection he'd made. He then hit a five-iron to within 150 yards of the green and a perfect seven-iron onto it, where he two-putted for a five, his first par of the day. Alan made seven. Now he was only four holes up.

The rhythm, the heartbeat of the match changed.

Craig had found his swing.

Alan, meanwhile, lost his swing. Intimidated by Craig's relaxed, casual, almost half-swing, Alan tried to overcompensate by booming the ball, trying to counter-intimidate with power and distance. The result was predictable — his ball started flying wildly all over the course, finding the rough right and left, the sand, anywhere but fairway and green. Now it was Craig's turn to gibber on about the Internet and how he was loving finding out about all of this new stuff and had Alan seen this website or that while Alan stomped in silence towards whatever hellish spot he'd hit into. Golf — those playing well blabbered on like they were on a fucking chat show while those playing badly were fuming mutes.

By the time they got to the thirteenth green Craig had won three holes in succession and Alan stood over a five-foot putt he had to hole in order to preserve his now slender one-hole lead. He hit it weakly and watched in horror as the

162

ball died just before it reached the cup. 'Unlucky,' Craig said, placing the flag back in and walking off towards his bag. From a seemingly unassailable five-hole lead the match was now tied. Now they had a game on.

Unlucky? You fucking smug little prick. You were sleeping in the fucking gutter a month ago, you ungrateful bastard. I took you into my home, I've lent you money, I'm trying to sort your miserable fucking life out and you come out here, on my golf course and —

'Alan?'

He looked up, snapping out of this vicious reverie, to see that Craig was waving to him from the next tee box. Tied with five holes left to play. *Keep cool, keep cool, keep cool. Just a bit of fun between two old pals. Who cares who wins really?*

Craig won the next two holes and Alan suddenly found himself on the sixteenth tee, a short par three, two holes down with three to play. The full horror dawned on him suddenly — if he lost this hole then Craig would have won the match.

Craig who had not played in God knows how many years.

Who had been eating from dustbins until recently.

Who was playing for the first time on a course Alan played week in and week out.

Who was using clubs he had never used before.

Dear God.

Craig teed off first: a seven-iron to a green

with steeply sloping sides running down into thick rough all around. He struck it sweetly with that punchy half-swing and the ball landed on the front right-hand side of the green, but not far enough on. It wobbled and then — and here Alan was thanking the Golf Gods — it rolled off the side and down the hill, bouncing off into the rough. 'Ach,' Craig said simply. He was eerily, maddeningly, calm.

Much more pumped up than was dignified to be, Alan took an eight-iron and swung with all his might. The ball soared high and was pulled a little to the left but it found the back left-hand quadrant of the green and stayed on there. Safe.

They left their bags at the side of the green and trudged down the hill to look for Craig's ball in the thick wet grass. After five minutes and no sign of it Alan began to allow himself to feel a faint rush of euphoria. *Lost ball, he goes back to the tee and hits another, two-stroke penalty, he's on in three, even if he sinks it all I have to do is make two putts and I win the hole.* He was so lost in these calculations that it took him a moment to realise what he was looking at, right there by his foot.

Craig's ball.

He knew it was Craig's because he'd given him a few used balls from his own bag — all of them Titleists marked with yellow highlighter pen. He looked over. Craig was about thirty yards away, his head down, searching, his back to him.

Instantly an angel with the face of Bobby Jones appeared on Alan's left shoulder and a devil with the face of Donald Trump appeared on his right.

'*Shout your man over,*' Jones said. '*Tell him you've found his ball.*'

'*Fuck that guy,*' Trump snarled. '*Do you want to WIN? I mean, come on. It's your course. You're paying for everything. 'Unlucky'? Can you believe he said that to you? That little prick . . .*'

Before he quite knew what he was doing, Alan had kicked Craig's ball underneath a thick tuft of grass and stomped the tuft down on top of it, burying it completely from sight.

Bobby Jones hung his head in shame.

'*Winner,*' Trump whispered. '*Yuuuggeee winner.*'

They both searched for a few more minutes before Craig sighed and said, 'Fuck it.' He went back to the tee and hit another ball, which missed the green to the right again. Alan won the hole.

He had sinned against all that was decent and holy. He would go to his grave with this mark upon his soul. But he would find a way to live with it — he was only one hole down with two left to play.

Alan won the seventeenth through sheer good fortune — his completely skulled chip shot somehow finished just a few feet from the pin and he managed to hold his nerve and sink the putt, meaning the match was now all square as they walked onto the final tee. Whoever won the hole would win the match.

They were both silent as they headed up to the tee box and Alan saw now what he'd missed before — for all Craig's nonchalance and his 'I

165

haven't played in years' and his whole 'it's just good to get a bit of exercise' crap, Craig really wanted to win.

Alan chose a five-iron for safety — if he lost a ball through a wild swing with the driver it was all over — and managed to put his tee shot in the middle of the fairway, but a long way back from the green. Craig hit the driver — straight and longish, a good way past Alan's ball. He was likely to make the green in three at the most the way he was playing now. Two putts for a five. Alan needed a par to win.

As he stood over his ball for his second shot he found that his vision was shimmering and his hands were trembling. He had to carry the ball nearly two hundred yards over a small moat that guarded the green. He took an almighty swipe with the five-iron and felt that sweetness at his core that came from a perfect connection. The ball sailed high and true, silhouetted for a moment against the low sun (it was almost 3 p.m.), before it dropped down, looking for an agonising moment like it was going to fall short and splash into the water. It cleared the moat by a foot or two and rolled forward, onto the green, finishing around fifteen feet from the pin. Easily the best shot he'd played all day. On in two, just when it mattered the most.

'Golf shot,' Craig said, the highest compliment in the game.

Suck on that, Alan thought.

Craig duffed his next one, sending it skittering some fifty yards up the fairway, leaving him with about a hundred yards left to the green. A wedge. He struck it sweetly and got on in three, but far from the hole.

Craig got down in two putts for a five.

Alan needed two putts for the four that would win the match.

His ball was about fifteen feet from the cup. A pretty straight putt.

A feeling of superhuman confidence came over him. He could do this. As long as he won it didn't matter how close it had been. He could still stride into the house and when the kids asked 'Who won, Daddy?' he could bashfully shrug and say, 'Who do you think?' Craig could protest all he liked about how close it had been but, at the end of the day, you won or you lost and that was that. He lined the putt up and pulled the trigger. The ball curved towards the hole, getting closer and closer, honing in on the target before, right at the last second, just grazing the hole and then carrying on . . . and on. It finished less than two feet past the hole, beyond tap-in distance, but certainly a 'gimme': a short putt that the other golfer, out of good sportsmanship, would simply concede.

Alan walked confidently towards his ball, waiting for Craig to say 'that's fine', or 'take it away'.

Craig said nothing.

What the fuck? He wasn't really going to make him putt a two-footer, was he? Alan had given Craig several putts around that length during the round. He looked up into Craig's face — and found a gaze as blank and pitiless as the sun.

He was going to make him putt it.

Boiling with rage, Alan did the thing many

amateur golfers do when confronted with a short, pretty much impossible-to-miss putt: he strode up casually and took no time at all, just nonchalantly (although there was nothing nonchalant about what was going on inside his head: in there it was the Great Fire of London, it was blitzkrieg, World War III) knocking it towards the cup as though it were a two-inch tap-in and not a wobbly two-and-a-bit footer.

He missed by an inch.

Alan blinked, unable to believe he was still looking at his ball.

'Shit, bad luck,' Craig said.

Five. A tied match. It wasn't as bad as losing, but, Christ, how had he thrown this away from a five-hole lead? Naturally he was already rehearsing in his head how he would justify his defeat in the clubhouse. '*Oh yeah, he said he hadn't played in ages, so I gave him seven shots. Bit on the generous side as it turned out . . .* ' But he knew all of that would bring him little comfort. You won or you lost and that was that. 'A draw then,' Alan said, reaching out to shake Craig's hand. 'Well played . . . '

'I don't think it's a draw,' Craig said.

'Eh?'

Craig took the scorecard out of his back pocket. 'I get a shot here, don't I?'

The horror.

'Surely not he — '

But Alan was already looking at his own scorecard. There it was — the eighteenth. Stroke index seven. The seventh-hardest hole on the course. How the fuck was this poxy par four the

168

seventh hardest . . . ?

It meant that with a stroke deducted, as Alan had agreed in the locker room, Craig scored a four.

It meant that Craig had won.

Alan looked up. Craig was blithely extending his hand and saying, 'Good game.' Incredibly Alan found himself shaking it, although he was so numb at this point he couldn't actually feel anything. He hadn't so much snatched defeat from the jaws of victory as climbed into the belly of defeat and taken up residence there. Alan looked at the putter still in his left hand and said simply, 'I see.'

He drew back his arm to its full extent, like a man about to throw a javelin, and hurled his putter as hard as he could. Its steel shaft sparkled and glittered as it twirled high through the air before landing with a distant splash in the moat he'd hit that perfect five-iron over just a few minutes ago.

When they got home Alan went straight upstairs to shower. He heard Sophie saying excitedly to Craig, 'Who won?'

He didn't hear Craig's reply but the next thing he did hear was Sophie shrieking and laughing as she shouted, 'DADDY GOT BEATEN!'

A few minutes later, his forehead numb against the smooth crackle-glazed tiles (Fired Earth, 120 quid per square metre), the stinging needles of the power shower driving into his back, he allowed a small strangulated cry of pain to escape him.

PART TWO

Spring

19

It came early. In the third week of March the magnolia and cherry trees were starting to bloom. As Easter week began, and British Summer Time officially started, Londoners were indeed walking around in shirtsleeves and eating and drinking on the pavements.

The huge family diary on the kitchen wall — the diary Alan was studying as he stood in jeans and T-shirt, sipping Monday-morning coffee alone in the blissfully empty and peaceful house — showed a busy few weeks in prospect.

Tom was up in Glasgow with exams on the horizon; hopefully he was buried under textbooks in the reading room.

Katie was already down in Cornwall with Melissa and Sophie, where they were renting a house for the Easter break with Vanessa and Jeremy and their kids. All of the kids being at eye-wateringly expensive private schools meant that their Easter holidays had already started a week ago, long before anyone else's, and went on for a week longer. (*The more dough, the less they go*, Alan thought to himself.) Alan had to stay behind because of some meetings in London. He'd be joining them at the weekend, so he and Craig had the place to themselves for a bit.

Incredibly, against all odds, the survivalist-hunting-and-cooking piece had actually come together.

Even though Bear couldn't now do it himself (he was rock climbing in Oregon with Obama) they had the celebrated food critic Miles Warren, the comedian turned increasingly successful US movie star Fergus Marks and Andy Jacks, the guitarist from Britpop legends Crush, who was now an organic chicken farmer and a crusader for sustainable food. They were going to be shown the hunting ropes by a Scottish gamekeeper type and the cooking tips by Tomas Wells, head chef at the hotel they'd be staying at. The schedule was quite tight because Fergus had to go straight back to Los Angeles to begin filming on his new movie. Alan had to go to Cornwall, then back home, then straight to the Highlands to do the piece.

He sat down at the kitchen table and leafed through his mail. Since all invitations to launch parties, openings, premieres and the like now arrived by email his post had been traduced to what most people's was: a hateful stew of bills and junk. In Alan's case this dreck was enlivened (or rather, further cursed) five or six times a month by a Jiffy bag containing the manuscript of some book a friend or an agent or a friend's agent's colleague was looking for a quote for. Alan now had three stock responses for these.

Biographies/Autobio: '*An incredible tale, movingly told.*'
Novels: '*An astonishing tour de force.*'
Cookbooks: '*Mouthwatering. I use this book all the time.*'

Craig, his payment being 'imminent', 'any day now', according to Tim, was in London, on one of his flat-hunting trips. Ealing had been optimistically mentioned. As had Chigwell, Epping Forest, Greenwich, Norbury and even something called Penge.

And this felt welcome. It was time. Even though he'd really been no trouble over the last four months, largely keeping himself to himself, Alan had found things starting to rankle here and there. A certain glance, a comment, a look. It was sobering, shocking even, to find that this could still happen. That, even though time and fate had done their thing and made Alan and Craig what they were, even though Alan had 'won' by any quantifiable measure, Craig could still make him feel small and uncomfortable. Somewhere inside him Alan knew that all the money and fame imaginable could never re-engineer how we come to define ourselves as teenagers. Success didn't make that part of yourself any easier. Not even the first five minutes when you walked into a party and didn't know anyone. Craig, he realised dispiritedly, would always have that power over him.

Alan knew he should really be glad about all of this, about the fact that his friend was returning to his old self after being pretty much a broken derelict four months ago. That had been the whole point, hadn't it? Alan certainly didn't feel the need to be treated like some Hemingwayesque patriarch. He didn't want everyone calling him 'Papa' or anything like that. But, at the same time, Craig had never really said 'thank you' for anything. For all he'd done. And there were incidents, little moments, like the other night, when they were watching the news and Alan made some comment about how the railways should be renationalised and Craig had said, 'The socialist speaks,' while gesturing vaguely at the ten-grand TV, the enormous room stuffed with expensive furniture they were sitting in, the house, and Melissa had sniggered into her tea and said, 'Exactly,' there were moments like that when Alan wanted to stand up and scream, '*WHO THE FUCK DO YOU THINK IS PAYING FOR ALL OF THIS, YOU DISRESPECTFUL LITTLE TWAT? YOU WERE SLEEPING ON A BIT OF CARDBOARD THREE MONTHS AGO! YOU SHOULD BE SUCKING MY FUCKING COCK ON AN HOURLY FUCKING BASIS!*'

Yes, there had been a few tiny moments like that.

But the flat hunt was progressing, out there in Cheam or wherever he was today, and the money was imminent, so all would be well and soon they could all get on with their lives and Alan (that golf ball excepted) could bask in the warm glow of a good deed well done and a man's life turned around.

And he felt for Craig, trying to live in London. Alan, having made his property pile in the nineties, felt for anyone trying to live there today. Back when he and Katie were in their twenties and early thirties everyone they knew lived in a broadish sweep from as far south as Batter sea to as far north as Hampstead, via the likes of Notting Hill, Maida Vale and Belsize Park. Back then places like Bethnal Green, Brixton and Barnes were considered exotic and far-flung, the final outposts of humanity. Now they were pretty much like Mayfair and Belgravia — unattainable hotspots of wealth for pretty much anyone under forty. It puzzled him why you'd want to do this — live in some small crappy terrace in a dreary suburb because you were still, just, technically, in London. Your trip to Soho required a walk, then a bus ride, then a long Tube journey. It took about an hour and a quarter from your front door to W1 and yet you still managed to convince yourself you were living large in the capital because your postcode was something like SE72.

His phone rang: 'CRAIG MOB' coming up on the screen. Yes, Craig had a mobile now. One of Katie's old phones, on a pay-as-you-go deal. 'Hey,' Alan said, 'how's tricks?'

'I just spoke to Tim,' Craig said, excited.

'Lawyer Tim?'

'Go on.'

'Thirty-two fucking grand.'

'Jesus, Craig, that's brilliant.'

'In my account today.'

'Fuck. Congratulations.'

'And maybe a wee bit more to come. Something called 'black box income'.'

'What's that?'

'Fuck knows. Something to do with the way cassettes were sold back in the day. Some tax that was never paid through to writers or something. I wasn't really listening at that point. Anyway — we need to celebrate.'

'Sure. Are you still in London? Should I jump on the train?'

'Naw. I'm at Marylebone on the way back.'

'Right, I'll put some champagne on ice.'

'Fuck that. I'm taking you out. I owe you, pal. *Thank you*. Come on — let's go hit downtown Marham.'

'Marham?' Alan almost never drank in the town.

'Aye. It's got pubs, hasn't it?'

'Well, after a fashion. OK then, I'll meet you at the station.'

Alan hung up, feeling like a bit of a shit. Craig was all right really. Yeah, he was pretty decent.

★ ★ ★

'CHEERS!'

'Cheers to you, mate,' Craig said again as they clanked pints. 'Thirty-two grand. I cannae believe it. It's just . . . unreal.'

They were in the Dragon, the oldest pub in the town, dating back to the late seventeenth century, and usually quiet as the gigantic Wetherspoon's round the corner offered buckets of cooking lager and three-course meals from, seemingly, incredibly, something like 2.99.

They had nearly finished their third pints, were just stepping over the fuzzy threshold between 'jolly' and 'pissed', when a girl came up to their table — they were in the beer garden by this point, both obviously smoking up a storm — and said, 'Excuse me, sorry to butt in, are you Alan Grainger?'

178

'Ah, I'm afraid so.'

'I knew it! HAHAHA, TOLD YOU, ROZ!' She said this to a table across the garden. Alan and Craig looked over to where a bunch of youngsters were watching. 'I read your column every week.' She was in her late twenties or early thirties, short dark hair, not unattractive. Definitely not.

'Well, thank you.'

It was usually a fair barometer of the kind of person you were dealing with, whether they knew you from books, newspapers or TV. As you went further down the social order one prime-time TV appearance equalled many thousands of book sales equalled your face in the broadsheets every Sunday. Alan had cousins in Scotland he only ever heard from via text whenever he made a minor TV appearance. ('HO! BAWBAG! SAW YE OAN JAMIE! M8 YER A FAT BASS! LOL!') Alternatively, he could have won the Pulitzer and the Nobel in the same week and the same cousins would have been none the wiser.

'Can I get a photo?'

She did the thing with her smartphone — arm around him, taken from above — while Craig sat there trying to pretend nothing was happening. (And of course Alan remembered, over twenty years ago, standing in front of King Tut's in Glasgow, the roles exactly reversed, although camera phones were part of the distant future, the three girls around Craig, one of them handing the plastic Instamatic to Alan and saying, 'Do ye mind?' Part of Alan boiling with

179

jealousy, thinking about screwing the photo up on purpose.)

Then the girl said, 'Why don't you come over and join us?'

Alan said, 'Oh, that's very kind, but we haven't seen each other for a while and we're just catching up.'

Forty-five minutes and another pint later and there they were — squeezing in at a table of half a dozen or so very drunk people. ('Alan Grainger! You're a legend, mate! *Legend*.')

Several pints into the drinking session with their new pals (they'd told them the reason they were out celebrating, which earned Craig many slaps on the back and heartfelt 'congratulations') and they started on the shots. Within an hour or so the scene resembled one of the lustier episodes from Tom's Instagram account. Alan was starting to get a glimpse of the hangover that would be coming his way tomorrow — was just at the stage of rationalising, *Oh well, Katie's away, once in a blue moon won't kill me, nothing on tomorrow anyway so I can just sleep it off* — when it happened. He became aware of Craig nudging his side. He looked down to see Craig's fist opening up underneath the table, and there, in the palm of his hand, was a glossy rectangle of paper. Alan looked at it and then up at Craig. '*Coke?*' he whispered out of the side of his mouth. 'Where did this come from?'

Craig shrugged. 'Bumped into a guy I know in Soho. Knew we were going out tonight. We've got an empty . . .'

Alan laughed. 'An empty.' The slang they'd

180

used as teenagers whenever someone's parents were away and they had a house to themselves. It was a ridiculous expression at their age. He looked again at the wrap. 'Nah, I haven't done coke in ages,' Alan said.

'Just a wee toot, come on. Let me say thanks for all you've done.'

'Probably not a good idea,' Alan said.

There was a loud cheering behind them and they turned to see another colossal round of shots being placed on the table.

Fifteen minutes later they were in the cubicle with the credit card and the rolled twenty. 'Shit,' Alan said, sniffing. 'When was the last time we did this together?'

'Fuck. Barrowlands? Around '92, '93?' Craig said, leaning in to snort his line. 'Ahhhhhh . . . ' He handed the note to Alan again.

Like the excessive drinking, cocaine really was a young person's game. Alan had dabbled a bit in his youth, but had pretty much given it up once he'd reached his forties. When he'd been young, back in the *Time Out* days, one gram would provide three or four of them with the necessary energy burst to fuel an extended drinking session, a couple of lines each keeping them going until the early hours. In fact, beyond a certain garrulousness, you wouldn't even have known they'd taken the stuff. Now, however? He saw it in his friends. One tiny whiff and you morphed into a cross between a stroke victim and a vengeful and determined sex offender, your jaw a rigid, wired atrocity, your eyes glassy orbs of lust. (Pointless lust obviously — that

181

same tiny line having instantly reduced your genitals to some kind of joke made by a toddler out of Plasticine.) The number of people he knew who had wrecked perfectly good marriages over an ill-advised cocaine session. Alan knew all of this, he was perfectly forewarned with all this experience, as he sat there in the springtime beer garden, coked up now, with the girl who'd wanted his photo, Amy, telling him about her own attempts to write in between asking him what Jamie Oliver/Gordon Ramsay/the Hairy Bikers were *really* like. Craig sat across from him, sandwiched between two blondes, smoking and talking and laughing. He felt the first flicker of cocaine anxiety, but rode it out by telling himself, *You're not going to do any more of that shit, you're going to have a couple more drinks, calm down, go home, make a sandwich and get to bed by midnight.* Damage limitation. *Damage limitation.*

20

Kitchen disco in full swing.

It was strange how enough alcohol and drugs could distort your perceptions to the point where the frankly incredible seemed completely reasonable. If Alan had walked into his own kitchen on any weekday morning to find the scene before him now he'd probably have fainted. Amy, Roz and another guy were openly smoking. (It would be fine. Fine. He had three days before he went to Cornwall and then a week down there before they all came back. Ten days to clear out the smell.) Two of the other girls (Jessica and someone?) were dancing sexily to the Stones doing 'Beast of Burden', at full volume through the Sonos. Craig was racking out more lines of powder at the kitchen table while he talked to one of the guys (Frank?). Alan was putting more white wine into the freezer to speed the chilling process.

Another guy, whose name Alan had completely forgotten, was leaning against the fridge telling Alan how nice his house was. 'Seriously, mate. Some fucking place you've got here.'

'Yeah, cheers . . . '

'Where's the wife and kids then?'

'Down in Cornwall for the Easter holidays. I had to stay for some work stuff. Gonna join them in a couple of days.'

'While the cat's away, eh?'

'Yeah, something like that. Sorry, it was . . . ?'

'Steve.'

'Steve! Sorry, mate.'

'No worries. Tell you what — ' Steve regarded the enormous Sub Zero crammed with food and drink — 'the old writing lark must pay all right, eh?'

From what Alan could gather the group of three guys and four girls were all colleagues at the local college (or 'university' as it was now laughingly called, like all of them. The Ronnie Corbett University of Shoplifting, or whatever) who had been out celebrating the end of term when their evening took the unlikely turn of events that led to them being here in Alan's kitchen.

'Yeah, keeps a roof over our heads and all that . . .'

'Alan!' He looked over. Amy was holding a CD case with half a dozen fat lines on it towards him and a rolled banknote. Christ. He leaned in and honked one up, unable to avoid staring at her cleavage as he did so. 'Come and sit down,' she said, patting the sofa beside her. The music had changed now, Rhianna. 'Craig was telling us about how you've helped him out. I think it's amazing what you've done for him.'

'Ach, anyone would have done the same thing, you know. What do you do, Amy?'

'I lecture in event management, at the uni? I used to work in the music business, in London. But we moved out here after we got married.'

'Ah. Is one of these your . . . ?' Alan gestured vaguely at the other guys in the room.

184

'Oh no,' she said. 'Just colleagues. We're separated, me and my husband.'

'Right. Well, sorry about that.'

'I'm not. He was an arsehole. It was one of those relationships that . . . ' She went on, plunging into deep detail about her marriage, why it hadn't worked, how selfish her husband had been, how thank God they hadn't had kids, but Alan wasn't really listening. Because that last thick, chalky line had kicked in and he was turning the corner from anxiety into full-blown cocaine paranoia — *What have I done? Why are they all here? Oh God, look at the mess. People are smoking. Fuck, it's nearly three o'clock in the morning, how am I going to get all of these people out of my house? What have you done, you fucking fool?*

Craig had someone's iPod and was changing the music now, to the Stooges or something from back in the day. He was explaining who they were to one of the other girls.

He became aware that Amy was looking at him, expecting an answer to something. 'Sorry?' he said.

'Are you doing any more television programmes soon?'

'Ah, no. All that stuff was just a bit of an accident really. I don't really like being on TV. Most writers don't. It was just to promote the books really.'

'But you're really funny on TV.' She nudged him. She was very close to him now; her thighs were brown, the denim miniskirt she was wearing exposing them quite far up.

'Ach, thank you.' He fiddled with the label on his beer bottle.

'Are you OK?' Amy asked.

'Yeah, fine. Back in a sec . . . '

He went all the way along the hall and into the downstairs bathroom across from his study, at the front of the house, the music and hubbub of conversation reduced to a distant roar — some disco track was back on and everyone was whooping and dancing. He gripped the sink. *What the fuck are you doing?* Suddenly what had all felt like fun and games an hour ago all felt very edgy and scary. His heart was thudding and his mouth was dry. There was also, and there was no denying this, a thick current of lust pulsing through him. He ran some cold water over his wrists and took a few deep breaths, doing his Vincent in *Pulp Fiction* — *Here's what you're going to do. You're going to walk back in there, turn the music down, tell everyone it's been great to meet them but you've got an early start in the morning, stuff to do, so you'll call everyone cabs, on your account of course (no, wait, Katie might check the cab account and think 'why were there cabs to the house at half past three in the morning?'), and thanks for a lovely time, maybe see you all around sometime. And then you're going to go to bed and jerk off and that's all you're going to do.* Drying his hands he looked at the framed award above the toilet: his Press Association Award, 'Best Food and Drink Writing 2010'. Like all writers looking to play down achievements, he underscored the vulgarity of having such things in the house by putting them up in the toilets. *Right, OK. Going in.*

He came out of the bathroom and saw the lights were on in his study. He went in. Amy. Holding a glass of white wine, looking at his bookshelves, her back to him. 'Everything OK?' Alan asked.

She jumped a little. 'God! Sorry!' she said. 'I was just having a nosy. What a brilliant room. I'd love to have an office like this. Are all these yours?'

She was pointing to the section of shelving where he kept all the international editions of his books — hardbacks and paperbacks from France, Germany, Italy, Scandinavia and America. She set her wine down on the shelf and picked out an Italian edition of *Pause Button*.

'Yep.'

'How amazing. You must be really proud.'

'Well, I think the French one sold about fifteen copies to be honest.'

She laughed and turned round, holding the book. 'You know I got this when it came out, as a present in my first year at uni.'

'Wow.' Alan did the arithmetic on their ages and suddenly felt very, very old.

'This was my favourite recipe, look . . . ' She stepped closer to him, holding it open at a page. Alan looked — it was the ragu recipe from *Goodfellas*, with the pork, beef and veal, with the garlic sliced very finely with the razor blade. He could smell her hair, just inches beneath his nose.

'Yeah? Great,' he began. 'Tell you what, you can keep th — '

187

Suddenly she was pressing her lips against his and all at once her tongue was in his mouth and her free hand, the hand without the book, was massaging his balls.

'I, look, Amy, fuck — ' he broke off, panting — 'I'm married!'

'Technically I am too,' she said, scrabbling at his belt. *Oh Jesus. Oh Jesus.*

'Yes, but — '

'Oh, come on, we don't have to, I . . . ' She'd dropped the book now and had one hand down the back of his trousers, the other down the front as she kissed his neck. 'Just let me say thank you . . . ' She was sliding down him now, going onto her knees, her lips brushing his stomach as he felt his boxers being tugged down and something already well on the way to full erection springing free. *Push her off. Just push her off. You don't want to . . .* and suddenly a hot warmth was enveloping him and he was closing his eyes and moaning. God, it was heavenly, he thought after a minute or so, the strangeness, of someone else, after so long with Katie. After . . . Katie. Suddenly her face came into his head, massive and unbidden, he saw her at the kitchen table, the knotted forehead of concentration she got when she was doing the crossword, or reading a difficult passage in a novel. And then, before he knew it, Alan was pushing her back, folding himself back in, zipping up. 'Amy, sorry, you're lovely, but . . . I just can't.'

'Wow,' she said, standing up. 'Now I feel terrible.'

'No, no. Look, it's just one of those things. If I wasn't . . . ' He pulled her in for a hug.

'OK,' she said, breaking it off. 'Look, I'll go back out there first.' She kissed him on the cheek and slipped out of the door. He sat down, breathing heavily, curdling lust already turning to concrete regret in his veins.

He looked around the room thinking, *Did that really just happen?* and the universe arranged it so that the first thing his eyes settled on was a framed picture on his desk: Katie and the kids, taken a few years back in the Caribbean. Katie with the girls wrapped up in a big towel, Tom standing behind her, grinning. Of course his eyes settled on that.

Alan crept quietly upstairs and rooted through Katie's top drawer in their bedroom tallboy until he found her small stash of Valium. He took two and crawled into bed, the digital alarm clock reading 3.52. He could just hear the distant noise of the kitchen disco.

In the morning. He'd deal with all of this in the morning.

21

He opened his eyes. A simple enough task normally. This morning, however, it felt like his eyelids had been sealed shut with Pritt stick or crazy glue and it took some effort to actually start blinking. It was 9.14. He'd been asleep for a little over five hours. Alan tried to move. Bad idea. Incredibly bad idea.

Wow. Oh dear oh dear oh dear. When had he last experienced this?

The cocaine hangover aged forty-eight.

It seemed that during the night someone had suctioned every last drop of moisture out of his body. His lips were stuck to his teeth and his mouth felt like there had been a hairdryer stuffed into it for several hours. This was probably due to the fact that there had been no question of breathing through his nose while he slept — his nostrils having been as thoroughly blocked as if someone had rammed two custom-sized ball bearings up them, forcing him to breathe only through his mouth, desiccating his throat in the process. There was a relentless stabbing head-ache living in the middle of his skull and every one of his limbs ached. He tried to lift a glass of water from the bedside table and found that it was like trying to pick up a bowling ball. Newborn kittens would have been looking at him going 'God, he's weak'. As an additional bonus there was a sour growling in the pit of his stomach which was implying that he might very well be sick soon.

But all of these physical symptoms, appalling though they were, were as nothing when compared to the metaphysical symptoms of his hangover, which now gripped him fully as the details of the night before descended upon him with clarity and horror: him standing on the rug in the middle of his study, fists balled at his sides, the powerful clamping at the centre of him, the wet, repetitive sucking sound. He shook his head in an effort to dispel the vision and found that his headache possessed powers that had only been hinted at so far. *In your own home too.* He'd have to burn his study down now. They'd have to fucking *move.* Metaphysical? This hangover could only get more metaphysical if John Donne himself crawled up Alan's arse right now and started declaiming verse from within his very rectum.

Inevitably, with comically perfect timing, his mobile trilled into life. He crawled to the edge of the bed, stuck his hand in the pocket of his balled trousers, and pulled it out.

Of course: 'KATIE MOB'.

Alan let it go to voicemail and went back to sleep for another two hours.

★   ★   ★

He finally got up and made his way downstairs in his dressing gown just before noon, still feeling awful, appalling, but at least capable of walking, a feat he was unsure he'd ever master again

191

when he'd first woken up. As he pushed the kitchen door open the smell of stale smoke hit him. Jesus wept. There were overflowing ashtrays everywhere, a Manhattan skyline of dirty glasses by the sink, opened, half-drunk bottles of wine strewn about all over the place and, on the kitchen table, two CD covers with a filmy residue of powder on them. He dealt with these first by simply throwing them in the bin. Thank God this wasn't a Petra day.

Working very slowly, and with many a sit-down to sip cups of weak, sweet, milky tea, he gradually managed to fill the dishwasher, pour the undrunk wine away, and take the bottles outside to the blue bin. (At least the bin men would be here while they were still in Cornwall, so all the evidence would be carted away.) Stopping only once to throw up, he scrubbed the kitchen table and mopped the floor. He inventoried the cocktail cabinet and wine rack for what would have to be replaced (*Oh God, oh God, oh God . . .*) and finally slumped down in an armchair with a bowl of cereal around 1.30. Which was about the time he heard footsteps on the stairs and then Craig was popping his head round the door.

'A'right?' he said.

'Well, not really, no.'

'Aye, bit of a big night, eh?'

'You could say that. I feel like fucking death. What happened? When did everybody leave?'

'Fuck knows, about five? Or six? It wasn't quite light when they went. What happened to you?'

'Eh? Oh, just suddenly felt absolutely fucked. Sneaked off to bed.'

'Did you manage to sleep?'

'A bit . . .'

'Ah wis grinding ma gears all night.'

'Why the fuck did we decide to get on the coke?'

'Ach, seemed like a good idea at the time. Don't beat yourself up.'

Oh but he was. Christ was he. He thought of Katie and the kids, on the beach down near St Ives. Ice cream and fish and chips and running around in the surf and . . . for a second Alan feared he might cry. He just wanted to be by himself. Wasn't this one of the definitions of hell? That you were forced to spend your time there in the company of the people with whom you'd committed your greatest sins? Forever staring guiltily into their burning eyes?

'You OK, Alan?'

'Uh, yeah. Just fucked. Been a long time since I did something like that.'

'Like what?' Craig said.

'You know . . . coke.' Alan swallowed. 'Partying until the small hours.'

'Right,' Craig said. 'The good news is I have the solution.' He held up the TV remote and a glossy leaflet he'd brought in with him. Domino's. 'We have Sky Movies and we have pizza delivery . . . '

Alan looked at him. 'Jesus. We're going to lie around all day eating Domino's and watching movies?'

'You got a better idea?'

193

'I guess . . . no.'

'Right then, leave it to your auld da here. Some painkillers, extra-large pepperoni, some chicken wings, Coca-Cola, get us through to about six o'clock and then a couple of wee glasses of red wine and we'll be right as rain.'

Jesus, Alan thought. *We might as well be watching Jeremy Kyle in our pants.* It occurred to him that of course Craig could handle this better than him. He'd been sleeping rough for ages. His tolerance for feeling like he'd been hit by a bus was that much higher. 'OK,' Alan said. 'You phone the pizza, see what's on TV, I'm just going to call Katie . . . '

He eased himself up slowly, with considerable difficulty, and hobbled towards the door. He turned back. 'Oh, by the way, it goes without saying that none of this happened. We went out for a few pints, turned into a bit of a session . . . and that's about it.'

'Course. I've got yer back, pal.'

Alan went upstairs, calling Katie as he went.

Lying to your wife 101.

1) Admit that something happened. In the same way that a shark can detect an egg-cupful of blood in a hundred square miles of ocean, she will be able to detect the tiniest strand of hangover in your voice. Do not attempt to sound bright and breezy and everything's-normal-nothing-to-see-here-please-move-along. Admit to a bit of a drink-up and a painful but manageable hangover.

194

2) Do not go into too much detail. Some broad strokes will suffice — you went out, had a few pints to celebrate Craig's money coming in, turned into a bit of a session, you came back here and got stuck into the single malt. Went to bed about two. Craig was smoking in the kitchen doorway so a bit of it might have wafted in. You're really sorry.

3) Do not, under any circumstances, feel the need to confess the fact that you got blown by a twenty-something fan girl in your study.

'Hey, darling,' Katie trilled.

'How's tricks?'

'Oh dear! Are you hung-over?'

The call went according to plan.

As did the afternoon and evening.

They channel-hopped and landed on a couple of old favourites on Sky Movies — *Wall Street* and *Jaws*. They munched their way through an XL pepperoni with jalapeños, two portions of chicken wings, some spicy potato wedges and a litre of full-fat Coke (Alan conservatively reckoned the calorie count of the meal to be something in the region of 5,000) before opening a bottle of Rioja somewhere around 6 p.m. A couple of glasses almost made Alan feel human again.

Tomorrow he'd feel better. And the day after that, when he had to go to Cornwall, better still. And soon enough Craig would move out and last night would eventually be, if not forgotten, reduced in potency to a manageable disgrace, a tolerable *ignominy*, buried in his memory bank as an unfortunate, never-to-be-repeated experience.

That's how it would all go.

22

Katie and Vanessa were in the vast kitchen of the rented house, chopping vegetables, with a second bottle of Sancerre well under way. The younger kids were running around crazy somewhere above them while Melissa was watching TV with Jamie, Vanessa and Jeremy's sixteen-year-old Tinder-using son. Jeremy was out picking up some more shopping. (They'd gone through an incredible amount of food in a few days.) Through the windows they could see the sea, just north of St Ives. The Easter holidays, half-term, summer — when parts of Cornwall were seemingly overrun by every ponce in north-west London with a few quid to rub together and children young enough to still constitute nightmares in airports. They'd gone for a walk through town last night: the amount of 'hellos' and 'how are yous?' It was like strolling along Regent's Park Road on a Saturday afternoon. The house was costing them the best part of ten grand for the ten days they were here. (However, as everyone reasoned, by the time you'd factored in flights to somewhere warm, it probably all worked out a bit cheaper.)

'Big session, was it?' Vanessa asked.

'Sounded like it,' Katie said.

'Does he drink a lot then?'

'Alan?'

'No! Trampy.'

'Oh, Craig? No, not really.'

'I just wondered, with living on the streets and all.'

'I don't think he was ever full alky man.'

Vanessa topped them both up, finishing the second bottle. They were making a whole leg of lamb with many side dishes.

'God, we're getting through it,' Katie said. 'Tell me Jezza's picking up some more wine?'

'It was on the list,' Vanessa said, slicing the stalks off some ruby chard now. 'And so this money's actually appeared then, has it?'

'Yep,' Katie said. 'Thirty-odd grand, would you believe?'

Vanessa was thinking. 'And he's going to rent a flat and generally try and get back on his feet?'

'That's the idea . . . '

'It's so mad you've had him living with you for, what, nearly four months now?'

'He's not really been any bother to tell you the truth. He's actually been quite helpful with the kids.'

Sophie ran in, the two younger boys in her wake, and levelled a finger at her mother as she yelled, 'YOU'RE A POO-POO-HEAD!' With this she brayed with laughter and ran back out, her tiny disciples following her, shrieking at her own Wildean bon mot.

'And you still haven't thought of working all this into your column? 'My life with Trampy' sort of thing?'

'Well, obviously I did, but I told you, Alan wasn't keen.'

Vanessa was sipping her wine, thinking.

'Here we go . . . ' Katie said.

'Well, I was just thinking, might be a good story now actually, now that you have a resolution to it. A third act, so to speak. Two old school friends, one becomes successful writer, the other ends up trampy man. Successful man helps trampy man get off the streets, reclaim his lost fortune and get back on his feet and all that. I'm thinking *Times* Family possibly.'

'Mmmm, maybe.'

'You think he'd be keen?'

'Craig or Alan?'

'Both. Either.'

'Could you pass me the rosemary please? I don't know. Ask Alan when he gets here.'

'Would you mind if I pitched it?'

'Not at all. I think you'd write it well. When were you thinking of doing it?'

'Dunno. Whenever.'

'Well,' Katie said, 'Alan does have the paperback of the second *Eating Out* coming out soon. Maybe it would work around that?'

'That'd be perfect, wouldn't it? I'll talk to him when he gets here.'

They clinked glasses.

The way things got done: Columnist Friend A had an idea involving Celebrity Pal B that they pitched to Editor C. Editor C approved idea and Columnist Friend A got paid and Celebrity Pal B got their book/film/TV show/ scent promoted and Editor C (hopefully) got their circulation figures or their click rate or whatever up a little and the whole happy circus moved on from town to town. It was a game played out in the roomy kitchens of north and west London and over drinks in spacious rented houses in Cornwall and in the private members' clubs of Soho.

They heard the scrunch of tyres on gravel and then keys in the door and Jeremy was coming down the hall and into the kitchen laden with shopping. 'Jesus,' he said. 'Bloody bun fight in Waitrose, I'll tell you. It was like chucking-out time at the fucking Groucho.' Jeremy was well built, not quite rugger-bugger physique. Fiftyish, with thick grey hair, he had been a lawyer to trade who now did something very senior in the legal department of the BBC. (Which meant, much to his irritation, that his salary was available for public viewing on their website. Katie had checked it out when he'd taken the job and had been surprised that it was as little as £160,000 per annum. Vanessa earned much more. Jeremy argued that, although poorly paid, it was far less stressful than working in the City, which was probably true.)

'Did you remember the wine, darling?' Vanessa asked.

'Duh,' Jeremy said. 'Loads more stuff in the car. Jamie! Come and give me a hand.' A faint teenage moan from the front room. 'It's Sky Plus. You can pause it!' his father shouted.

'Melissa, you help too!' Katie shouted.

More low teenage grumbling and then the sound of clumping out to the car began.

23

Alan checked his reflection in the milky light of the bathroom on the first-class sleeper train to Inverness. He looked well: tanned and rested from a week by the sea with the kids, where he'd been eating healthily and doing a bit of surfing, which was certainly good for the old waistline. He turned and regarded the small single bed behind him dubiously. The idea of getting the sleeper had felt brilliantly romantic a few weeks ago but now, standing there in the swaying carriage as they rolled slowly out of Euston and through the tunnels under north London, he was less convinced about how much actual 'sleeping' would get done in here.

The photographer and his assistant were already up there.

Fergus Marks was flying into London from Los Angeles, then another plane to Edinburgh tomorrow and then being driven up to the hotel.

Miles Warren was holidaying in Scotland and would make his own way there.

Andy Jacks had to be in London tonight 'for a thing' and, fairly incredibly, would be flying himself up tomorrow in a light aircraft belonging to a friend. 'No, really,' Pandora had said. 'He's a proper pilot and everything'

He was giving Pandora a 'lift' in the plane, something she sounded very excited about. *Well, each to their own*, Alan thought. He'd about as soon slather his nuts in ground beef and dangle them into the maw of a starving Dobermann than fly in a tiny plane piloted by a rock star. But apparently Jacks was a much changed man from his cocaine-snorting nineties heyday. He had six children and an enormous organic chicken farm to run. He'd followed the traditional rock-star curve — from going to bed at 6 a.m. to getting up at 6 a.m., largely existing on a macrobiotic diet of bark and leaves and mineral water.

Alan checked his watch: time for dinner and a few drinks before he turned in for the night. He made his way along the wobbling corridor and into the first-class restaurant car. It was completely empty and softly lit by spots at each table. Ideal. Alan took a seat, ordered a Talisker and soda as an aperitif, and put his laptop, notepad and the novel on the table.

The mooted reason he was getting the sleeper in the first place, other than the fact that it popped you out straight in the heart of the Highlands, was so that he could 'have some peace and quiet to do some work'. He still had to finish writing the 5,000-word essay on modern restaurant culture that was going to preface the new edition of *Eating Out*. Finish writing it? He hadn't *started* writing it. Part of the reason for this was that, while he had certainly agreed to write this essay (over a lot of Chablis and a fifty-quid piece of Dover sole in Scott's with his editor), when it actually came to properly contemplating it, he found the words '5,000-word essay on modern restaurant culture' made him physically ill.

After scribbling a few phrases like '*the molecular gastronomy trend, while looking to be the sun, turned out to be a black hole*' and '*future generations will scratch their heads as they contemplate the culture of the pop-up restaurant*', he closed the notepad and did what one should properly do on a long train journey: he drank and looked out of the window, at the blackness of what he guessed was now Hertfordshire sliding past the window. A waiter drifted by and placed a menu in front of him and Alan ordered a second whisky while he perused it, feeling the pleasurable tingle of a man used to living in a household of three children who was about to enjoy a meal alone with a decent book to read — surely one of the most routinely underrated pleasures in life?

He ordered — the Rannoch Smokery duck followed by the Highland beef and Docharty potato casserole with seasonal greens and then the cheeseboard, along with a half-bottle of their Pinot Noir — and sighed contentedly as he opened his book.

He had just finished his main course ('overcooked beef struggling in a sauce thick enough to tar battleships') and was slicing a piece of Tain Truckle Cheddar when his mobile rang. 'CANTERS', his accountancy firm. At eleven o'clock at night? This was odd. Had they forgotten to pay the VAT bill this quarter or something?

'Hello?'

'Alan? It's Bill. Sorry to call so late. Can you talk?'

'Ah, I'm on a train to Scotland, but yeah.'

'It's a bit of a weird one. I got a call at the end of today and I just wanted to review a few things before I rang them back but, the thing is, you're going to be audited.'

'Audited?'

'By HMRC. Last year's accounts. The ones we submitted in January. It does happen now and then.'

'Christ. Why?'

'Well, they say it's random, but who knows really. It's a pain in the arse frankly. We'll have to go right through all your receipts, all your invoicing.'

'Is it, I mean, is everything OK? Do we have anything to hide?'

'No. Not really. There's always little things like when you're away for business and you stay in a hotel and you claim the whole bill as a deductible expense while, in reality, you're only allowed to claim 'subsistence', which means food really. Tea and coffee. Not alcohol and cigarettes and stuff like that. I've had a couple of cases with clients in the past where they've gone right through the individual bills and made us take off every single gin and tonic from the minibar and every pack of fags from room service and stuff like that.'

'Fucking hell.' Alan looked at the receipt on the table for £56.86, for his dinner and drinks, a bill he had been about to automatically stuff into his wallet where it would live for a few days until it was transferred to the box in his study where he kept his receipts until, every quarter, they were mailed to Canters so they could do his VAT return and then file the receipts away for his annual tax return. 'Do I actually have to do anything, Bill?'

'Not right now, no. We'll get into it. You'll probably have to come in for a meeting at some point, so we can go over some stuff, but I just wanted to give you a heads up.'

'Right. Thanks. Shit.'

'Like I said, it's a pain in the arse, but we've been here before with other clients. We'll handle it. Try not to worry and have a good trip. What are you doing up there?'

'Oh, a feature for the Food Quarterly thing.'

'Great. Well, have fun. I'll keep you posted.'

Alan hung up. Christ, it was true what they said. When you were young the bank manager was the demonic figure in your financial life. As soon as you started making some real money he faded into the background, only to be replaced by the even more terrifying figure of the taxman.

Alan finished the last of the wine (scoring it out of the receipt) and wove his way back along the corridor to his cabin, where he tossed and turned in the swaying bed for a good while before he fell asleep, somewhere in the Lake District in the early hours of the morning.

24

'What was Alan like at school? What was Alan like at school?' Craig scratched his stubble and thought some more as he repeated the question.

They were having lunch in Dean Street Townhouse. Vanessa's iPhone sat on the table between them, the voice-recording app doing its thing while Craig scratched his chin and considered the question, trying to land on a witty sound bite of an answer. He used to be good at this sort of thing. But it had been a very long time since he'd done an interview. (The late nineties, in some bar in Glasgow with a kid from either *M8* or *Tennents Live! News*, one of the Scottish music papers of the time. A doomed attempt to promote his final, independently released solo record.)

'Ach, he was a'right, you know?' Craig laughed self-effacingly. 'Sorry, Vanessa, been a while since anyone sat me down in front of a Dictaphone. Christ, no even a Dictaphone now. iPhone. Whatever.'

Vanessa laughed too. 'Well, how did you meet him? The first time, you know?'

She topped him up. They'd had a good half-bottle with the starters, trying to loosen him up a bit. Craig thought and looked through the stained-glass window, out onto Soho.

Just a few months ago he'd found a good place to sleep along there, next to that Guinness pub off Soho Square, an unlocked gate leading to a wee basement entrance to an empty office. Got a few good nights in there before some fucking junkies found it and started coming down to smoke rocks. And now here he was: drinking ten-quid glasses of wine, surrounded by cunts. 'I dunno. He was just always around, from when I was thirteen or fourteen.' He remembered something, that fucking armband. 'Aye, that's right, about the time we all started getting into punk, thirteen, fourteen, he turned up wearing this really shit Crass armband, you remember Crass?'

Vanessa shook her head.

'Mad anarcho punk band. Anyway, Alan turned up once with this really shit home-made Crass armband. I think his granny had made it for him or something. Some of the boys ripped the piss right out of him and he went home crying. He was, you know, he was a bit of a plastic.' Craig laughed, saying the word for the first time in God knows how many years.

'A plastic?'

'A plaso. A plastic punk.'

'What on earth is that?'

'Just, someone who's trying to get into it but they're a bit rubbish, ken?'

'Like, an imitator?'

'Kind of. Just . . . slightly the wrong clothes and that. Anyway, that's when I remember him starting to hang out with our crowd a bit. Coming to gigs and things. UK Subs at Ayr Pavillion, SLF at Killie Town Hall, Anti-Pasti up at Tiffany's.' Craig was now literally speaking Swahili as far as Vanessa was concerned. 'Be about 1982, I think, once we were all getting into forming bands and stuff like that, he bought a bass, the instrument nobody wants to play, right? And he was always trying to join in until finally I thought, fuck it, and he was in my band for a bit.'

'Was he any good?'

Their main courses arrived: mince and potatoes for Craig, Caesar salad for Vanessa.

'Fuck naw. He was shite. But Alan was always . . . organised. Really organised. Sometimes ye need someone like that, y'know? But at the end of the day he couldn't really play and that's all right for a while but then ye start getting serious about it and — '

'Was he surprised back in the early nineties when you became successful? With the band?'

'Don't know. You'd have to ask him.'

'Do you think he was bitter?'

'Bitter? It wasn't like Pete Best. Like we kicked him out just before we made it big. He was only in a band with me for about a year or so, when we were about sixteen or seventeen, kinda mid-eighties time. It was all the Pastels and the Mary Chain and Creation stuff by then.' Again — Swahili. 'We didn't 'make it' — whatever that means — until years later. So naw, I think he was just pleased for us. Said he was. Mind you, you never know, do you?'

'How do you mean?'

'Well, you know, like Morrissey says, 'we hate it when our friends become successful'.'

Vanessa laughed. 'And how did you feel about him, later?'

'How do you mean?' Craig wiped gravy from his mouth.

'When he became successful.'

'Ach, I kinda missed a lot of that, you know? I had other things to deal with.' They had already covered Craig's descent into alcoholism and destitution in the noughties in the early part of the interview.

'But now, say. How do you feel about it now?'

'Well, he's helped me out massively.'

'That's not quite what I asked though, is it?' Vanessa said.

Craig met her eye. There was a pause and then he said, 'Obviously I'm pleased for him. He's done really well for himself.'

'Great. Here, just let me pause that,' Vanessa said, reaching for her phone. 'Just going to pop to the loo.'

In the downstairs toilet Vanessa checked her make-up and washed her hands. Very often the tone, the attitude, of a piece was decided long before it was ever written. For instance, no matter how appallingly the interviewee behaved, if you were writing for, say, Condé Nast, you wouldn't put the boot in because the tone of interviews in those kind of lifestyle publications was generally one of 'aren't we all great, isn't this great, it's all lovely, here's some adverts for watches'. Even if the interviewee actually tried to rape the journalist it would be covered in an aside saying they were on 'exuberant' form. Similarly, the piece Vanessa was writing was for the *Sunday Times* Family section. The piece she'd pitched to her editor was a life-affirming one, where old bonds triumph over adversity. Where the protagonist goes through some tough times but, basically, where friendship conquers all. So it wouldn't be appropriate, she wouldn't be mentioning, what she thought she'd just seen: the set of the jaw, a certain hardness in the eyes and the flatness of tone when Craig met her gaze and said, 'Obviously I'm pleased for him. He's done really well for himself.' No, Vanessa thought, *whatever's gone on there, I think we'll keep that out of it.*

It did make her slightly sad, however, the realisation — common to many jobbing journalists who must routinely deliver copy crafted to suit many different publications — that lurking beneath the piece she was going to write about the life-affirming powers of friendship, there was another piece, a different piece, a better piece. One about the strange currents and deep, dark pools that hide beneath the surface of many lifelong friendships, especially ones that have involved dramatic reversals of fortune. Yes, there was definitely something to be written on that . . .

25

A car was waiting to collect Alan at Inverness Station. The drive to the hotel near Grantown-on-Spey went past Loch Moy and took just over an hour.

They were going through a valley with towering grey-stone Highland mountains rising up above them, springs of water coursing down the rock face, swirls of mist hiding the peaks. The beauty of this part of his own country never failed to amaze Alan, although he still struggled to connect the scenery he was looking at now with the words 'his own country'. He watched the sun split the crags between the mountaintops and reflected that the vista he was looking at seemed to have about as much in common with the concrete new town he and Craig had grown up in as a Rembrandt in a gilt frame had in common with the picture of a tennis player scratching her arse. He sighed contentedly, just about managing to sweep the tiny grain of worry about last night's news under a rug in his mind. An audit — so what? He hadn't been doing anything illegal, had he? Some perfectly legitimate tax avoidance no doubt, but nothing approaching tax evasion. As always when you've found some contentment within the universe, the phone rang with some bastard intent on shattering it.

He looked at the screen — 'PANDORA

211

MOB'. Probably ringing to crow about the awesomeness of private air travel.

'Pands,' he said. 'How's tricks? I'll be there in — '

'Alan,' she began, and immediately he could tell this was not good. 'Are you sitting down?'

'Oh God . . .'

'It's Andy Jacks.'

'What the fuck's happened?'

What had happened was this.

At 6 a.m., as agreed, Pandora had arrived in reception at the Groucho Club to collect Andy, who had been staying there the night before after finishing some interview duties to promote his new book. The plan was to jump in the car she had waiting and drive the hour and a half out to the private airfield in Essex where the Cessna prop plane (on loan from Pink Floyd's Nick Mason) would be waiting for Andy to fly them to Inverness, where they were due to land around 10 a.m. It all seemed so reasonable.

Pandora's fears had begun when the receptionist at the club had been unable to rouse Andy by telephone. Pandora had convinced the guy to just let her go up and knock on the door and get him moving. Much joking about bloody-rock-stars-not-known-for-their-early-starts-are-they? She took the tiny lift to the second floor and started walking down the narrow hallway to Andy's room. Here her fears had been allayed when she distinctly heard music coming from behind his door. He was at least up. Probably couldn't hear the phone for the stereo. She'd knocked crisply, cheerfully, on the door and after just a few seconds it had swung open and Pandora's fears had gone from 'simmering' to 'off the charts' in half a second.

Andy Jacks stood there, naked save for his boxer shorts. He had a glass of something in his hand and a cigarette dangling from his lips. Indeed the air in the room was so thick with cigarette smoke it was like someone had opened the door to a steam bath. Music, disco, blared from behind him. 'Room service?' he said, perfectly pleasantly.

'Ah, Andy, no. It's Pandora from Food Quarterly? The —'

'Come in, come in!'

Pandora advanced tentatively into the small room. The curtains were closed against the weak dawn now rising across Dean Street. Andy reversed to allow her entry and in doing so fell over a small stool and went crashing to the floor, sending his drink flying. 'Hi . . .' Pandora said weakly, terrified, to the three figures on the bed. There were two girls and a man, a skinny, squirrelly-looking fellow who said 'All right, love?' without looking up from the enormous pile of cocaine he was shaping into lines on a picture that had been torn from the wall. Indeed, many of the surfaces in the room — the TV stand, the bedside tables, the coffee table — were covered in a film of white powder, like someone had been dusting for prints. Any available surface area not covered in a film of powder was littered with glasses or bottles: half-drunk bottles of wine and beer, champagne, whisky and vodka.

Clearly Andy had suffered 'a regression'.

He got back to his feet, laughing. 'Spilt my

bloody drink. Pandora, can I get you something? Vodka and tonic?' He made the offer in a perfectly charming and debonair way, as though he were offering tea and biscuits at 4 p.m.

'Ah, Andy,' she began gently, like she were talking to a madman, to Colonel Kurtz in his cave, 'we're going to Scotland? For the feature?'

'Eh? What feature?'

Oh God.

One of the girls on the bed got up and staggered across the room, knocking a few glasses to the floor as she went; she tumbled into the bathroom and began noisily vomiting into the toilet. The guy chopping the cocaine laughed and said, 'You bloody lightweight, Tara.'

Andy, a model of good manners, grinned sheepishly and closed the door.

'You're meant to be flying us there?' Pandora said. 'In your friend's plane?'

'Is that . . . did we . . . ?' Some light seemed to come on in his eyes. 'Shit, I thought that was *next* week.'

'But — '

'Here, Andy,' the guy on the bed said, passing over the picture and a rolled note. Andy took it, leaned down and smartly cracked a huge line of cocaine up his nose. He then offered the mirror to Pandora.

'Not for me thanks,' she said.

'To be honest, I'm not sure I should be flying today,' Andy slurred. *No shit*, Pandora thought. She doubted he'd even get into an *airport* like this, much less into the cockpit of a plane. 'Yeah, last night turned into a bit of a . . . celebration.

214

Hadn't been out in town for a while and all that. So — what's plan B?'

'Jesus,' Alan said, trembling hand pressed to his forehead in the back of the car as he took this in. 'Where are you now?'

'In an Addi Lee on the M4 to Heathrow. I managed to get us on the 11 a.m. BA to Inverness. He's in the back fast asleep. He took a handful of Valium and passed out the minute he got in the car.'

'Fuck. We're meant to be *hunting* this afternoon. He's got to shoot a fucking pheasant or a rabbit or something.'

'Alan, I cannot stress how bad an idea it would be to put a shotgun in the hands of this man right now.'

'Maybe we can see if one of the other guys will do the shooting and he can fish or do the veggie one. Fuck. FUCK. How late are you going to be?'

'Should be at the hotel by 1.30-ish?'

'Right, OK. I'll feed the others some bullshit. We'll have to start a bit later than planned. Let me know how he is when he wakes up. Fuck. Sorry, Pandora.'

'Hey, rock and roll.'

Alan hung up. Never work with children, animals or rock stars, who were pretty much a combination of the first two elements.

They were pulling up at the hotel now: a five-star Victorian lodge of pale sandstone set in many acres of grounds. As he got out he could see Archie the photographer and Danny (one of the bods from digital who'd be filming for the

215

website) smoking on the front porch, talking to an elderly man in tweeds and deerstalker hat. (A resident?)

'Alan! How's tricks?' Archie said as Alan came up the steps. 'What a place! Sensational!' He flapped a hand at the scenery. The tweedy man eyed Archie with some suspicion as Alan tried to place Archie on his own personal Flaming Meter: probably about a six right now. Two drinks and he'd be telling the story about how he let one of DiCaprio's agent's assistants blow him at a party at the Beverly Hilton last year.

'Hey, Archie. Yeah. Your first time in the Highlands?'

'No no, darling. I was here about ten years ago. Shooting Kate. Can't remember a fucking thing obv. Listen — ' he turned and swept an arm over Tweedy Man — 'this is Fintan, our gamekeeper! Isn't he adorbz?' Archie clapped his hands together as if introducing a cute tiny puppy at a dog show. Fintan the gamekeeper advanced, his eyes downcast, hot with shame.

'Ah, hi there, Fintan,' Alan said, extending his hand. 'I'm Alan, the editor.'

'AyerichtenuffpleastaemeetyeAlan.' This was spat out so fast that even Alan, the only Scotsman in the group, struggled to piece it together as 'Aye, right enough, pleased to meet you, Alan'.

'Bear speaks very highly of you,' Alan said.

'Ochhe'sfullo'itthatwan.'

'Miles is in the bar, Fergus is having a nap,' Archie said. 'I take it you've heard about Pan?'

'Yeah. They're, uh, running a bit late. Surprise surprise.'

216

Archie rolled his eyes.

'Right,' Alan said, clapping his hands together, trying to get into 'taking control' mode. 'I'll go say hello to the guys then we can have an early lunch and run over things . . . '

★　★　★

Miles Warren was indeed in the bar. 'Hey, Alan,' he said, looking up from the tea he was pouring — green tea, Alan noticed — as Alan entered.

'Miles, nice to see you again. Thanks so much for doing this.'

'Yes, tell me, exactly what the fuck are we doing today?'

O-Kaaay.

'Tiny change of plan actually. I think you were meant to be salmon fishing, but how do you feel about shooting?'

'What, shotguns?'

'Yep, gonna try and get some rabbits.'

'Fine by me, but when do you think we'll be done?'

'Uh, well, obviously we're already running a bit late.'

'Andy?'

'Ah, yeah. Bit of a delay there, I'm afraid.'

'So I heard. Thing is, I really wanted to try and get back to London tonight.'

'Really? I thought you were on holiday up here?'

'Weather's been miserable. Jane went home with the kids yesterday.'

'Ah. Well, we're probably not getting done till

the light's gone now. Which is what up here, eight o'clock-ish? I thought we'd all have dinner here, few drinks.'

'Not drinking at the moment, I'm afraid . . . ' Miles topped his green tea up as though to reaffirm this.

'Really? Right. Well, let me get Pandora to look into getting you on a flight out of Inverness tonight.'

'Ta. Do I have to wear that awful tweed suit someone's put in my room by the way?'

'Well, it was part of the whole idea. Scottish-gamekeeper-look kind of thing.'

'Christ.'

'You hungry? I thought I'd get some lunch in. The others should be here soon and we can go over the game plan. I've heard they do excellent game here.'

'On a diet at the moment, I'm afraid.'

Jesus. Let the party begin, Alan thought.

'Hello all!' They turned to see Fergus Marks entering, refreshed by his nap. Alan and Fergus embraced, then Fergus. Everyone knew each other a little bit because of chat shows and parties and green rooms. 'What happened to Bear?' Fergus asked.

'Oh. Hiking with Obama again.'

'The cunt,' Miles said, although it was unclear whether he meant Bear Grylls or the former president of America.

They ordered sandwiches and soup and whatnot. Archie came in and snapped some casual shots of the three of them chatting for half an hour or so until there was the crunch of tyres

218

on gravel from outside, voices, and then Pandora was walking in trailing a sheepishly grinning Andy Jacks behind her. 'So sorry we're late!' Andy said. 'My fault.'

Alan's first thought was how extraordinarily well he looked. A few weeks back, on the night of disgrace, when Alan had done pretty much (if Pandora was to be believed) a quarter of what Andy had done the night before, Alan had wound up spending forty-eight hours in the foetal position. But here was Andy — laughing and shaking hands and hugging Fergus, ordering himself a Bloody Mary and generally being the life and soul. Alan pulled Pandora towards him, a little way off from the main group. 'Jesus, Pan. I was expecting a corpse.'

'I know! It was nuts. He banged the Valium, slept all the way to Heathrow, then sort of sleepwalked through security, he blagged both of us into the Concorde lounge, fell asleep again until we were walked onto the plane, slept the whole flight and then slept all the way here in the car. He's fine.'

'Christ, I'd be on a drip.'

'I know, right?'

Alan checked his watch. They were meant to have left hours ago. 'OK, folks,' he said, walking over and perching on a chair. 'Here's the plan . . .'

They were going to be ferried by Land Rovers to a stretch of the estate that bordered Loch Moy. There the ghillie was going to set Fergus up fly-fishing in one of the best salmon spots. Miles would be taken further along the bank to shoot

219

for rabbits, while Andy would be taken deep into the woods by April the forager to hunt for wild mushrooms, sorrel, edible flowers and the like. ('Fair enough,' Andy grinned, 'I've earned the demotion . . . ') Archie's assistant would snap a few shots of Miles blasting away with the 12-bore, and a few of Andy, well, foraging, while Archie remained with Fergus most of the time, because they'd need 'action' shots of him actually landing a salmon.

Contingencies were in place of course. A couple of rabbits and a whole salmon (all caught by Fintan the gamekeeper that very morning) were already packed in ice in one of the cars, ready to be pressed into use should the celebrity hunters come up short. April had pre-foraged some bits and pieces should the woods prove resistant to giving up their treasures. Tomas the chef from the hotel had prepared a variety of recipes depending on what the day actually yielded. Maybe trout instead of salmon, maybe wood pigeon instead of rabbit. He'd packed a gas stove, pots, pans, cutlery, seasonings and condiments into the second Land Rover. There was also a pretty impressive selection of wines in there too. All being well they'd be cooking and eating on the banks of the loch by just before dusk that evening, Archie snapping off some shots as the sun went down, the whole thing filmed for the website by the two kids from digital who were staying at a much cheaper B&B down the road.

Finally, after Miles had negotiated just wearing the tweed jacket with his jeans, after Andy had ordered and downed a second Bloody Mary, and after Fergus had finished an urgent conference call with someone in New York, they all packed into the cars and drove off towards the loch, the whole thing definitely having the air of a school trip by this point.

26

Late afternoon, the London skies beginning to turn to lead as, slightly unsteadily, Craig wound his way out of Dean Street Townhouse, along Dean Street and then left onto Old Compton Street. He'd left Vanessa chatting to some friends at the bar. They'd put away two bottles of wine during the lunch/interview. The girl could definitely drink, no question.

Almost unconsciously he found himself wending his way towards Denmark Street, the guitar-shop epicentre of London. He had done this walk many times during his homeless years and it felt strange and unnerving to be doing it now, when he was able to actually buy something, when he had the cash card for his new deposit account in his pocket. (He hadn't been able to get a credit card or a current account yet as he had no credit rating, but he had a debit card with the Visa symbol on it, the first time in over a decade that he'd possessed such a thing.) There was just under thirty thousand pounds in there, the money he had left after paying his lawyer and paying Alan back for his short-term loans. He took his mobile (Katie's old mobile) out of his pocket and rang Katie. 'Hi, Craig,' she trilled. 'How did it go with Vanessa then?'

'Aye, fine. She's lovely. Felt a bit weird, mind. Doing an interview again after all these years.

Listen, Katie, I'll not be home tonight. Got some flats to look at later and then again first thing in the morning. So I thought I'd walk up to Bloomsbury and book a wee hotel for the night. OK?'

'Sure.'

'Just wanted to let you know in case you were cooking or something.'

'No problem.'

'Any word from our friend in the North?'

'Just a quick text. Apparently some problems with Andy Jacks running a bit late.'

'Oh aye. I bet. OK. I'll see you tomorrow afternoon, I guess. Bye.'

'Bye.'

Craig wandered up and down Denmark Street, looking in the shop windows. The guitar shop — where dreams began. Yes, it was definitely an odd feeling, knowing he could go into one of these places and buy pretty much anything on the wall. He'd been enjoying playing Tom's wee Tele copy through his practice amp. It had been such a long time since he'd done it. The physical sensation of playing electric guitar — it was a very specific thing. You didn't get exactly that feeling from anything else. He hadn't realised he's missed it until he'd done it again. Like you don't realise you've missed tropical holidays until you go on one again.

From Denmark Street he wound his way north along Tottenham Court Road and then made a right towards Tavistock Square, towards the Tavistock Hotel, one of those old, slightly down-at-heel London hotels beloved of the budget-conscious tourist. He wandered into reception and had a chat with the girl behind the desk. Yes, they did have a room available for the night. There were only twins left but she could give it to him for the single-room rate of £83 without breakfast. That would be fine.

Craig lay his knapsack containing fresh socks, T-shirt, notepad and his new laptop on one of the beds and lay down on the other. It was quiet. It was nice.

It felt like a while since he'd been on his own. He needed some time to think. To plan. He reviewed his journal and checked the pages he'd bookmarked on the laptop.

27

'Fucking hell, this is tricky,' Fergus said.

He was whipping the long, thin fly rod above his head, trying to cast it out over the deep swirling pool just as Fintan had shown him earlier. ('*It'sawinthewristnowson.*') Fergus was wearing dark green waders and standing up to his hips in the river. Archie was balanced on a rock, snapping away. 'Looks great, darling,' Archie said every few seconds. From downstream they heard *crack crack*, two sharp reports as Miles blasted away at scampering rabbits. Andy was deep in the woods somewhere. Alan sat on a rock by the stream and lobbed the odd question at Fergus. '*Yeah, we eat a lot of fish . . . living in LA you can get pretty much anything you want any time food-wise . . . I love to, cook . . . not done too much of the killing it first part, though . . .* '

In the clearing behind Alan, with a good photo background of the river and the heathery moorland beyond it, chef Tomas had a fire going and had set up his portable gas range. '*I grew in Buckinghamshire,*' Fergus was saying. '*It's pretty much as far from the sea as you can get.*'

Alan looked nervously at the sky. It was nearly five o'clock. They only had a couple more hours of daylight in which to catch, kill, prepare and eat the food. And lavishly photograph all this happening. 'Grub's up!' a voice trilled from the

225

trees as Andy and April appeared from the undergrowth, Andy swinging a wicker basket. 'Well, we won't go completely hungry, let's say that. Any luck?' he shouted to Fergus in the river.

'Not a bloody sausage, mate.'

Alan and Archie looked in the basket — a load of mushrooms, bunches of wild garlic, sorrel leaves, sprigs of wild thyme and rosemary, and some bluish flowers Alan didn't recognise. Andy flopped down, knackered, sweat on his brow. 'Well played,' Alan said. 'What do you reckon, Tomas?'

'I'm thinking a wee mushroom stroganoff with herbs as a side dish. Maybe stretch it into a main course if we have to . . . ' He glanced towards the fishless Fergus in the river.

'I heard that,' Fergus said, casting again. One of the kids from digital was filming him from the opposite bank.

'Ah ha,' Andy said. 'As the only one who's actually scored some food so far I think I've earned this . . . ' Alan looked over. He'd spotted the wine-crammed cooler bag and was already rooting through it. *What the hell*, Alan thought. It was after five.

'Go on then, Andy, pour us all one.'

'Ooh, Chablis,' Andy said.

'That's really to go with the salmon,' Tomas said.

'What fucking salmon?' Andy replied.

'Ha h — ' Fergus went to reply. But, before he could get the second 'ha' fully out he modulated into saying 'fucking . . . HELL' and suddenly the

226

rod was twanging and bowing in his hands. 'I've . . . get the gamekeep, wassisface?'

They all turned just in time to see a huge fish jump out of the water and crash back down with a great splash.

'FUCK!' Archie said, scrambling for his camera and running towards the bank.

'Keep filming. You — go and get Fintan!' Alan yelled to the digital kids on the far bank, before turning back to Fergus and saying, 'Easy, easy, don't pull too hard, let it run a bit.'

'Shit!' Fergus said. Archie was right down there, snapping away; the look on Fergus's face was pure adrenaline, pure excitement. *Oh, this is gold*, Alan thought to himself. The fish broke the surface again and then dived for the bottom. Alan could see its milky-white underbelly. It was *big*. Andy scrambled onto the rock behind Fergus, shouting encouragement and abuse, swigging from a bottle of Chablis. The reel ratcheted as Fergus let the fish run, line playing out.

'Watch you've got enough line!' Andy shouted.

'Reel him back a bit!' Alan shouted.

'FUCK OFF!' Fergus shouted.

The sound of feet stamping and they looked up to see Fintan the gamekeeper sprinting into the clearing with a speed far beyond that of a man in his seventies. Miles arrived just after him, panting, out of breath, with the shotgun in one hand and two dead rabbits held by the ears in the other.

'Miles!' Alan said. 'He shoots, he scores!' Miles waved a hand at him, too out of breath to reply. Fintan had already grabbed the landing net and was wading into the water, regardless of the fact that he wasn't wearing waders, quickly up to his waist as he got right beside Fergus and started helping take the strain off the rod. 'Heresonlockitaffnow.' He popped a catch on the reel.

'Jesus, he's strong,' Fergus said.

'Ayelookstobenoabadweefishnow,' Fintan said.

'Wee?' Fergus said.

Fintan was scanning the pool with a practised eye. 'Aye, aboottenpoundah'dsay.'

'Ten pounds?' Fergus said. 'What's the biggest you've caught?'

'Ochaboutthirtyoddpound.'

'Jesus.'

'Carefulsonhe'sgonnay — '

The fish leapt clear of the water again, springing about four feet in the air, crystal beads of water spraying off it as it shook its head furiously from side to side, trying to dislodge the hook in its jaw, making a last, desperate bid for freedom.

Everyone's — Andy, Miles, Fergus, Alan, Tomas, Pandora, the digital lads — jaw was dangling as the fish crashed back down into the water. Everyone's except for old Fintan, who already had the landing net going in under the salmon as it splashed down, netting it and hauling it out of the water and, seemingly in one swift motion, swinging it over and safely onto the bank where it writhed and juddered swathed in the green netting.

Everyone burst into applause as Fergus held

his hands above his head in triumph, all of it lovingly photographed by Archie who had been snapping away throughout.

Behind him Alan heard the pop of a cork — Pandora, opening a bottle of Bollinger. Everyone was crowding around the flapping salmon, Andy Jacks, tall, swaying a little on his heels as he bent over to inspect it, the fish's spectacular mottling glinting green, blue, black and silver in the early-evening sunlight shafting through the trees above them, bits of dry leaves and pine needles sticking to its slick, oily skin. Alan saw Miles accepting a glass of champagne as Archie helped Fergus out of the water and onto the bank.

The general hubbub of celebration was broken by Fintan saying, 'Achthat'stoobadshe'llhuvtaego-back.'

'Eh?' Alan said.

'What?' Fergus said, flopping down, exhausted. 'Back in the water? Why?'

'Illegallyhooked . . . ' Fintan turned the salmon's head round to face them, holding the long, curved jaw tightly in his hand. There it was — the black-and-red fly Fergus had been using, it was hooked into the outside of the fish's jaw, not inside it.

'What?' Pandora said. 'What's wrong with that?'

'It means,' Tomas said, 'the fish didn't take the bait. The hook just went into its jaw as it swam past.'

'So?' Archie said.

'Illegal,' Fintan said simply.

'Oh, come on,' Alan said. 'Who's going to know?' Fintan just stared at him and, in his face, Alan saw an old man of decency and rules. Surrounded by an already half-drunk pack of London media types.

'Bollocks,' Fergus said, flat on his back, panting.

'Fintan's the gamekeeper,' Alan said. 'His call . . .'

They watched sadly as Fintan gently took the hook out of the jaw. He let Archie take a couple of photographs of Fergus with it and then he carried it back to the bank, got down into the pool and lowered the salmon into the dark water. It hovered just below the surface and then, with a flick of its powerful tail, vanished.

'Well,' Tomas said, 'I'd better get plan B from the cool box.'

'Fuck it, let's get pissed.' This was Miles, who Alan saw was pouring himself a second glass of champagne.

'I thought you weren't drinking?' Alan said.

'Hey,' Miles said, pointing to the two rabbits lying on the ground, 'I'm the only one who's actually caught anything. I think I deserve a drink.'

Glasses were clinked, more bottles were opened and a party atmosphere began to descend around the campfire as Fintan first showed Fergus how to gut the reserve salmon that had been brought up from the Land Rover and then began showing Miles how to skin a rabbit. Andy Jacks was slicing and frying the wild garlic, helping Tomas make a base for the sauce for the rabbit stew.

Pandora took Alan off to one side. 'Mmm,' she said. 'This does present us with something of an ethical dilemma.'

'How do you mean?'

'Well, we've got all that footage of Fergus catching the bloody thing. Do we just cut it into him then gutting and cooking it and pretend it was the one he caught or do we come clean in the piece and admit the whole 'here's one we prepared earlier' thing?'

'Well, we'd need everyone on side to do that . . . '

'It's hardly Watergate, is it?'

'Mmm. Lemme have a think. Here, pass us the Chablis.'

The smell of frying garlic filled the clearing as the sun got lower in the sky, sinking into the loch.

* * *

Twilight now. They'd managed to get through most of the case of wine. Andy threw another log onto the fire. God, they'd eaten well.

After Miles and Andy had skinned the rabbits (well, Fintan had done most of the actual skinning but the guys helped enthusiastically enough) and gutted the salmon, all three of them had pitched in with the cooking. Tomas had poached the salmon with handfuls of the wild herbs in the fish kettle he'd brought. They'd dusted the pieces of rabbit in seasoned flour, fried them off in butter and then simmered them in red wine and garlic. There were side dishes of

231

mushroom fricassee and a sorrel salad. Music was playing from the open door of one of the Land Rovers, some compilation of Pandora's. Fintan and Tomas sat off to one side, bitching about estate politics, while the three celebrities did their own version of the same thing: telling scurrilous tales of the worst people they'd ever worked with, who had crippling booze and drug problems and who was banging who. Archie, as ever, topped everyone with a truly staggering sexual anecdote involving Gianni Versace, some rent boys and an ounce of cocaine.

Miles seemed to have forgotten about making the last flight out of Inverness so they'd all be heading back to the hotel soon and leaving first thing tomorrow.

Yes, a weird scene and no mistaking out here in the middle of the Highlands. 'Better be setting off before it's properly dark,' Alan said to Pandora, both of them stretched out by the fire. 'Do you want to head back with the guys and I'll hang around and help clear all this up?'

'Sure. Well done us, by the way. The piece is going to look great.' Behind Pandora the kid from digital was still filming away, getting some mood footage of everyone chatting and drinking.

'HEY! CAREFUL, SON!' Alan heard Fintan bark, a note of urgency in the gamekeeper's voice he hadn't heard at any point that day. Alan turned in time to see a fairly drunk Andy Jacks with the shotgun pressed to his shoulder, taking aim at something in the trees. 'No way you can hit that,' Fergus said. There was a wood pigeon on a branch around fifty yards away. Alan was

232

just forming the words 'Don't be silly, Andy' when three things seemed to happen at once.

The pigeons flew up into the darkening sky.

Andy stumbled over a log.

The gun went off.

And then there was screaming and everyone was running and shouting and the words '*get an ambulance*' were echoing around, and over on the other side of the clearing, where he'd been emerging from having a piss, it became clear what had happened. It took Alan a moment or two to truly comprehend the full horror of the situation.

Andy Jacks had shot Miles Warren.

★ ★ ★

He saw the story breaking almost by accident on the laptop he'd bought himself, in the early hours, sitting up in bed in the cheap hotel. Not that he wasn't almost obsessively following anything to do with Alan on social media these days anyway. It'd been amazing how quickly he'd caught up with the world of the Internet. The Grainger kids had helped a lot. Melissa, Tom. Even the wee one knew more than him. When he started to see the headlines — 'SHOT . . . AIRLIFTED . . . TRAGEDY' and so on — he immediately sensed this might be good timing. Throw chaos onto chaos. Christ, this was too good. A gift from the gods. He almost felt bad for the guy. Almost. From what he was reading events would certainly be detaining him up there. Tomorrow. Tomorrow morning.

233

28

Katie was making breakfast, cracking eggs into a bowl, when a bright ping alerted her to a new email. She switched from Word document to Safari and went into her Gmail account. There it was, in her junk mail, the bold black type of a new message. The heading 'KATIE YOU SHOULD SEE THIS'. There was an attachment. She didn't recognise the sender's address, flibbertigibbet@mac.com.

Katie hesitated. It could be classic spam. A virus. The attachment looked like a video. She was caught between curiosity and prudence. After a few sips of tea and an attempt to start a new paragraph of her column, curiosity won out. She clicked on 'accept' and then 'play'.

The video clip was only thirty seconds long. Her blood turned to antifreeze, but she still watched it twice, just to make sure.

Then she went into the futility room off the kitchen.

She didn't want the children to hear her crying.

29

How fast does modern media move? It was a question Alan found he sometimes had to ponder, at talks and on panels at literary festivals and the like. He was pondering it right now as he sat slumped and glazed in the taxi taking him home. The sky was as grey as the featureless scrubland beside the M40 blurring past him. Every few seconds his phone buzzed in his pocket as yet another newspaper, radio or TV station tried to get hold of him for a comment.

The answer to the question was — insanely fast.

It turned out that one of the kids from digital had not only been filming the entire time but had been idiotic enough to send a clip to his mate. Who had sent it to a mate who had sent it to a mate ... suffice to say that in the forty-eight hours since the incident, before they managed to have it taken down, the clip 'ANDY JACKS SHOOTS MILES WARREN' had been viewed 3.8 million times on YouTube. It was the lead item on all the TV breakfast shows that morning and had made the front page of every single national newspaper: many of them using the same photograph of an ashen-faced, handcuffed Andy Jacks being led into Inverness Police Station.

Alan had spent the last forty-eight hours in, respectively, Inverness General Hospital, Inverness Police Station, Inverness Airport, the paper's offices, the offices of the paper's lawyers in Bloomsbury and finally the Royal Free Hospital in Hampstead. He'd had perhaps three hours' sleep in all that time.

Andy Jacks had been arrested for attempted murder. After much wrangling the charge had been amended to one of reckless endangerment and Andy had been released on bail. He'd spent the night in the cells, where he'd had all his blood work done. God alone knew what the toxicologist's report was going to show.

Miles had been airlifted to Inverness hospital first, where he was operated on before being transferred to the Royal Free that morning. The blast had hit him in the left shoulder, breaking his clavicle and peppering him with buckshot from his left nipple up to his neck. Incredibly it had missed his lungs. Safe to say Miles was not in the best of moods and they were waiting to hear from his lawyers.

Fergus Marks, along with everyone else, had been detained so long for questioning by Inverness police that he had missed his flight back to LA, thereby missing his start date. Studio lawyers were now making lots of noise about this.

Alan had just endured two hours of his editor, the chairman, Graham and their chief legal counsel basically screaming at him: '*Who lets a bunch of drunken fucking celebrities wander around in the dark with loaded fucking guns?*'

He'd been told on no account to speak to anyone in the media until the paper had a clear legal line thought out. On the back seat of the cab next to him was a haystack-sized bundle of the Sunday papers. Looking for relief from his own story he began flipping through the supplements — business, sport, money — and incredibly found his own face scowling back at him from the family one, a picture of him and Craig as teenagers, trying to look moody against the wall of a pebble-dash council house in the mid-eighties: it was Vanessa's piece about Craig's incredible story of fame, homelessness and rehabilitation. Alan skimmed it. There was a potted biography of their twinned histories — Craig's early success, Alan's struggle (somewhat exaggerated), Craig's descent and Alan's ascent — then their meeting in Soho last November.

A couple of Craig's quotes rankled a little. '*Alan? He was just this wee guy who tried to hang out with us*' and '*Musically? Naw, he was shite!*' But then he did say, later on, '*he's really helped me turn my life around. I hope I can pay him back.*'

Then, at the very end of the piece, there was some information that was new to Alan, that Craig was apparently planning a solo show in London. He'd noticed since he'd starting using social media that there was still a bit of interest in the band, interest that might be rekindled by the recent turnaround of events in Craig's life. The piece ended with another quote from Craig: '*I've had some very dark times. But it's nice right now. It feels like I can finally see some light at the end of the tunnel.*'

So this was interesting, Alan thought as the

taxi delivered him up the gravel drive of his house, Craig was in the back half of the Sunday papers beaming about the light at the end of his tunnel while Alan was spattered across the front pages, embroiled in a hellish darkness of 'celebrity firearm mayhem'.

The first thing that struck him, as he closed the front door behind him and dropped his bag in the hall, was how unusually quiet the place was. It was late on a Sunday afternoon, normally a day of maximum chaos: cooking well under way, Sophie running around, TV blaring. He went down the hall and into the kitchen.

Katie was sitting at the kitchen table, her laptop, as ever, in front of her. 'Where're the kids? Craig?' he asked.

'All out. How are you?'

Alan laughed as he sat down. 'Fucked. Absolutely knackered. It's . . . the whole thing's a shitshow. God knows what's going to happen next. I think Miles is suing Andy. Might be suing us too. It's all just . . . '

'OK,' Katie said. 'Well, I'm sorry about the timing of this, but it is what it is, I'm afraid . . . '

'Eh? The timing of what?'

Katie turned the laptop around, leaned over, pressed 'play' on the video clip.

Alan watched.

He felt his scalp burning.

His insides were turning to water.

Beads of sweat were popping out on his forehead.

There, on the screen, in grainy camera-phone footage, was Alan, standing in the middle of his study. He had his eyes closed and his hands on the dark hair of a girl whose head was rhythmically bobbing up and down. There was a sheen to the footage, like it had been filmed through a windowpane.

Alan tried to speak and found that he couldn't. He buried his head in his hands and let out a low moan.

He heard the scraping of a chair. When he looked up Katie was walking back across, pulling something behind her. A wheelie suitcase.

His suitcase.

30

It wasn't so bad. At any rate, he found he could just about cope with it, if he remained fairly drunk most of the time.

Like now, stretched out on the bed with a plastic bathroom tumbler brimming with off-licence whisky, feeling almost expansive in the cocktail-hour glow of his second drink. It seemed like everything in here was plastic. Alan scanned the now familiar items (it had a small sofa and coffee table in an adjoining room so they had the giant, hairy balls to call it a 'suite'), the plastic TV remote, the plastic kettle, the tiny plastic cartons of UHT milk. The light in the bathroom felt plastic. His heart felt like it was made of plastic, something synthetic, unreal, which was doing a job of sorts in his chest, pumping, keeping him alive, but that was about it. It felt like he couldn't *feel* any more.

There was his suitcase propped up on the wee folding stand thing. There was, of course, the Corby trouser press on the wall near the door. (Alan wondered — how many men's lonely vigils have been monitored by the flat, brown, uncaring face of the trouser press? How many tearful Scotches, how much sad masturbation had it witnessed?) There was the bureau underneath the window with his laptop on it. Through the window he could just see the edge of the minty-green (plastic) 'H' that formed the first letter of 'Holiday Inn'. Beyond that, further off in the night, you could just make out the traffic boom of the motorway. Five minutes on that motorway, just along to the next turn-off, would have taken him home to the home he no longer had.

He was a week into his stay now and was starting to be on nodding terms with most of the staff. As he walked into the bar every evening sometime between six and seven for his pre-dinner drink Dennis the barman already automatically reached for the Glenfiddich. Alan hated Glenfiddich — but it was the only malt they had.

It had not been an uneventful week.

The Miles Warren case was rolling along. Miles himself was recovering and back home now. He'd have some permanent scarring. His lawyers were still 'formulating their position' but it seemed likely that he'd be suing both Andy Jacks and the newspaper. Meanwhile Andy Jacks's lawyers were hinting that they too might counter-sue the newspaper for putting their client in proximity to a loaded firearm when he was clearly in no fit state to be responsible for such a thing.

Alan sat up and lifted his mobile off the bedside table. As he called Craig's mobile again he saw that it was his sixteenth attempt in the last week. What the fuck? He needed to speak to him about that night, about the atrocity, about who could possibly have filmed him.

Alan had gone the other obvious route of trying to figure this out: he'd hung around every

241

pub in town trying to see one or other of the people who'd been there that night. It was no great feat getting in touch with Katie — the paper ran her work email address and her Twitter account details right underneath her column every week. It had clearly been filmed through the side window of the study by someone who'd wandered into the garden. The problem was he couldn't even remember the name of the girl from that night, let alone anyone else who was there. Maybe Craig could. He'd seemed to handle the drugs and booze better than Alan had. But, again, Craig's phone was ringing out, just Craig rather tersely saying 'Leave a message'. Where the fuck was he? What the fuck was going on? Alan stood up, hanging up. He sighed and looked at the clock under the TV. Nearly seven o'clock. Bath time for Sophie. He imagined Katie walking down the hall towards the bathroom, the water running in the background, Katie shouting ' Come on, Sophie!' as Sophie dithered and played in her room. Katie had probably opened some wine. There'd undoubtedly be Sophie's tiny vest or pants lying on the stairs somewhere.

Suddenly the specific image of this, of all that had been rent from him, was too vivid, too sudden, to bear and Alan found he had to sit down and press a thumb and forefinger into his eye sockets to try and eradicate the vision. It didn't work and, before he quite knew it, he was calling the house. Three rings and then a breathless Sophie picked the phone up. 'Hello, Daddy!' she trilled.

242

'Hey, Sophs,' Alan said, doing his very best to sound bouncy and upbeat. 'What's going on?'

'I'M PLAYING *MINECRAFT*! I BUILDED A NEW BEDROOM!'

'Right, good work. You not having your bath yet?'

'No. Cleo's running it.'

'Cleo? Where's Mummy?'

'Out. In London.'

'Oh. Right. I didn't . . . OK. Is everything OK, darling? Where's Melissa?'

'Doing homework in her room. Are you working, Daddy?'

'I . . . yes. Daddy's working. Look, I've got to go right now, Soph, OK?'

There was a tiny sob at the other end, then Sophie saying, 'Please come home, Daddy. We miss you.'

Alan gripped his phone tighter, got a hold of himself. 'Soon, darling. I'll see you later this week after school. We'll go for sushi.'

'YAY! SUSHI!'

'Tell Mummy I called. OK? I love you, darling.'

'Bye, Daddy!'

He hung up and drained his glass.

'*I can't even look at you just now*,' Katie had said in her last email. They'd agreed not to say anything to Sophie and Melissa just now, until Katie figured out what she wanted to do. The girls had been told that Dad was 'away with work' for a while. He was fine to see them once or twice a week, collecting them from school and taking them for dinner. Hence his current location at the Holiday Inn nearest to the house. Tom, at twenty and living away from home, was a different matter. He was coming down next weekend for the Easter holidays, and Katie had decreed that Alan should be the one to tell him that they were having a 'trial separation'. She'd leave it up to him as to how much detail he wanted to give Tom. Alan kept trying to run a version of this conversation in his head and found he could never get very far with it before he was reaching for the whisky bottle. He'd just have to be fairly drunk come the time. (*Not a problem*, he thought.) Well, he'd heard about stories like this. He knew of them from life and from literature: the husband who strays and ends up in the sad hotel, the bedsit, the one-bedroom flat. He'd heard about them and now he was living in the middle of one. He looked at the clock again. It was just after 7 p.m. now. Oh well, there was at least one person who'd be missing him, who'd be wondering where he was.

He reached for his jacket hanging over the back of the chair and headed downstairs, for the bar, for Dennis and the Glenfiddich.

31

Katie had gathered her war council on the tiny smoking terrace out the back of the members' club upstairs at Quo Vadis. Along with Vanessa, Camilla and Emily she was smoking her head off, their highballs of iced vodka and tonic marking four towers at each corner of the small table.

'Oh my God, how awful. How awful for you, Katie,' said Emily.

'That fucking bastard,' Camilla said.

'Mmmm, indeed. But it doesn't quite add up now, does it?' said Vanessa.

'How do you mean?' Katie asked.

'How *awful*,' Emily repeated, even managing a sob this time.

'Yes,' Vanessa said. 'Do shut up now, Emily darling. Let the grown-ups talk. Now — ' she turned back to Katie — 'you've no idea who sent this video?'

'No. Except that it had to be someone who was there that night, right?'

'Not necessarily,' Vanessa said, stubbing out a Marlboro Light. 'Someone who was there filmed it certainly, but they could have shown it to someone else who then decided 'ah ha!''

'And you can definitely tell that it's Alan?' Camilla asked.

'God yes. Plain as day.'

'Which is most puzzling,' Vanessa said.

'How so?'

'Well, obviously Alan's not Benedict Cumberbatch or Wayne Rooney or anything like that, but he's been on the telly a fair bit. He's kind of known as being a married man with three kids and stuff, you know . . . '

'You mean . . . ' Emily said. '*Blackmail?*'

'Duh,' Camilla said.

'Well, it crossed my mind,' Katie said. 'But — '

'But why show your hand in advance? Why send it to you when they could presumably have tried to get some money out of Alan to make sure you *never* got to see it?'

'Exactly,' Camilla said, whirling her index finger in the air over the table while smiling at the waiter who'd just popped his head out of the door in the time-honoured 'same again' manner.

'What's Alan's version of what happened that night?' Vanessa asked.

'He went to the pub with Craig and got absolutely steaming, they got some coke from somewhere, Alan wound up inviting a bunch of randoms back to the house, more drink, more coke, he ended up getting . . . well, that's that.'

'Mmmm. Does sound plausible.'

'Vanessa!' Emily said. 'It sounds terrible!'

'Well, it's certainly not what you want to picture from the father of your children, is it?' Vanessa conceded. 'Coked-up mess with his willy in the mouth of some slag who's kneeling on your lovely carpet?'

'Vanessa!' Emily shrieked again.

'But let's try and keep some perspective, eh? It's not like Alan has a rich history of this kind of behaviour. And there were . . . influencing factors.'

'Craig?' Katie said. 'Actually Craig was very contrite about the whole thing. And you can't blame him for Alan's behaviour. He's a grown man.'

'Mmm. Quite. But I'm just saying, it's been an odd time, with Craig living there. No?'

'Well, yes, I suppose so.'

'I thought he'd moved out now?' Emily said.

'Just the other day,' Katie said. 'He's renting in Hackney.'

'Hackney?' Camilla said. 'Not cheap.'

'Also not dignified,' Vanessa added. 'He's hardly twenty-three.'

'I think it's all a bit *I'm back: bright lights big city*,' Katie said. In the week since Vanessa's piece had run a lot of interest in Craig seemed to be bubbling up. He'd been asked for a lot more interviews and a gig had been announced.

'Are we all going to his gig?' Camilla asked. 'It's at XOYO, in Shoreditch. Craig is happening.'

'Really?' said Emily.

'Well, happening might be stretching it,' Camilla said, 'but there's definitely some nostalgia interest.'

'Christ, Camilla,' Vanessa said. 'It really is disturbing that someone your age still knows about all these places.'

'Ah, but I don't look my age,' Camilla said. 'Anyway, it was your profile that started this off for him.'

'Yes, I am rather known for career resurrection,' Vanessa said, before turning back more seriously to Katie. 'All I'm saying is, darling — be careful about junking a twenty-three-year relationship because someone got off their head and did something stupid.'

'Still too angry for perspective,' Katie said.

'And there's been nothing else?' Camilla asked, clearing space on the table for the fresh round of drinks that was approaching. 'No follow-up emails from whoever sent this?'

'No.'

'It is all a bit bloody weird.'

'That's one word for it,' Katie said.

'Poor Alan,' Emily said. 'Living in some Holiday Inn on a bloody roundabout.'

'Poor Alan?' Katie said. 'You've changed your tune!'

'No no — I think he's an utter shit,' Emily said. 'But still . . .'

'Well, he definitely needs a good slap,' Vanessa said. 'I think we can all agree on that. But, do think on, Katie. Is the issue that Alan is now an unhinged, serially unfaithful scumbag, or is it just plain old Alan who, under the influence of drugs and booze and someone from a previous life, had that old tabloid classic — a moment of madness?'

'Mmmmm,' Katie said, stirring the lime around in her drink.

'It's just awful,' Emily said.

'Right,' Vanessa said, 'well, as some ancient Greek or other said, the first thing we do with a piece of evidence is to question the motives of the person presenting it.' She was rummaging in her red ten-grand Birkin. 'So we need to try and

248

find out who that is. Here, this fellow is quite good. A friend of mine used him on her second divorce . . . ' She was handing Katie a business card.

'Really?' Katie said.

'Really,' Vanessa said.

32

East. Alan hadn't been east in a long while. When he'd first come to London in the early nineties you'd sooner have walked through Brixton in full Ku Klux Klan regalia — with your cock out and a sign saying 'SUCK THIS, DARKIES' taped to it — than wandered about Hackney at night. The only thing you'd have travelled to Hackney to buy when Alan was in his twenties was drugs, ideally without leaving the safety of the taxi. And now look at it: flat whites, handmade brogues, artisanal fucking bread. Following the directions he'd tapped into Maps on his phone he turned right and headed up Hackney Road, towards a large block of what looked to be recently refurbished Georgian houses, all now clearly converted into flats.

He'd finally got hold of Craig — '*Shit, sorry, Alan,*' he'd said. '*The old phone's dead. I got a new iPhone and I couldn't whaddya call it, port the old number in from the phone you gave me. Sorry. I thought I'd given Katie the new number . . .* ' — and had been rewarded with an invite round to his new place. Strangely, and for no good reason, Alan found that he was nervous at the prospect of this meeting. He hadn't seen Craig in a few weeks, true. On the other hand, he thought, it might simply be the nameless dread that came from it being nearly six o'clock and, very contrary to his recent habits, he hadn't had a drink yet.

He had a few minutes to spare. Fuck it. He turned into the pub he was passing, out of the unseasonably warm April heat, fought his way to the bar, and ordered a Stella. Sod it. Stella and whisky chaser. Alan handed his card over and turned to regard the locals, sipping his beer. There was a gathering of Amish gentlemen at the end of the bar. At a nearby table a gay couple — one of whom was dressed in what appeared to be knickerbockers, a polka-dot bow tie, braces and a waxed, pointed moustache — were having a flaming argument. A girl wearing a diaphanous body stocking and covered head to toe in tattoos was conducting a loud Skype call on her iPad. Some kind of lurid techno pumped deafeningly. Alan did a relatively 'cool' job. He didn't think of himself as an 'old' 48-year-old. But, in here, he might as well have been dressed as a regimental sergeant major or a High Court judge. He looked over into the corner and caught the eye of an octogenarian man, clearly someone who had been coming here since around the 1950s, who was sitting alone, sipping his pint. Alan nodded towards him, in a gesture meant to signify some kind of drinkerly solidarity. The old boy just looked away, clearly figuring Alan for some gay pickup artist whose kink was the over-seventies.

'Sorry, sir.' Alan turned to see the barman, who was also dressed as an Amish farmer, holding the card machine towards him, his debit card sticking out of the bottom of it. 'Do you have another card? This one's been declined.'

'Declined? That's not possible.' Alan felt his face reddening. When had this last happened? It was an instant flashback to student days, or his early years in London, when a declined card was a monthly, if not weekly, occurrence. 'Can you try it again . . . is it your machine?'

'I don't think so. I've already tried it twice.'

'Oh for fuck . . . hang on . . . ' Alan fumbled in his pockets, found a twenty-pound note and a ten and handed the ten over. 'Here, just keep the change.' What fresh hell was this? There was plenty of money in that account. Had he been using the card too much? Activated some kind of red-flag nonsense? Maybe something to do with the hotel? This was the card he'd given them when he'd checked in over a week ago. Could that be it? He'd have to call the bastard bank in the morning. He drained his pint, threw the whisky down and, blinking in the sunlight, regained the pavement and crossed the road. *'Top Floor Flat, 248 Hackney Road.'* There it was, the buzzer already had his name on it — *'C. Carmichael'*. Alan pressed the button and a few seconds later there was Craig's voice saying 'Alan. A'right? Come on up' and the door was clacking open and Alan was ascending the stairs.

It took him a moment or two to adjust his focus as he came out of the dark of the stairwell onto the light of the landing, to recalibrate his vision and convince himself he was really seeing what he was seeing.

Craig was standing in the doorway, bathed in bright summery light from behind, holding a glass of some clear, iced liquid in his left hand

252

while holding the door of the flat open with his right. It had been nearly three weeks since they'd last seen each other, granted, but this . . . Jesus. Craig was wearing blue jeans and a crisp white shirt. There was something wrong, something . . . Alan couldn't locate it, fumbling for words even as he extended his hand to shake. Craig's skin looked brown, tanned. He'd gained some weight and was clean-shaven, sporting a new, expensive-looking haircut. But that wasn't it, no. There was something else. Something had happened in the middle of . . . Craig was smiling as he said, 'You found it. Come in.' Finally it hit Alan.

'Craig. You've had your teeth fixed.'

'Oh, yeah.' Craig grinned sheepishly, revealing a flash of gleaming crowns on his upper front, where the blackened stumps had been, all the teeth around the new ones polished or whitened to the same lustre. 'A couple of weeks back.'

The surreal pageant continued as Alan followed Craig into the flat. There was a big living room — perhaps thirty feet by fifteen — with three large Georgian floor-to-ceiling windows flooding the place with light. A sleek sofa faced a glass coffee table. The floorboards were painted white, adding to the shimmering brightness of the whole thing. There was a dining area at the far end, in front of a fireplace. There were piles of books everywhere, there were throw pillows and paintings and a thick rug in a kind of burnt-orange colour. A Martin acoustic guitar sparkled on its stand in the corner.

'Drink?' Craig was asking.

'I . . . whatever you're having,' Alan said. 'Fucking hell. How much is this costing you?'

'Guy wanted two grand a month, furnished,' Craig began, busying himself at the far end of the room, 'but the second bedroom's tiny. Cheers . . . ' Craig handed him a glass, ice and lime floating in it.

'Cheers,' Alan said, before sipping the drink and saying, 'Grohhhhgghh — what the fuck is this?'

'Soda water,' Craig said. 'Sorry, you said 'whatever I was' . . . see, I'm not really drinking right now.'

What the fuck is happening? Alan wondered. He recognised something in the corner, a kind of lime-green swivel armchair. 'I used to have a chair like that.'

'It is yours,' Craig said. 'It was in your garage. Katie said I could . . . you know.'

'Oh, right.' The first mention of the unmentionable.

'Look, we can go out for a drink if you like?'

'Please,' Alan said, handing his glass to this strange apparition that used to be Craig.

They went to some bar on Columbia Road, along from the flower market. It was a slightly more restrained, tasteful version of the pub Alan had popped into earlier. Craig continued to sip iced soda water. Not wanting to look like a total alky, and in deference to the warm spring night, Alan made do with frequent pints of white-wine spritzer. He could have a real drink later. After they'd caught up on Alan's recent celebrity-shooting-related trials and tribulations, they got down to the real business.

'Jesus, Alan, I was as wrecked as you were that night. I can barely remember anyone. But it's simple enough, isn't it? One of them either figured out the two of you had sloped off together, or they just wandered off outside, for a fag or a piss or whatever, saw you in your study getting . . . you know. They got their phone out and filmed you and here we are.'

'Still doesn't explain why they sent it to Katie.'

'You reckon?' Craig said. 'I think that's the easy part. He or she's got this on their phone, they're in the pub steaming drunk one night, Katie's written some column that's pissed one of them off, her email address is right there at the bottom, and one of them says, 'Hey, let's teach this cow a lesson — send her that video of her husband getting blown.''

Alan nodded, thick with drink. This did sound plausible.

'Where are you at with Katie now?' Craig asked.

'I'm at the Holiday Inn, Junction 4 off the M40.'

'Fuck. She'll come around, Alan. You fucked up, it's a nightmare, but she'll come around.'

'I miss the kids,' Alan said hopelessly.

'Christ, aye.'

'Anyway, here, I'll get them in — '

'Sorry, I've got to go, got to practise a couple of songs. Early start in the morning.'

'Eh?'

'I'm doing this thing on 6 Music, on Shaun Keaveny's show? To promote the gig. Got to be there by eight.'

'Oh, right. OK. Another night then.'

'Aye. Course. Sorry.'

They stood up and hugged awkwardly. 'I'll just stay and finish this . . . ' Alan said, indicating his drink.

'Alan,' Craig said. 'Are you . . . are you OK? You don't look great, pal.'

'Well, you know, it's been quite a couple of weeks, with one thing and another. Probably putting it away a bit too much.'

'Look, take it easy. Katie'll come round.'

'Yeah.'

'Right, see ye.'

'Hey, what time are you on tomorrow morning? On the radio?'

'Oh. About nine, I think?'

'I'll tune in.'

'Great.' Craig turned to leave.

'Oh, shit, Craig?' He turned back. 'Fuck, my card got declined earlier. Must be some fuck-up at the bank. Do you have . . . ?'

Craig was already reaching into his pocket, almost as though he had anticipated being asked this very question. 'Here,' he said. 'There's about a hundred there, is that enough?'

'Yeah, plenty. Thanks. I'll pay you back later in the week.'

'Don't be daft — I owe you.'

'Right, well, good luck tomorrow morning.'

'Night, Alan. Get on home now.'

Alan watched him go, out into the street, through the twilight throng of drinkers and then whistling off down Columbia Road in his fresh white shirt. He looked at the money in his hand, then he looked at his watch — east London, 7.30 on a mid-April evening. If he left now he could make the 8.15 from Marylebone back to the hotel. He thought about the hotel, about the trouser press staring blankly at him. 'Hey.' He found himself cocking a twenty at the barman and saying, 'Double Jameson's and ice please.'

33

It took him a few minutes to realise where he
was — the same awful room at the Holiday Inn,
already hot with sunshine and the traffic noise
filtering in from the motorway. He sat up and the
scale, the magnitude, the sheer vindictive power
of his hangover made itself known. Christ. He
slaked himself with the stale glass of water by the
bed and tried to reconstruct the previous night's
events. He'd walked round to Shoreditch House,
drinking whisky sours, hoping to bump into
someone he knew but gradually realising there
was no one much over thirty in the entire place,
that he was starring in some hipster version of
Logan's Run. He'd got a cab into Soho and had
tried the unholy Trinity — south to north along
Dean Street, from the Groucho to upstairs at
Quo Vadis via 76 Dean Street — hoping to find
someone he knew but finding only strangers and
more booze. He'd finally run out of cash in 76
Dean Street but had come up with the perfect
solution — he put his card behind the bar and
sat out on the patio, smoking and drinking neat
double Scotches until midnight and then
feigning stunned surprise when they brought the
bill and his card didn't work. It being Soho
House they were, of course, very understanding,
and Alan promised he'd call tomorrow with
another card and settle the whole thing.

He walked to Marylebone, just made the last

train and had stumbled into bed around 2 a.m., having first (the evidence on the writing table across from him was saying) savagely punished the bottle of Talisker he had in his room.

Alan supposed that this was the kind of thing that tended to happen when you didn't have work to do, or children to attend to. The kind of thing that was all fun and games if you were nearing thirty, sad and tragic if you were nearing fifty.

Jesus Christ, he winced as he swivelled round and gingerly put his feet on the carpet. He picked up his phone and noted with alarm that he had seven missed calls: all in the last two hours or so, one from Katie, two from the paper and no less than four from Canters.

He tried Katie first, but she was engaged. He called Canters and asked for Bill. The alacrity with which Bill came on the line immediately worried Alan. 'Alan,' he said. 'Bad news, I'm afraid.'

'What?'

'I . . . I have to say I'm as surprised as you will be about all of this, it — '

'For fuck sake, what is it?'

'You're being formally investigated by HMRC on suspicion of tax evasion.'

'*WHAT?*'

'I know, I know. It just landed yesterday. They've frozen your bank accounts pending a resolution.'

The declined card. Alan felt his insides curdling. 'They . . . they can do that?'

'I'm afraid so.'

259

'Well, what have . . . have we done anything wrong?'

'No! Well, not wrong as such. As you know we've played a bit fast and loose now and then with what can strictly go through the company, and if they want to play hardball they can. But I don't want you to worry because . . . ' Bill talked on.

'Who . . . why is this happening?' Alan had the edge of tears in his voice.

'I don't know.'

'Jesus Christ! And they can do this? Freeze my accounts? How . . . what am I meant to live on?'

'If you come by the office I can arrange to get you an advance from petty cash every few days. Tide you over until we get this sorted out. Though I have to warn you — it is going to cost a few bob.'

'Jesus Christ, Bill. This is a fucking nightmare. What's the worst-case scenario here? I mean, could I go to fucking jail?'

'No no. I shouldn't think so.'

'*You shouldn't th —* '

'Look, let me crack on here and try and find out some more, OK? I'll get back to you.'

Alan hung up and stared out of the window, at the sizzling asphalt of the M40 a few hundred yards away. What had happened here? One minute he had a lovely wife, family and home and the next he was penniless and living in a fucking Holiday Inn. It was like a *Hold My Beer* gif: he was the guy reversing a forklift in a warehouse, all fine, then he nudges a shelf and, two seconds later, it looked like someone dropped the bomb. It looked like Ground Zero.

Could I go to jail? No no.

He felt no reassurance from Bill's words. As a child growing up, Alan had always assumed that the world was filled with adults full of know-how and can-do. Then, when you got there, the scales fell from your eyes and you realised that the adult world was filled with fakers, bodgers and buffoons. The mechanic who opens the boot expecting to find the engine there. The dentist who wrecks your mouth. The gas engineer who blows your house up and cheerfully hands you a bill for several thousand pounds. *The accountant who says it's all fine, all the way to jail.*

Alan realised he needed a second opinion on this. He needed know-how. He needed to talk to a grown-up. But he only really knew one grown-up and Katie wasn't talking to him at the moment.

There was a knock at the door. He pulled a sheet around him and stumbled across the wrecked room to answer it. 'Ah, sorry to disturb you, Mr Grainger — ' the guy, some kind of assistant manager, tried his best not to look shocked at Alan's terrible face, the room, his undoubtedly reeking breath — 'but, as you know, once a week we have to run your bill through and there seems to be a bit of a pr — '

'Problem with my credit card?'

'Oh. You kn — '

'Yes. I'm sorry. I'll sort it out by tonight.'

'Great. Thank you. Sorry to dis — '

Alan closed the door.

As he sat back down on the bed his mobile

phone beeped its 'scheduled meeting' alarm call. By this point he was actually terrified to look at the screen for fear of what it might bring. He picked it up to see that his phone was informing him that he had lunch with his son, Tom, later.

Ah good, he thought. *Perfect. Just what I need today. I need to have lunch with my son and tell him that I've been unfaithful to his mother. That I've had to move out of the house and that we might be getting a divorce, oh, and by the way, I'm broke and can you lend me the money to nay for lunch?*

Alan tossed his phone onto the bed and looked at the clock beneath the TV: 8.30. He looked at the Scotch bottle. He looked back at the clock. He looked back at the Scotch bottle and then he started having a discussion in his head — *well, sun's over the yardarm, it's five o'clock somewhere and all that.* With a great effort of will, he thought something along the lines of — *no, I am not ready to be that guy.* He got up, walked past the whisky and into the bathroom and turned the shower on. Recrossing the room, naked, waiting for the water to run warm, he remembered something.

Alan turned on the digital radio that sat on the bureau beneath the window, turned the dial, and got the tail end of laughter, male and female laughter intertwining in coils of happiness.

'Right, oh dear,' Shaun Keaveny was saying, 'well, thanks for that, Craig. Craig Carmichael, who's been with us for this morning, formerly of the Rakes — way, way back in the day — who's now returned to making music after a long and,

262

as you've just heard, a fairly colourful time out. Craig, you're playing XOYO in London on, is it — '

'The 20th. This Friday.'

'Friday. And I believe the gig's sold out now, is that right?'

'It is Shaun, aye.'

'It must feel a bit weird that all this stuff — radio sessions, sold-out shows — is suddenly happening for you after, well, in your case I think it's literally fair to say, a few years in the wilderness . . . '

'It does. It really does. I was thinking that on the way in here. I walked up Regent Street and I was thinking — 'Wow, just last summer, I was sleeping over there.'' Craig sounded slick, professional, as though he'd just come off a six-month promotional tour of the US. 'So, aye, it's all been a bit crazy and brilliant and I dunno . . . I'm still trying to take it all in really.'

'Well, we wish you all the best, Craig. Now, what's the last tune you're going to play for us today?'

'Ah, some of your older listeners might remember this, Shaun. It's called 'Daybreak'.'

'I certainly remember it, Craig, and I'm not *that* old. Well, maybe that's debatable. Anyway, been great having you on the show. Craig Carmichael with 'Daybreak'.'

The sound of Craig's acoustic guitar filled the small hotel bedroom. He sounded good. 'Yes, I see,' Alan said.

He reached for the Scotch bottle.

34

'Fuck sake, Dad . . . '

He'd arranged to meet Tom in the Cottage for
a pub lunch. It was in fairly terrible proximity to
the Dragon, the pub where the outrage that had
brought him here had begun. They sat in the
corner, their heads lowered over their pints, pies
and chips and lasagnes being carried to tables
around them. As they'd agreed, Katie had told
Tom the bare bones of the situation: Alan had
been unfaithful to her and this had precipitated
the separation they were currently undergoing.
(Katie had hinted that Melissa, and no fool her,
was starting to ask difficult questions too.) She
hadn't gone into detail about the video and stuff.
Still, Tom continued, 'I mean, *for fuck sake.*'

'I know.' What else could he say? It was
difficult being spoken to like this by your
twenty-year-old son, but Alan knew he had to
take it. That he had no choice.

'What were you fucking thinking?'

'I wasn't, son. I was drunk. It was the most
stupid thing I've ever done in my life.' He sighed
and rubbed his temples. He'd crunched a few
Polo mints on the way here, to take the tang of
whisky off his breath, and the mint was mixing
with the lager to create a horrible, chemical wash
in his mouth. Christ, he felt like shit. As though
reading his mind Tom said, 'Dad, you look like
shit.'

Alan nodded. He'd probably have to check out of the hotel tomorrow. He'd have to find somewhere to . . . Christ. All of his friends were married, with kids. Could anything be grimmer? 'Uncle Alan is staying in the spare room for a while, children.' The freshly scrubbed young faces, eating their cereal in the morning when you stumbled in, hung-over and reeking. 'How's your mum?' he managed to say to his son.

'Angry. Not sitting around crying or anything like that. She's been out in London a fair bit. Well, last night I thought I heard her crying.'

Alan thought about this, about what he had made come to pass — about his children lying in bed in the home he had made for them and listening to their mother crying because of what he had done. He felt his shoulders about to give and it took an incredible effort of will to stop the sobs from coming. Crying in front of your children — quite the Rubicon to cross. Alan had done it before of course: in front of the TV or at the cinema, where most visits for him involved tears at some point, even to — almost especially to — the average kids' film. He could still recall his restrained sobs during *Inside Out*, or his racked chest-heaving as Jessie sang 'When She Loved Me' in *Toy Story 2*. (When Tom, sitting next to him now with a huge fist wrapped around his pint, was just four, slurping his Coke and patting Alan's hand. *'Is OK, Daddy.'*) He thought of all the times his children had wept in front of him, of the tears of various stripes and hues: of pain from the grazed knee or the cut

265

finger, of frustration at the cancellation or denial of a promised treat. Tears of fear, or tiredness or confusion. *You have always been the minister of tears, it has been jour job to salve them. It was your job, for many, many years, to put jour arm around the sobbing child and say, 'There, there. Come on. It'll be all right. Everything'll be OK.'* And now, here in the quiet corner of this pub, this strange reversal was happening: Tom's arm going around his father's shoulder as he said, 'Come on. It'll be OK, Dad. It's going to be all right . . .'

'I'm sorry, son.'

For the first time Alan had a sense of . . . something out there. Of forces ranged against him. The sense that his idiotic blunder had somehow precipitated not only Katie's actions but the fiasco in the Highlands, the revenue investigation, everything. '*I'm so sorry,*' he said to Tom again, his head buried in his hands, unable to face his child at this moment. Alan got a hold of himself. He breathed in deeply, managing to expel the salty tide rising in his lungs. 'Jesus, Tom, I'm . . . it's just been a hell of a couple of weeks.'

'It'll be OK, Dad. I . . . we all still love you.' As befitted someone just out of their teens, Tom had to lower his voice and look at the ground in order to say this last part. Tom was also receiving a milestone moment in education here, a true marker between adolescence and adulthood. As children we think adults walk in a sunlit grove of reason and sanity. At some point we come to realise just how narrow that grove is, how easy it can be for some people to stumble off it and into the shadows beyond.

Tom paid for lunch and lent him the train fare into London.

35

Monday: accounts frozen by HMRC.

Tuesday: nervous breakdown in front of your son.

Wednesday: officially homeless.

Thursday: board meeting at the newspaper.

Alan entered the conference room at the newspaper feeling absolutely no fear, no terror. Partly because he was already, obviously, slightly drunk, but mainly because fear — terror — is the apprehension of terrible things happening. And Alan was way past that now, he was living in a world of horror. Full slack-jawed horror. To use the analogy of a plane crash, he was way past gripping the armrests at each new bump and bang of turbulence, of staring fixedly at the 'Fasten seat belts' sign, and now well into the stage where a chunk of the fuselage has been torn off and you're heading for the mountain — sitting there watching your fellow passengers get sucked out of their seats and hurled one by one into the blistering air. He'd had to check out of the hotel that morning because he no longer had a functioning credit card. Apparently he could buy a kind of prepaid card and load the cash he was collecting from the accountants onto it. It all sounded like a bit of a palaver to be honest. The hotel was storing his stuff for him though, until he sorted something out.

He came round the corner and looked into the

glass-walled conference room (until recently scene of so many lovely meetings. *Ah, Pandora! Rory! Why had I not known happiness when I had it? Why had I not known how green my valley was when my only problems were things like disaparaging the idiocy of Clarkson cooking a full English breakfast on the bonnet of a sports car?*) to see, arranged around one end of the table as though in a courtroom, Greg his editor, Rose the managing editor, good old Graham from Legal and Business Affairs (who was obviously trying very hard not to catch Alan's eye) and a woman he didn't recognise.

'Alan, thanks for coming in,' Greg began as the hand-shaking went on. 'You know Rose, Graham . . . and this is Fiona from HR.'

Ah.

He sat down in the chair that had been placed facing them, putting his Costa Coffee cup on the table in front of him, the coffee cup he'd poured a good slug of whisky into from his hip flask on the walk from the Tube station to here.

'Right, well,' Greg went on. 'The good news is I think we're going to be OK with Miles. He seems to have calmed down. We're going to have to pick up all the medical bills and whatnot, he'll have a little bit of scarring, but I think we'll be in the clear there. Same thing with the Andy Jacks nonsense.'

'Great,' Alan said.

'The only thing that's an utter pain in the butt is the studio about Marks. Bloody Americans. You know what they're like with litigation. I'm afraid it looks like we're going to have to settle there.'

'How muc — ' Alan began.

'Seven hundred grand,' Rose said flatly.

'Jesus.'

'They wanted millions,' Greg said. 'We've managed to talk it down to a goodwill payment, without prejudice and all that stuff. But — '

'But someone has to be held accountable,' Rose cut in.

'Yes, clearly,' Alan said pleasantly. The quartet facing him had no idea that horror week held no more horror for him. It would just have to run its course. 'So you're firing me.'

'Well, yes,' Greg said. They all looked at him.

'Is there anything else?' Alan said.

They all looked at each other, perhaps more alarmed by his equanimity than they would have been by his smashing the place up.

'Well, would you like to discuss this?' Fiona from HR was saying.

'No.'

'I'll need to get you to sign a couple of things, Alan,' Graham was saying.

'Sure. Stick it in the post. Look — I've got to get off actually.' He was already rising. 'Thanks, guys.'

Rose shrugged and shuffled her papers. Fiona looked vaguely disappointed there hadn't been a scene. Greg got up and extended his hand again. 'Look, Alan, in the future, once all of this is buried, who knows. Maybe we can look at — '

'Yeah, sure. Thanks, Greg. See you.'

He walked briskly to the lift. Yes, from the way certain heads dipped down into their cubicles as he passed, word had certainly got out about the main event taking place in the conference room today. As he reached the lift he heard a voice saying 'Alan', and turned. Pandora, standing there, in her little black cardigan and jeans.

'Pan — ' he began, then he saw she already had tears in her eyes as she came in to hug him. He also saw in her expression a reflection of how shocking he looked.

'I'm so sorry,' she said.

'It's OK. No one died. Well, Miles nearly.'

Pandora attempted a smile at this. 'I should never have brought Andy up in that state.'

'No, don't do that. I asked you to.'

'Do you want to get a drink later?' She wiped away a tear. Pandora, who he could probably have fucked and didn't. Maybe he could have told Katie this. That was the thing with not fucking people though, wasn't it? It was very hard to bring up, in the context of an argument over infidelity, a list of people you *didn't* fuck. It was impossible to gracefully drop into a conversation, like having a first or a ten-inch penis.

'Maybe. Text me.' He heard the lift doors opening behind him. 'Look, I've got to run, OK?'

He pecked her on the cheek and, carrying a whiff of her perfume with him, was quickly descending.

'*I've got to get off . . . Actually, I've got to run.*'

Until recently he had said these things and they were true. He had a job — several jobs in fact — and a family. There was always something to do, somewhere to be, someone to pick up, an

271

errand to be fulfilled. Now he had nothing to do. Was this how it went for those who reached middle age and found themselves childless? Just oceans of free time expanding on all sides, reaching the horizon? Did those activities like food and sleep and exercise, things that got pushed to the margins of life when you had work and a family, did they become the central events? Where did Alan have to be right now? Nowhere. The pub. And you couldn't very well go around saying that, could you? *Without women, life is a pub.* Where had he read that?

He sipped his Irish coffee from the paper Costa cup as he crossed the sunlit atrium of the lobby and again it came. '*Alan, Alan!*' He turned to see Graham, half running from the bank of lifts to catch him up. He was holding an envelope. 'Here,' Graham said. 'You might as well take these. Sign and initial where marked and post them back and, look, I'm sorry, mate. Rose was really fucked off.'

'It's OK, Graham. I get it.'

'Listen, I heard about the HMRC business.'

'Yeah. Fucking nightmare.'

'Have you looked into it?'

'Well, the accountants are dealing with it.'

'Sounds odd to me. I mean, things like this, it's usually . . . ' Graham looked around and then lowered his voice, as though there might be revenue agents all over the place. 'It's usually because they've had a tip-off.'

'Really?'

'How bad are things between you and Katie?'

'Oh fuck off, there's no way.'

'OK, OK. Look, I know a couple of people who've been through this. I'll ask around.'

'Thanks, Graham.'

'No problem.' Graham put a comforting hand on his shoulder. 'One thing though, Alan, for fuck's sake have a shave and cut back on the boozing, eh?'

Alan smiled. 'Yeah.'

'OK. Chin up,' Graham said and then he was gone.

Alan walked out into the sunshine. It really was hot now. He wandered through the little park near the offices, looking for a free bench, but there were none. In the end he took his jacket off, spread it beneath him, and sat down on the grass. He drained the last of his Irish coffee and set the cup down in front of him, noticing as he did so that he'd managed to get a couple of sizeable coffee stains on his shirt. Oh well. He looked around at his fellow Londoners: pensioner couple, gay couple, office workers sharing sandwiches, bike courier, media types.

It occurred to Alan that he had no idea where he was going to spend the night. When had this last been the case? 1989? Interrailing around Europe during his second year at uni? He had a couple of hundred in cash on him. King's Cross just along the road, bound to be somewhere there. The full absurdity and horror of this idea struck him — living in some toilet hotel in King's Cross that allowed you to pay by the day in Cash. He almost laughed. He was brought out of his reverie by a cardboard-sounding 'plop' and looked up to see a young girl, a student, walking

273

past him, looking back and giving him a funny kind of smile. A kind of head tilt. He looked down at the empty Costa cup. Well, not quite empty now. There it was, at the bottom, glistening gold in the sunlight — *decus et tutamen*.

Now he laughed.

He pocketed the quid, took the hip flask out of his pocket and took a good pull on it, got up and started heading towards the Tube station. He knew where he was going. He had kind of known it since he left the hotel that morning. It just felt too right, too symmetrical, to be avoided.

36

'Fuck, are you OK?' Alan had rung ahead. Craig stood back to let him into the flat.

Alan flopped onto the sofa and told Craig about the last seventy-two hours, about the revenue, about his sacking. He even told him about the girl dropping a pound coin into his Costa cup earlier.

'Jesus,' Craig said, biting at a clean, manicured nail. (Another improvement. Craig was like Terminal 5, every time you turned around they'd made some minor improvement.) 'Nightmare. Hey, I'll tell you something, when I *needed* a pound I'd sometimes sit there for hours with nothing of the kind getting handed over. You must have a good face for it.'

'A good face for begging?'

'Aye. Some people do, ye know.'

'Well, maybe that's what the future holds.'

Alan had never thought of begging as requiring talent, natural ability, but perhaps here, as in so many other things, he was wrong. Maybe he'd been wasting his life pursuing something he was ill-suited to when his natural path — begging — was written all over his face.

'Don't talk shite,' Craig was saying from the far end of the room, where he was busying himself with the tea things. 'Look, you'll get all this sorted with the tax stuff, I'm sure you and Katie can work things out, and you can still

275

fucking *write*, eh? They cannae take that away from you for fuck's sake.'

'Thanks,' Alan said, accepting the tea. 'But I'm not a *writer* writer. I write fucking restaurant reviews. You need someone to print them and pay you. What am I going to do? Post them on the Internet? Put them on Yelp? TripAdvisor? Print the reviews myself and stand giving them out on street corners?' For a second Alan amused himself with an image of himself standing on the corner of Old Compton Street and Dean Street — the path dozens of his friends took hourly en route to the Groucho, Soho House, Quo Vadis or Dean Street Townhouse — filthy and terribly dressed, holding out a grubby sheet of public-library photocopied A4 called 'The Alan Times'. Containing his new review of, what? McDonald's? Dumpster food? The sandwiches Pret give to the homeless? They sipped their tea.

'I nearly cried in front of Tom yesterday.' He still hadn't cried. It was odd. It felt like . . . when he'd been constipated.

'Shit. How is Tom?'

'He . . . it's a headfuck for him.'

'Aye, I spoke to him briefly the other day.'

'You did? How come?'

'He wanted the guest list for tomorrow night, for him and a couple of mates.' Tomorrow night — Craig's show. 'I meant to ask,' Craig said. 'Do the girls know yet?'

'Nah, but Melissa's starting to suspect something's up. Katie doesn't want to say anything until she's decided what she's going to do.' He thought of Sophie's tiny wee face, trusting and loving, and how the news of what he had done would smash it in, defile it. He pushed the thought away, experiencing with it a physical pang for strong drink. He sipped his tea instead and asked — 'Anyway, how's you? How you feeling about tomorrow night?'

'Shiteing it. We're properly sold out now.' Alan had noticed a few times how Craig had started to refer to himself using the royal 'we'. *We got a good review. We're doing that show.* Maybe, to be charitable, it was a hangover from having spent so many years in a band with other people.

'That's fantastic. What's the capacity?'

'Five hundred?' Craig shrugged.

'Really? I — fuck.'

'You sound surprised . . . '

'I, no, I just, I suppose I don't know what I expected.' In Alan's mind he'd imagined the place as a tiny pub back room, like one of the dives Craig used to play back in Ayrshire, when he was starting out. When *they* were starting out. 'Wow. That's amazing, Craig. I'm really pleased for you.' He was too, within limits. Alan didn't subscribe to the whole credo of *it is not enough that I succeed, others must fail.* He wasn't one of those people who believed in *we will forgive our friends anything except their success.* At the same time, he wasn't stupid, he wasn't a maniac. He'd rather good fortune could have been befalling him rather than Craig here. But, if good fortune was going to elude him for a while, then it may as well alight on Craig.

'You're coming tomorrow night, right?' Craig asked.

'Oh God, I don't know. Look at me. I'm hardly in a state for public presentation right now. Katie will no doubt be there. Vanessa. All her mates, looking at me like I'm a fucking bastard. Tom and his pals. Maybe it's better I don't go.'

'Fuck sake, you made it happen.'

'Nah.'

'You did. All this.' He gestured around at the flat.

'Ach. We'll see.' Alan yawned. The shadows were lengthening on Hackney Road, outside the three tall windows. What was he averaging on the sleep front at the moment — two hours a night? Maybe three? Not bad, considering. 'Look, Craig, sorry. I'm fucked. Do you mind if I . . . ?'

'Naw, come on.'

Craig opened the door. 'Like I said, it's not huge.'

It was a box room, about ten feet by six, the dimensions of a prison cell. A small window with a thin curtain faced out onto the brickwork of the next building. A couple of cardboard boxes in the corner, Craig's guitar case. A single mattress with no bedding on it and Craig was saying, 'Aye, sorry, I don't have another duvet but here . . . ' Craig was handing him something blue and rolled up. 'It's not been used since Petra washed it for me.'

'OK. Cheers. See you in the morning.'

So it was that Alan lay down to sleep in Craig's spare room, in the sleeping bag Craig had used to sleep in the streets on, the one that

Alan's cleaner had washed for Craig when they took him in, in what felt like another lifetime now.

37

'When's Daddy coming home?' Sophie asked for the seventh or eighth time that morning.

'Yes, when is Father returning?' Melissa asked in more measured, searching tones.

'For God's sake, you two, I told you — Daddy's working and I don't have time for this this morning. Eat your cereal. Now where did I put my effing purse?'

They were in the kitchen, having breakfast, a family routine that had been played out literally thousands of times, but now with one of the key performers missing. Another performer, Tom, was sleeping soundly somewhere above them. *Bloody university holidays,* Katie thought. *Comes home, bags of washing, treats the bloody place like a hotel. Hardly ever does a bit of work. Sleeps until lunchtime. How many more weeks of this? Why didn't he have a holiday job? What happened to those bloody shifts at Waitrose he was getting?* No. She stopped herself. She wasn't going to go down this road. Wasn't going to turn into her mother.

'I noticed his column wasn't in the paper this week,' Melissa said. God, she was sharp, Katie thought.

'Oh did you now?' Katie said, buying herself a few seconds to think. 'It's not unheard of for columnists to get the odd week off.'

'Daddy never takes a week off. He even writes

it when we're on holiday.'

'Yes, well, Daddy — Sophie, please sit down and eat your breakfast — Daddy's had a fair bit on his plate this past couple of weeks, what with all that trouble in Scotland.'

Melissa didn't quite say 'harrumph!', because no one in human history ever has, but she did push herself up from the table and stalk out of the room, eyeing her mother as she said, 'Something's afoot.'

'Oh, stop being so melodramatic, Melissa. And brush your hair. Where is the fu — the flaming thing?' She was looking for her purse in the vegetable rack now.

'Mummy,' Sophie said.

'Yes . . . darling?' Katie just managing to keep the edge out of her voice.

'Why is something afoot?'

'No no. Everything's fine, darling. Melissa's being silly.' She was about to call Petra — who was, as ever, ironing in the futility room, she was in pretty much every day at the moment, what with everything, more bloody money — and ask her if she'd seen her fucking purse when she saw it, peeking out from under the folds of the school blazer Sophie had carelessly thrown on the kitchen table. 'Ah!'

She got her phone out. Her Twitter page was open and Katie saw that the last thing she'd retweeted to her sixty-odd thousand followers (some of them very odd indeed) was Craig's last tweet about his gig tonight. (Craig, she'd noticed, now had nearly nine thousand followers on Twitter — not bad going in a month or so.)

281

'But why is something afoot?'

'Why is what afoot, Sophie? Nothing's afoot.'

'But . . . we all have feet.'

'What?' Looking up from her phone now — a missed call — genuinely confused.

'Melissa said something was a foot!' She saw Sophie was genuinely distressed, close to tears.

'Oh, right. It's just an expression, Sophs. It means something's going on.'

'What's going on?'

'NOTH — nothing, darling. Please. Go and brush your teeth.'

Sophie stomped off and Katie hit the button to return the call, picturing the phone ringing in that rather sterile office off Piccadilly Circus, picturing the small, well-mannered man answering it.

'Ah, Mrs Grainger. I was about to try you again. How are you this morning?'

'Ah, fine thank you. I was, do you have some . . . some information for me?'

'Indeed I do, yes. I was wondering if it would be opportune for us to meet again? As a rule I try to avoid discussing a client's affairs over the telephone and there may be some back and forth required, in the form of questions and answers that would be best done face-to-face, so to speak. I could easily travel to you if we can agree a time that is, as I said, mutually opportune.'

'Actually, I'm in London tonight,' Katie said. 'Could we meet early evening do you think?'

' Certainly. The sooner the better. Are you able to come to my office?'

'Sure.'

'Say six thirty?'

'See you then, Mr . . . ' She had to think for a second. 'Ames.'

'Very good. I look forward to it.'

Katie hung up. Where on earth had Vanessa dug this guy up? 'Sophie darling, don't you think it would be much better if you put your school things in your room after school, rather than just scattering them ra — ' She had to stop herself saying 'randomly'. 'Random', along with 'literally' and 'like', was on her list of banned words, words overused by Melissa and her friends. 'Just scattering them around the house, mmm?'

'OK,' Sophie whined dutifully.

'And don't whine, darling, it's very unbecoming.'

38

Christ, when had he last gone to a gig? They'd gone to see Springsteen a while back, but that had been in a box, at Emirates, a freebie courtesy of the paper. But a gig like this? Coming up from Old Street Underground he'd seen people heading towards the venue, mostly much younger than him, but a few oldies scattered here and there, people who knew Craig from the first time around, rather than because of his renaissance, if you will. Of course he hadn't been going to the gig at all. No way. He hadn't been going to drink that night either . . .

He'd been stretched out on the sofa all day, watching Jeremy Kyle. Well, why not? Why not fully embrace the cliché? He would normally have been writing something, but he had no one to write for at the moment. He'd normally have just got back from doing the school run, but there was no school run to do any more. At the very least Katie would have been pottering around the house, which would have shamed him into going into his study and writing *something*. But there was no Katie to potter around now. Just him and the day, stretching empty and uselessly ahead of him. 'But, Steve, Steve,' Jeremy was saying, while the audience booed and catcalled behind him, '*you* did this. You caused all this! You *have* to take some responsibility here . . .'

'No, mate, listen . . . ' Steve tided to interject. Steve was bald, covered in tats, and looked to weigh in at about eighteen stone. His speaking voice sounded like he had just learned to talk that very morning. From what Alan could gather Steve seemed to have slept with his ex-partner's two daughters (i.e. his own stepdaughters) as well as a couple of his neighbours. There was clearly some pocket of the world out there where Steve was regarded as a good thing, a catch. The woman and her two daughters sat across from Steve, arms folded, jaws set. 'He's a dirty bastard . . . ' this fine matriarch said to Steve, the last word being beeped out. 'I'd only take him back if . . . '

Alan tried to recast this scene in his own milieu. Having been busted sleeping with two of his stepchildren, Katie then comes home to find him balls-deep in Theresa from next door. He somehow manages to calm that down and then he only goes and fucks Andrea, their neighbour on the other side, too. He had to say, watching this, he kind of felt like calling Katie up and saying, 'Really? I'm the bad guy? Have you seen Steve?' And there was also that 'I'd only take him back *if* . . . ' Steve had a chance. There was a caveat in there, true, but he had a shot at getting back with Karen — who was possibly even heavier than Steve, he now saw — if he could just toe the line a bit and stop banging her kids and everything else in sight.

He had looked at his phone — 10.45. Barely half the morning gone. Could it really be taking that long? 'You can't help oo you fall in love wiv,

285

can you?' Steve was saying on the TV. 'Yes, Steve, but look. Look at what you've done to this family,' Jeremy was replying. Alan walked over to the window and looked out at Hackney Road, being swept now with spring rain. Buses splashed through puddles with rings of iridescent petrol in them, rings the colour of a pigeon's neck plumage. There was the off-licence across the road, its yellow-and-green sign already promising release come evening. This was the insoluble problem: if you didn't drink in the evening you felt anxious all evening. If you drank in the evening then you felt anxious all the next morning. The only solution he could see to this was to stay drunk the whole time, but what lay down the road? Could the terrible symmetry increase to the point where, in a couple of years, Craig was stepping over Alan in a Soho alleyway and saying, 'Uh, Alan? Alan Grainger?'

Hackney Road. Follow that all the way west to the Euston Road, all the way along to Marylebone Station, thirty minutes on the train, hop in a cab and five minutes later he'd be walking up his drive, to the grand house, everyone in the kitchen. Tom still home, lying on the sofa, doubtless scrolling through his phone. Melissa probably whining. Katie pounding out her column. Sophie having her tea. Tiny Sophie, sitting at the table, the cutlery comically oversized in her little fists, the great, exaggerated precision with which she cut her food. The milk moustache on her lip. Oh God . . . he had to shake his head violently from side to side in order to clear the vision of his youngest child from his head. He looked across the street to see a man — black, maybe in his thirties, stripped to the waist — ranting and raving to himself in the rain while he rooted through the rubbish bin next to the bus stop. Oh well, this was one of the therapeutic benefits of living in a big city like London. Whenever you felt like you were going crazy all you had to do was look around you.

Anyway, he'd hung around the flat all afternoon, watching daytime television, eating rubbish and drinking Diet Cokes. And then, as afternoon gave way to evening, he'd started glancing with increasing frequency towards that yellow-and-green signage. Finally, around 6.30, he'd crumbled and wandered across through the traffic to buy a bottle of fairly disgraceful Chardonnay. A little over an hour later he was back there for another one. (What was the white wine/red wine deal? Red wine: you sipped a single bottle of that all night, had a piece of cheese and went to bed. White wine: you drank three bottles in the space of two hours, smashed the house up and then went round and fucked the neighbour. You went full Steve.)

By 8.30 he was in the pub down the road nursing a Stella. (He often found himself uselessly remembering the old German drinking adage — '*Beer on wine, das is fine. Wine on beer — das is fear.*' Uselessly because whatever way round he was doing it, by the time he remembered the phrase he found he didn't care.) By 9 p.m. his thought process had come around to 'fuck it'.

So here he was after all.

The guy with the guest list did the usual thing of scanning up and down the page forever before finally, grudgingly, locating his name. He got a little stamp on the back of his hand, an envelope with a stick-on ACCESS ALL AREAS pass in it, and then, with a slightly quizzical look from the bouncer (or was he just being paranoid?), was ushered into the place. He followed the sound of music down a hallway and into the room itself. It was packed, loud, a DJ playing some nonsense or other. The stage was bare except for a single spotlight shining on the one microphone stand and an acoustic guitar on its stand. Alan wove his way to the bar and elbowed in, grateful for the fact that it was very dark in here and everyone seemed fairly drunk. Waiting for his lager with cocked twenty, he became conscious of eyes upon him. He turned to his left and saw Vanessa, just a few feet away, also waiting to be served. They looked at each other and Vanessa smiled first. Alan gave up his place and moved over next to her. 'Hello, Alan,' Vanessa said. 'How ghastly is this?' Meaning the crowd, the venue, the fact that she was further east than Centre Point.

'Yeah,' Alan said. 'Can I get you a drink?'

'Don't be silly, I'll get yours, I'm already getting a round in . . . ' She gestured and Alan looked across the room. A few yards away, clustered around a pillar, were Emily, Camilla and a few others he didn't recognise. Camilla raised an eyebrow at him. Emily just looked away.

'Oh fuck,' Alan said.

'Well, yes,' Vanessa said.

'Stella, thanks, V.'

'Alan, darling, I hate to say this, but you look absolutely terrible. You've lost so much weight.' He knew this. He'd been drunk every day for what now? More than two weeks? Still, he wondered how much longer he could openly walk about in public with this face.

'I suppose you think I've been a bit of a shit,' Alan said.

'To put it mildly,' Vanessa said. 'And a pint of Stella please.' Turning back to Alan. ''A fucking idiot' would be another way of putting it.'

'Is Katie with you guys?'

'She's meant to be. Texted earlier to say she's running a bit late. Some meeting or other. Well.' She turned her full gaze upon Alan now. 'What are we to put it down to?'

'What?'

'Your escapade. A 'moment of madness', was it?'

'Yes.' He looked at the floor.

'Just so you know,' Vanessa said, passing him his drink, 'I'm batting for you, but I'm a bit of a lone voice at the moment.'

'Thanks, Vanessa.'

'You want to come and say hello? Get it over with? Emily will probably blank you.'

'Maybe later. I'm going to go further down the front, get a good view.'

'Yeuch. Rather you than me, darling.' She pecked his cheek and disappeared into the crush towards her gang, cradling four half-pint tumblers of vodka and tonic.

Alan fought his way through and got about

289

halfway towards the stage before it became too difficult to continue. He sipped his lager and looked up at the dust motes moving through the ice-blue beams of light that criss-crossed the stage. It used to be smoke, in his day. Everyone, just pounding cigarettes indoors, happily puffing away, thinking the party would never end. How many times had they stood in crowds like this when they were young, him and Craig? At gigs in Glasgow, at Tiffany's, Night Moves, the Barrowland. That electric tingle of anticipation. He missed that. Maybe it was just one of those things you found you could get along without when you got older. He wondered how Craig was faring, somewhere behind that stage, in a wee tiny dressing room, probably trembling with nerves. Walking up and down and shaking his arms as though expelling energy through his fingertips, as Alan used to see him do in the old days. Just as he was musing on this Alan became aware of a change in pitch within the crowd, of cheering breaking out down near the front and then applause, starting at the front and drifting all the way to the back of the room. There, onstage, in a white shirt and suit jacket, was Craig, a guitar already strapped on as he made his way to the microphone. Being onstage had already done its hallucinogenic thing of making him look taller, of lending him gravitas and charm. 'Good evening, London,' Craig's voice boomed through the PA to cheers. 'Christ, I just realised it's been over twenty years since I said that . . . ' He'd clearly rehearsed this line, but it got more cheers. 'Anyway, I'm Craig Carmichael. It's nice to be back and this is an old song some of you may remember . . . ' He went into the first track from the Rakes' debut album. To his surprise, even though he hadn't heard it in many years, Alan found that the whole song came rushing back to him at once. He even remembered Craig writing it, Alan being amazed that someone his own age could do something like that. He watched Craig — his eyes scrunched shut, his mouth pressed tightly against the mike like he always used to — and mouthed along with the words '*we were so young, so dumb* . . . ' It was a song Craig had written when he was nineteen, full of embarrassment and affection for the way they were when they were fifteen. Four years being a lifetime at that age. Not what it is now — an afternoon. A lunch hour. God, Craig was good, his voice strong and clear, his guitar-picking nimble and precise; like all great pop songs it was full of yearning and regret beyond the years of the person who had written it. Yes, it was apparent to Alan now. The universe was simply righting itself. Craig had always been the truly talented one. He had been a hack, a hack who'd got lucky, who'd married well, who had ridden the property train well, buying at the right times in rising markets. Who'd published flippant, sarky columns and books, who'd never written a song, never really risked anything of his soul. Yes, standing there as his childhood friend's voice filled the air, drifted out over hundreds of people, it felt like a great and long overdue correction was taking place. He was not so drunk as to be unaware of the fact that he was very drunk, but Alan felt that this correction

291

was only fair, that it would be churlish of him to stand in the way of it. It felt appropriate that Craig's return to his natural place in the world had to be accompanied by Alan's diminishment. Things would work out. He'd declare bankruptcy. He'd somehow scrape together the money to rent a flat — a room even — as close to Katie and the kids as possible. He'd get through. Nothing would ever be great again but the world would not end. He'd manage. And finally, bathed in Craig's music, lost in this crowd, the tears came. He didn't care. They rolled down his face, soaking his cheeks. Gone, transported in this aching reverie, he did not immediately realise that someone was tugging at his sleeve. He turned round and found himself face-to-face with his wife. How beautiful she looked. How much love he felt for her. How absolutely *pissed* he was. It took him a moment to see there was something wrong with Katie's face. Her eyes, the blotched mascara; she'd been crying too. She pulled him towards her now and he felt that she was trembling as she placed her mouth next to his ear and began to shout above the music. She kept repeating three words over and over. And then Alan was turning, looking up at the stage in amazement and then turning back to Katie, who was just nodding at him, her mouth hanging open, and then Alan was stumbling backwards, pushing through the crowd, looking for an exit, finally finding it, and then he was careering down a concrete corridor, heading for the door at the end of it, a bouncer saying 'HEY' and then stepping back as Alan waved the AAA pass. Through

292

the doors and down another, narrower, corridor, running past flight cases and beer crates and things, the music, Craig, growing momentarily quieter and then louder again, but in a different way, sharper, clearer, and then he was screwing his eyes shut as blinding spotlights cut into him, hot on his face as he came through the heavy curtain, conscious of another 'HEY', of an arm grabbing at him as he went by, of a last-ditch attempt to stop him, and then the curious sensation of hundreds of pairs of eyes upon him, such as he felt now and then when he walked onstage at a book event, or a literary festival, that weird sensation of nakedness, and then Craig was turning round just as Alan reached him, Alan moving at a full run now, Craig still playing his guitar, strumming away as they locked eyes for a split second and then Alan was screaming 'YOU FUCK-ING CUNT!' as his fist made the connection with Craig's jaw and Alan went down on top of him, the acoustic guitar splintering between them with a boxy crunch as Alan got in blow after blow, Craig, incredibly, *laughing*, before Alan's thumbs were digging into his windpipe and he was squeezing as hard as he could, Craig's eyes bulging and people in the crowd screaming, saliva dribbling from Alan's mouth in fury and then the sound of heavy boots somewhere behind him, several pairs of hands grabbing him, Alan flailing, trying to fight, trying to get back on top of Craig, but he was being lifted up and then he was dropped and the back of his head hit the stage and then that was that.

39

He became conscious of being awake. His eyes were still closed, although he could tell by the quality of light pressing against them that it was not early. He turned onto his side and his head gave an explosive jolt of pain. Christ . . . it came back to him. Banging his head on the stage. The fight. And only now did he think to ask the question: *where am I?*

Alan opened his eyes. He was in bed, somewhere unfamiliar, not the awful hotel, not the box room at Craig's. A voice was saying 'Alan?' and another voice saying 'Daddy?' He turned carefully, sitting up. Katie, Melissa and Sophie were in the room, his daughters sitting on the end of the bed, Katie in the chair next to it. 'I . . . hi,' he said, his voice papery and cracked. Katie brought him a glass of water and he drank gratefully.

'Are you OK, Dad?' Melissa asked him, with something in her voice he hadn't heard in a long time — genuine concern.

'I, yeah. I think so. Sore head.'

Sophie came scampering up the bed saying 'Daddy!' as she threw herself against him. 'Ow!' Alan cried as the impact rippled through his heachache zone.

'OK,' Katie said. 'That's enough, girls, let's give Daddy some peace.'

'No, it's OK,' Alan began. He realised now

where he was — he was in hospital.

'Melissa,' Katie was saying, 'go and tell Dr Khan that your dad's awake. Then take your sister and go and find Tom in the canteen.'

'Come on, numpty,' Melissa said to Sophie.

'I hope you feel better, Daddy,' Sophie said to Alan.

'Here, just a sip,' Katie said, sitting on the bed, handing him the water again. 'So, what do you remember?'

'I . . . being on top of Craig? Hands grabbing me? What happened after that?'

'You got knocked right out. Ambulance came and brought you here. Do you remember any of that?'

A vague recollection, gliding on his back under bright lights, floating. 'Not really.'

'You've been asleep all night. They gave you some Valium in the drip to help. The doctor said you were close to alcoholic poisoning, total exhaustion.'

'It . . . it's been quite the time.' Alan tried to remember when he'd last felt happy. On the train to Scotland, sipping that first glass of wine before dinner.

'I know,' Katie said. She sat down close to him and brushed the hair out of his eyes. Human contact — how he'd missed it. How much your body craved it, like it craved water and food. 'You're all over the Internet by the way.'

'Eh?'

'How many people with camera phones do you think were at the gig? There's clips of you beating the shit out of Craig that have got twenty-odd thousand views since last night.'

'Jesus . . . '

She smiled at him and then, behind her, the door was opening and a doctor, Asian, quite young, was entering.

'Good morning. And how are we feeling?'

'Bit of a headache.'

'I'm not surprised. You've got a nasty bump there. You were incredibly dehydrated too, so we'll keep you on the drip for now.' He was shining a light in Alan's eyes now, pulling the lids back. 'We're just going to run some tests this morning and if all is well you should be able to go home this afternoon.'

'Home?' Alan said, but not to the doctor.

'Home,' Katie said firmly, taking his hand.

'Try and drink plenty of water too,' Dr Khan was saying. 'I'll be back with the consultant in a little while.'

'Thank you, doctor,' Katie said, getting up to close the door behind him. 'So.' She came back towards the bed. 'How much do you remember of what I told you? At the gig?'

Those three words — *it was Craig. It was Craig.*

'Craig. Craig sent you the video.'

'This chap Vanessa put me on to. He does a lot of electronic detective work. Traced the email to an IP address, a new laptop Craig had bought himself. It got me thinking about the other stuff recently, the tax stuff, how it all just seemed to happen at the same time? So he broke into Craig's flat and — '

'He broke into his flat?'

'Oh, they do this stuff all the time. Obviously we can't use anything we learn that way in court but, you know, I just wanted to know. He broke in and hacked into his laptop. Not only did he find the video he sent to me, he found some other emails too, to the Inland Revenue.'

'I . . . you mean . . . '

'Craig shopped you. For tax evasion.'

'I mean, what made him even think to get on to this?'

'Well,' Katie said, 'that might have been my fault. I remember, last year, not long after he came to stay, having a conversation with him in the kitchen, about limited companies and stuff. It must have got him thinking. Now I've — '

'Jesus,' Alan said.

'I've been over all the tax stuff with Daddy's people. I've been telling you for years your accountants are bloody useless. And, yes, there's been a bit of underpayment going on, nothing criminal, and if we repay them a chunk of what we're calling 'overenthusiastically claimed business expenses' then it'll all go away.'

'How much is 'a chunk'?'

'Oh, fifty or sixty grand.' Katie tossed this off lightly, as those from money do.

'Fuck. Where's Craig? What happened to . . . ?'

'You didn't hurt him too badly. Black eyes, those new teeth of his knocked out. He disappeared. Just legged it from the venue. He's deleted all his social media accounts. God knows where he's gone. Camilla went to his flat later that night, it's not far from hers, but no one home. I imagine he'll go to ground for a bit.'

'It's just . . . why? Why did he do all this?'

'I don't know. I just don't know. You must have pissed him off somehow.'

Alan sat back to process this new information, information he felt wasn't really new, that, in some way, he'd always kind of known, and then the door was opening again and his children were coming in, all three of them, led by Tom, who was grinning, holding his phone up, pointing at his father and saying, 'Legend.'

★ ★ ★

The footage was extraordinary, Alan had to admit. There was Craig, eyes screwed shut, singing. He stepped away from the mike just as the dishevelled figure of Alan crashed into the spotlights (and here the camera work of the person filming on their iPhone — someone called Giggyl997 according to their YouTube handle — stumbled as they panned across to take in the rough beast slouching towards centre stage). By the time Craig turned round Alan was upon him in a blur of fists. The acoustic guitar breaking, the cartoonish *ka-twanng* of strings snapping. The beating went on for a good few seconds before the bouncers managed to drag him off. There were a fair few screams and 'OhmyGods' and stuff, as well as some laughter from a few audience members who seemed to think it was all part of the act, perhaps some GG Allin-esque performance art. Alan hadn't recalled being midway through screaming '*you fucking bastard*' when the bouncer carrying his shoulders dropped him and his head smashed into the stage. Yes, all in all, it had been quite the entrance. The clip — with the admittedly unflattering title 'Nutter Stage Invasion' — had now notched up 28,203 views. The best thing about watching it, though, was that he was watching it in his own bed. He was watching it *at home*.

Home.

How glorious that word sounded to him now. How much we devalue it. *'I'm popping home.' 'I'll just be at home.' 'Oh, nothing much. Stayed home.'* When you don't have one for a while, how magical its sound becomes.

He'd been ordered to take a few days' bed rest, not so much from the bang on the head, more because of the absolute punishment he'd given his body in his two weeks of itinerant living. Alan had certainly gained a new-found respect for the people of the streets. Brothers, sisters of the pavements, how did you do it? The stamina, the dedication required to stay drunk all of the time. To get up and do it all over again day in and day out. He lay there, on this the third morning of sobriety, listening to the sounds of home all around him: the back door banging as Katie came and went to do bits of gardening, the murmur of a TV downstairs, music from somewhere above him, probably Melissa's room, the occasional garbled English/Russian exchange between Petra and Katie, a toilet flushing, Radio 4 from the kitchen, the pump of the shower running — all of it as sweet to him as a symphony now.

There had already been other developments

too. Katie had pulled the trigger on the one family weapon Alan was always loath to utilise — her father.

He'd come round to see Alan yesterday and Alan had explained the situation at the paper. 'Oh dear, that Rose?' his father-in-law had said. 'No no. This won't do. Let me see what I can do.' They'd made polite chat, skirting around the subject of Alan's recent moving out ('Ah well, things go on, don't they? Between men and women. Not my business. Family. That's the important thing. You'll put all this nonsense behind you') until, as the old man was leaving, he turned round, his hand on the bedroom doorknob, and said, 'Just one thing, before I sort all of this out for you.' He had looked directly at Alan and asked, 'It was you who broke our bloody lavatory, wasn't it?'

'I'm afraid so,' Alan said, without shame. He was all out of that for the time being.

'*I knew it!*' the Duke said fiercely, and with that he was gone.

Something came back to Alan, a moment from that night, *Craig, jumping into the toilet before him, coming back out with a cheery 'All yours!'*

The Duke was as good as his word though. A swish of his chequebook took care of the back-taxes situation (they'd sort it out down the line, a drop would simply come out of Katie's inheritance) and a single phone call rectified his employment situation. He'd be back at the paper next month. How did Alan feel about this blatant nepotism, about grubbing at the family trough? Fine. Right now he felt absolutely fine about it.

There were only two issues outstanding.

Craig had simply disappeared. Yesterday Katie had gone with Vanessa to the flat in Hackney to find no Craig but instead a young couple who had moved in the day before having answered an advert in the local newsagent. The diminutive Mr Ames was already on the case. As for the other outstanding issue . . .

It had been one night out of the something like eight thousand they had spent together. 'A moment of madness' as Vanessa had urged Katie to view it. He would have to work to make Katie forgive him.

And he would.

40

Five Months Later

The flat countryside of north Ayrshire rolled past the car. How long had it been since he'd been back here? Shortly after his mother's funeral, to attend a niece's wedding? Seven or eight years ago? Something like that. Alan changed up from fourth to fifth gear as a decent stretch of road opened up in front of him, still getting used to driving a non-automatic car for the first time in a while. All they'd had at the Avis desk at Glasgow Airport.

It was mid-September, and the weather was doing that thing it does in Scotland: finally giving you your second week of summer nearly four months after you had the first week of it, somewhere around the end of May. He had the window down, the skies above blue and cloud-less, the Firth of Clyde sparkling beneath them. As he approached Ardgirvan familiar landmarks started appearing to him: the maternity home where he was born. The old Volvo factory on the edge of town where many of his friends' fathers had worked. Then Ravenscroft Golf Club was coming up on the right, the eighteenth tee, the seventeenth green, the sixteenth tee, the fifteenth green: the last four holes packed tight together, running straight up and down. Ardgirvan Golf Club on the rights, then the school. Now past all of that and onto the main road towards town, the turn-off to where he'd grown up, to where his mother had lived until she died, coming up on his left, the petrol station on the corner still there, where he'd filled the tank of his dad's car for the first time after passing his test, way, way back in time. Driving past the grand Victorian houses, the grandest in the town, mostly hotels or care homes these days, before he was over the roundabout at the Annick bar (where you would famously get served in the snug at about fifteen) and then parking behind the high street.

He turned the engine off and looked again at the scrap of paper, at Mr Ames's small, precise block capitals. He knew exactly where it was, right in the town centre, right at the Cross. He paid and displayed and walked through one of the alleyway shortcuts and came out on the high street. A little over thirty years ago this had been his whole world. Safe to say the years had not been kind. Charity shops and 'we buy your gold' and cheap frozen-food retailers. He passed the Boot pub, another favourite teenage haunt. Next to the Boot stood the only sign of modernisation Alan could see: a large, spanking-new branch of Costa Coffee. He checked his watch — 9.37 a.m. He went in and bought a large Americano with hot milk to go with the copy of the *Guardian* already tucked under his arm, picked up at the airport, to accompany him on his vigil.

He found a bench at the Cross, the spot where the four main roads of the town intersected, and sat there sipping his coffee, with the newspaper cracked out across his thighs. He replied to

303

Katie's *'How's it going? x'* text, saying, *'Here. Waiting. Will keep you posted xx'*, and watched the comings and goings in this small Scottish town he had not lived in for over thirty years. Everyone in shirtsleeves, relishing what was likely the last of the sun for many months. Given that it was a school day there were a surprising number of kids going back and forth. Then he recalled the many days they had spent 'dogging it', back in the day. Mornings or afternoons spent at someone's house while their parents were at work, endless cups of tea and biscuits and watching horror films on VHS tapes — *The Bogeyman, I Spit on Your Grave, Cannibal Ferox* — rented from Target Video, another casualty of the high street, which, he now realised, used to be on the site of the Costa. Old people congregated in clumps here and there, the men outside the bookies or smoking outside the Bam — famously the hardest pub in Ardgirvan — and the women outside the supermarket. In fact there only seemed to be the very old or the very young in evidence here. He guessed it was another reason the town centre was almost dead now: anyone of driving age was in their car, headed to the retail park down towards the harbour, where all the brand names lived: Starbucks, KFC, McDonald's, Frankie and Benny's, Tesco and Sainsbury's and Asda. The high street was left with the distinctly off-brand: a boutique called JENNYS (no apostrophe) whose wares would doubtless have reduced, say, Vanessa to helpless tears of mirth, a bakery called COFFEE TIME, one of those shops that 'sold' TVs and fridges to people at the bottom of the socio-economic heap at interest rates approaching 2000 per cent per annum. Lost in this reverie, he almost missed him. Had to look back up sharply from the *Guardian*. There he was, across the street, walking with his familiar head-down, slight limp, wearing sunglasses and a dark hoodie and holding a paper bag and a Costa cup; they must have just missed each other. Alan got up, aware that his heart was thumping in his chest, aware that he had no idea what way this might go, but that he had to try. *Zachto? Et tu?* He hurried across the road and was coming up behind him just as Craig was turning his keys in the door, the doorway between Ronnie the Barber's and JENNYS. He sensed someone's presence behind him and turned just as he pushed the door open, the dark tenement hallway visible behind him.

'Craig,' Alan said.

Craig looked at him, his eyes unreadable behind the sunglasses. A beat, Craig still with one hand on the keys in the lock, the other cradling the coffee cup and a bag of what Alan now saw were crusty rolls. 'Come on then,' Craig shrugged, heading into the hallway, leaving the door open behind him.

The flat was one floor up. And 'flat' was overdoing it. It was a room. A sink in one corner, a single bed in the other. No bathroom he could see. There was a small sofa and an armchair with a coffee table between them, a minibar-sized fridge and the inevitable Belling hotplate with two rings. All of the furniture looked to date from about 1985. The walls were dirty, the plaster cracked, the windows that looked out onto the high street covered with filthy net curtains. A stale smell in the air, like damp digestive biscuits. Craig tossed the bag of rolls onto the coffee table and sat down in the armchair. Alan remained standing just inside the doorway.

'Bit different from your last place,' Alan said.

Craig didn't reply. He'd sat down and was neither looking at Alan nor pointedly not looking at him. Alan hadn't exactly thought Craig would be scared of him, but he'd expected some level of anxiety, surprise, guilt. *Something.* As it was he seemed completely cool. Almost bored. As though Alan was keeping him from greater things. Craig took his sunglasses off.

'Aren't you wondering how I found you?' Alan asked.

'Naw. Private detective, I suppose.'

'How's your face?' Alan said.

Craig shrugged. There was silence for a moment and then Craig said, 'You're here because you want to know why I did it, aren't you?'

Alan sat down across from him. Craig looked at him for a long time then shook his head. 'You're such a fucking *dick*, Alan. You've always been a wee dick. From the first time I met you.'

Truth. It was almost a relief to hear it. Most lifelong friendships go a lifetime without it ever having to rear its head.

'Even after all — ' Alan began before Craig cut him off.

'After all you did for me? You patronising cunt. You just wanted to show me how great your fucking life was. Like I didn't know that already.

306

Your smug fucking pus in the papers all the time, on the telly. Crapping oan about fucking salads and partridges and all that fucking shite. You know how long I watched you cunting about Soho before ah decided tae speak to ye? Fucking ages. Aw aye — take the homeless guy tae the Groucho for a fucking laugh. But ye couldnae stop there, could ye? Couldnae just have had a few drinks, bunged us a couple of quid and fucked off. Ye had tae show me the big house, the wife, the cars, aw that shite. You were fucking *nothing* when ye met me, ya wee fanny.'

'So you planned all this?'

'Up tae a point. After you were bragging about all your 'limited company, screwing the revenue' shite ah thought ah'd just drop ye in it there. Then, that night, after the pub, back at yours, coked aff yer tits, ah knew you'd end up firing intae wan o they birds. And that ah could maybe wreck yer finances and yer marriage. But then, aw that carry-on you got into with those idiots shooting each other on that daft photo shoot? Losing your job? That was a bonus. That was too good.'

'One other thing — the toilet, that night at Katie's par — '

Craig laughed. 'Aye, that was a belter, eh? Improvised that on the spot. Dodgy plumbing, the amount of Ex-Lax you'd been banging. Ah saw ye twitching in yer seat . . . '

Alan got up and went to the window. He looked out at Ardgirvan high street. 'Why here?' he asked. 'Why come back here?'

'Because I'm no like you.'

'What does that mean?'

'I'm no a self-hating prick. I didnae have tae marry some posh English bird, change ma fucking accent, send ma kids tae some poxy private school . . . all the shite you've done just tae try and distance yerself fae here. And one other thing — yer writing's shite and ye know it. That fucking 'novel' ye wrote. Jesus Christ. How the fuck did that even get published? I know you're not thick enough tae actually believe you're any good now, are ye? Because . . . '

Craig talked on, saying all the things friends should never say to each other. Alan wasn't really listening any more. Some of what Craig was saying was, of course, absolutely true. And Alan remembered the pangs, the deep, physical pains, that had racked him all those years ago, back in the early nineties, when, for a couple of brief years, it looked like Craig was going strato-spheric, like Craig was going to leave him behind, with his sell-out shows in New York and his music on the radio and his face in the papers, and Alan there with his schlocky little job at the old *Time Out* office on Tottenham Court Road, taking the Tube everywhere and renting that tiny room in Seven Sisters. He thought of all the quotes — *it is not enough that I succeed, others must fail . . . we will forgive our friends anything except their success . . .* And then Craig sank too far, too fast, too hard. While Alan rose, swimming up into the world of money and success, dappled sunlight glittering on the surface of the lagoon where he now basked, while Craig flailed, sinking down into the terrible cold and darkness, weeds enveloping him on the bottom while he looked up — at Alan's kicking heels. Alan realised his instinct had been right, that first night Craig stayed at the house, at the dinner table, laughing at him with Melissa. With men, the dynamics are fixed early on. It didn't matter how much money he had, how much success. It didn't matter if he was standing there in a suit of solid gold and Craig was lying naked in a gutter. Alan would always be trying to impress Craig. And Craig would always despise Alan. Even sitting here, with Alan about to drive back to Glasgow Airport, then sit in the BA exec lounge, and then fly back to his (gradually recovering) near perfect life, leaving Craig in his hovel, the only mail on the doormat a tragic pile of low-grade credit card offers and takeaway food menus, even with all that, there was no doubting where the power lay.

'Were we ever friends?' Alan asked, from the doorway.

Craig shrugged. 'You just get stuck with people, don't you?'

He walked back along the high street, towards where he'd parked the car. He took a good look around, at the grimy Victorian buildings of the town, at a seagull eating a chip, knowing that he would never be back here. Across the street, now boarded up, covered with fly posters, was what used to be the Annick Hotel. He stopped and looked up at the windows on the first floor, where the function room had once been. The last time he'd been in that room came back to him, unbidden and complete in his mind.

★ ★ ★

You hurried up the stairs, the carpet sticky under your feet, your guitar case in one hand and a plastic bag with leads and effects pedals in the other. Craig had left them at rehearsals. You could hear it before you pulled the door to the function room open, the regular, rhythmic thud-thud-thud. As you came in you saw Andy on the small stage, behind the kit, heard the hippy guy who owned the PA system shouting 'Aye, right, now the snare' and a rat-tat-tat replaced the thud-thud-thud of the bass drum. You crossed the wooden dance floor, towards where a few of the others stood. Craig had his back to you and was talking animatedly over the sound of the snare drum. One of the others nudged Craig as you drew near and he turned, saw you, and said, loudly, 'Aye, that'll be fine.' The others looked at the floor. The sound of the brakes going on, of someone screeching the conversation to a halt mid-sentence and changing direction. 'Whit were ye talking about?' you asked.

'SNARE, KICK AND HI-HAT TOGETHER!' the PA guy shouted now. Andy started playing — 'Reel Around the Fountain'.

'Nothing,' Craig said. 'How come you're late?'

'You asked me to get this,' you said, holding out the bag of pedals.

'Oh aye. Right. Cheers.' Craig took the bag and walked over towards his amp. The others moved away too, towards chairs and tables, towards their own guitar cases.

No one talking to you. You could see a couple

310

of smirks being hidden as their backs turned and you knew, you just knew.

You stood there on the small dance floor, your face burning, the drum kit ringing around the empty room, the smell of stale beer and bleach. Somewhere behind you Craig plugged his guitar in and started playing along with the drums.

It was 1986.

We do hope that you have enjoyed reading
this large print book.

Did you know that all of our titles
are available for purchase?

We publish a wide range of high quality
large print books including:
Romances, Mysteries, Classics
General Fiction
Non Fiction and Westerns

Special interest titles available in
large print are:
The Little Oxford Dictionary
Music Book
Song Book
Hymn Book
Service Book

Also available from us courtesy of
Oxford University Press:
Young Readers' Dictionary
(large print edition)
Young Readers' Thesaurus
(large print edition)

For further information or a free
brochure, please contact us at:
Ulverscroft Large Print Books Ltd.,
The Green, Bradgate Road, Anstey,
Leicester, LE7 7FU, England.
Tel: (00 44) **0116 236 4325**
Fax: (00 44) **0116 234 0205**

THREE THINGS ABOUT ELSIE

Joanna Cannon

There are three things you should know about Elsie. The first thing is that she's my best friend. The second is that she always knows what to say to make me feel better. And the third thing . . . Might take a little bit more explaining. Eighty-four-year-old Florence has fallen in her flat at Cherry Tree Home for the Elderly. As she waits to be rescued, she wonders if a terrible secret from her past is about to come to light. And if the charming new resident is who he claims to be, why does he look exactly like a man who died sixty years ago?

DALILA

Jason Donald

Irene Dalila Mwathi comes from Kenya with a brutally violent personal history. Once she wanted to be a journalist, but now all she wants is to be safe. When she finally arrives, bewildered, in London, she is attacked by the very people paid to protect her, and she has no choice but to step out on her own into this strange new world. Through a dizzying array of interviews, lawyer's meetings, regulations and detention centres, she realises that what she faces may be no less dangerous than the violence she has fled . . .

THE LIGHTKEEPER'S DAUGHTERS

Jean E. Pendziwol

Elizabeth's eyes have failed. She can no longer read the books she loves or see the paintings that move her. But her mind remains sharp, and music fills the vacancy left by her blindness. When her father's journals are discovered on a shipwrecked boat, she enlists the help of a delinquent teen, Morgan, to read to her. As an unlikely friendship grows between them, Elizabeth is carried back to her childhood home — the lighthouse on Porphyry Island, Lake Superior — and to the memory of her enigmatic twin sister Emily. But for Elizabeth, the faded pages of her father's journals reveal more secrets than she anticipates . . .

THE COTTINGLEY SECRET

Hazel Gaynor

Cottingley, Yorkshire, 1917: When two young cousins, Frances Griffiths and Elsie Wright, announce they have photographed fairies at the bottom of the garden, their parents are astonished. The girls become a sensation; their discovery offering something to believe in amid a world ravaged by war . . . One hundred years later: When Olivia Kavanagh finds an old manuscript and a photograph in her late grandfather's bookshop, it sparks a fascination with the story of the two young girls who mystified the world. Delving deeper into the past, and the truth behind an innocent game that became a national obsession, Olivia begins to understand why a nation once believed in fairies. But can she find a way to believe in herself?

THIS IS NOW

Ciara Geraghty

Martha wants a drink. There are six reasons why she shouldn't have one; she wrote them down over a year ago. Two of the reasons are the same. A name. Of someone she didn't think she'd ever see again . . . Roman, a fourteen-year-old Polish immigrant, is on the run. He understands now what it means to be caught between a rock and a hard place . . . Tobias, old and alone, lies in a hospital bed in Dublin where the memories of Dresden are insistent visitors . . . And for Cillian, a police detective, the past is like a current, pulling him back, reminding him of all he's lost. Each is running from the moments that brought them to a place where the past cannot be undone and the future cannot be known — a place called now.

THE NINTH HOUR

Alice McDermott

On a gloomy February afternoon, Jim, an Irish immigrant, sends his wife Annie out to do the shopping before dark falls. He seals their meagre apartment, unhooks the gas tube inside the oven, and inhales. Sister St. Saviour, a Little Nursing Sister of the Sick Poor, catches the scent of fire doused with water and hurries to the scene: a gathered crowd, firemen, and a distraught young widow. Moved by the woman's plight, and her unborn child, the ageing nun finds Annie work in the convent's laundry — where, in turn, her daughter will grow up amidst the crank of the wringer and the hiss of the iron. As the decades pass, Jim's suicide reverberates through many lives — testing the limits and the demands of love and sacrifice, of forgiveness and forgetfulness.